A GENTLEMAN UNDER THE MISTLETOE

THE LORD JULIAN MYSTERIES—BOOK SEVEN

GRACE BURROWES

Cover image by Cracked Light Studio

Cover design by Wax Creative, Inc.

DEDICATION

To the elves in our lives
who consider joy ample compensation
for their many benevolent gifts to us

CHAPTER ONE

"What in the name of Good King Wenceslas was I thinking?" I muttered this query for the third time in an hour as a footman leaned too far from his ladder and went tumbling into the snow. Ropes of greenery came down after him, along with a few whoops from the balcony above and a dash or two of profanity.

"You all right there, Young Jamison?" somebody called down.

Young Jamison sat up, snow atop his head, greenery about his shoulders. "Right as a trivet what's got a pot of toddy keeping it warm. Oh, didn't see your lordship there on the terrace. Happy Christmas, sir!"

A bit too happy, and Christmas was still weeks away. Clearly, the day's portion of toddies had already found its way from the pot into the staff.

"Carry on, Young Jamison." I should have assisted the man to his feet, should have returned the cheery salutation. My dear father would have done both, my brother Harry would have been up the ladder himself, and Arthur—the present duke—would have good-naturedly ignored the whole ridiculous business.

Papa and Harry were dead, Arthur was cavorting about Munich

or Salzburg in anticipation of a remove to Vienna—his letters were nearly incoherent with joyous plans and amazing sights—while I bided at the family seat and doubted my sanity.

Happy Christmas, indeed.

I returned to the warmth of Caldicott Hall, which would be spared decking with boughs of any sort until later in the month.

"Julian, there you are." Dorothea, Her Grace of Waltham, made a cheery picture coming down the grand staircase. She was attired in Father Christmas green, which went nicely with her red hair and Celtic complexion. "I vow you have been least in sight for the past fortnight. Did I, or did I not, just see Young Jamison plummeting from the heavens outside the library?"

"Mama, good day. Jamison came off a ladder and is none the worse for losing his balance. He might well be the worse for drink, however."

"Nonsense." Her Grace swanned down the remaining steps. "A tot to ward off the chill never addled anybody's wits. Ginny has sent word that she'll be here tomorrow. Declan has a slight cold, so they will tarry an extra day in Town."

My youngest sister, Virginia, had two children—a boy and a girl. I was godfather to the boy, Declan, whom I had last seen when the lad had still been a gurgling bundle of joy held securely in the arms of his adoring papa. His younger sister was a stranger to me.

With the arrival of Ginny and her offspring, the holiday onslaught would begin in earnest. "I shall endeavor to contain my disappointment at the delay. I assume Lord Kerrick is accompanying his wife and children?" He'd better be, or my brother-in-law and I would have *words*.

"Of course. Kerrick adores the holidays as much as I do."

Lachlan, Earl of Kerrick, adored my sister, and she returned his affection in scandalously full measure. They had been a love match, and I hoped they still were.

"Mama, might you have a word with Mrs. Gwinnett about the toddies?"

Her Grace peered at me. "If she made them any stronger, the peace of the realm would be imperiled."

"Precisely. The peace of Caldicott Hall has been shattered since Stirring Up Sunday. Some restraint with the rum is in order. The kitchen being a feminine domain, and Mrs. Gwinnett being a sensitive soul, I will leave it to you to request that she moderate her generosity."

The duchess's expression took on that considering aspect mothers aimed at a child who had just possibly blundered onto the verge of vexing them.

"Are you coming down with something, Julian? An ague? A megrim? You grow cranky when you are stalked by illness."

I am not perishing cranky. My mother and I were navigating a gradual thawing of relations after years of polite distance. That she would set a verbal trap of the classic maternal variety should have been reassuring.

"I am in the pink of health," I replied, starting up the steps, "though somewhat short of sleep. I will leave you to negotiate with Mrs. Gwinnett while I tend to the day's correspondence." I bowed slightly and resumed my progress up the steps.

"Arthur never complains about the holiday toddies."

Arthur, His Grace of Waltham, seldom complained about anything. I loved my surviving brother fiercely and of late resented him in equal measure, even as I gained new sympathy for the burdens he so stoically carried.

"Of course Arthur didn't comment on the toddies, Mama. He was too busy shoveling himself out from under a daily deluge of reports, letters, invoices, and parliamentary epistles. I will now do my feeble best to impersonate him lest his duchy fall to pieces on my watch. I bid you good morning."

Mama waved a graceful hand. "Very well, then, be on your way. Tend to business in the Caldicott male tradition, and I won't tell you my news."

Fiend. I came back down the steps. "Unfair, madam. If my mood has suffered because I was nearly potted by a tipsy footman, you cannot blame me. The Christmas pudding has barely begun soaking, and the lot of them are teetering on the brink of riot."

The maids abetted their confreres, lingering beneath the mistletoe dangling from every doorjamb and crossbeam in the Hall.

I could not honestly say I missed Spain, where I'd spent several hard years in uniform mostly on reconnaissance. I'd been good at my job, to the surprise of both the enlisted men and my superiors, and to my own surprise most of all.

I did miss the simplicity of that life and the sense of having an occupation at which I was competent. This business of serving as steward of Arthur's dukedom was irksome in the extreme, and yet, I'd nearly demanded the job when I'd exhorted His Grace to see some of the world. That Osgood Banter, Arthur's devoted paramour, traveled with him meant the duke's eventual return was in doubt.

Merry Olde was murderously intolerant of those who preferred the intimate company of their own gender. Arthur and Banter were safer on the Continent, and thus I'd sent them traveling with heartfelt best wishes.

"What is your news?" I asked while Her Grace fiddled with a red ribbon dangling from the kissing bough suspended from the foyer's chandelier.

"The news is happy, for the most part. To see old friends and distant family is always a happy occasion, or it should be."

"Mama, I am honestly overwhelmed by the sheer volume of work required to maintain Arthur's correspondence. He could glance at some parliamentary report and know whether it required reading, skimming, or a summary toss into the flames. I must attend to every word, and my eyes... What is your news?"

I need not remind my mother of my weak eyes. Since the day a mortar shell had landed on a powder wagon in my general vicinity, my eyes had been sensitive to excessive light. I wore blue-tinted spectacles in bright sunshine and when my vision otherwise bothered me, which was frequently of late.

"Hire another secretary," Her Grace said. "Hire three. Arthur would not want you ruining your sight over the price of turpentine or sailcloth."

Both were vital issues to the Royal Navy. "Your news?"

"Uncle Terrence will join us for the holidays this year."

I weathered this blow as I might have weathered the news that my much-treasured personal mount, one Atlas, was colicking, which was to say, badly.

"Merry Uncle Terry is inflicting... rather, visiting us for the holidays?"

"He's mellowed, Julian, and he did worry so about you and Harry."

Uncle Terrence was neither merry nor in the strict sense an uncle. He'd been a friend of my grandfather's from Grandfather's four-in-hand days, though Terrence was years Grandfather's junior. The march of time had nonetheless turned Uncle Terrence's disposition from salty to sour. Some of my most bewildering boyhood memories had been of Uncle Terry sitting glum and silent at the Christmas feast, or stalking around the Boxing Day open house like some sort of bad fairy at a storybook christening.

"You are the hostess of this gathering, Mama. If you choose to add Uncle Terrence to the guest list, I will welcome him graciously as well. Now, if you'll excuse me?"

"Have you paid a call on the nursery yet today, Julian?" Her Grace asked the question a bit too casually.

"I will stop by after I have reviewed the morning mail." I'd said the same thing yesterday, with predictable results. I'd finished my afternoon apologizing to my young nephew for my neglect—again.

"Of course you will. Truly, Julian, you are failing to enter into the spirit of the holidays. One would despair of you but for the fact that you are pining for Miss West."

With every fiber of my being, I missed Hyperia West. "She and I do not dwell in each other's pockets. I look forward to her eventual arrival at the Hall." Had dear Perry not agreed to spend her Yuletide with us, I'd likely be swilling toddies, tumbling off ladders, and adorning myself in greenery too.

Hyperia West was my friend, fiancée, and the lodestar of my honor. *Love* was too pallid a term for the esteem in which I held her, and yet, the date of her arrival was still undecided.

"Well, then, away with you," the duchess said, tucking the red ribbon into the kissing bough. "Back to your turpentine and sailcloth, and Leander will simply have to accommodate your more important duties."

Mama took few shots, but she aimed each one for the bull's-eye. "Good day, Your Grace. I'll see you at luncheon."

"No, you won't. I'm meeting with the committee to discuss prizes at the Boxing Day fête. You will take a tray in the study, which you will ignore, and then you will eat half the offerings cold, and Mrs. Gwinnett's feelings will be hurt, and I will have that to deal with well as your disdain for a hearty toddy."

She blew me a kiss and sailed off in the direction of the conservatory while I contemplated ordering myself a whole pot of toddies.

Arthur's correspondence was important, never-ending, and infernally boring. When I should have gone directly to the study and locked myself in with a vow not to emerge until every piece of mail had been dealt with, I instead marched to the family wing and climbed to the nursery suite.

Leander was five-going-on-sixish, my late brother Harry's by-blow, and recently commended by his mother into the keeping of the ducal side of the family. The boy was coping with a lot, and somebody had best warn him that the holiday mêlée would include Uncle Terrence.

The mail, despite all my wishes to the contrary, would still await me in another quarter hour.

I found the lad with his nose in a book, some tale about King

Arthur and knights and dragons. "No soldiers today?" I asked as the nurserymaid scurried off for a much-deserved cuppa in the servants' hall.

"I played with them already," Leander said. "Unless you'd like to play with me?"

The child could reenact a number of Napoleonic battles with frightening enthusiasm. "If you've dismissed the men to their barracks, it would be a shame to muster them out again for a mere skirmish."

"Because you are busy." Harry's ghost peered out at me through Leander's reproachful eyes.

I joined the boy on the toy chest where he'd perched. Not the most comfortable seat for a grown man. "Christmas is coming. The whole house is busy. I vow I've never seen so much cleaning and dusting and polishing in my life. I shut the door of the study in part just to get some peace."

Leander peered up at me. "You could take a nap."

"Then Her Grace would worry that I'm sickening for something." Was Leander still taking naps? I did not know, and I was his legal guardian. "Have you been to the stable today?"

He had his father's love of horses. My land steward was in the process of buying a pony that I'd present to the lad on Christmas morning. We'd dickered and dithered with prospective sellers until ponies had been trotting through my dreams. The chosen beast was awaiting his fate in the livery stable at the estate village, though precisely who had bought the pony for whom was cloaked in utmost secrecy.

"I visited Atlas after breakfast," Leander said. "Young Jamison took me, because Nurse said you were busy."

The child needed a proper governess, but Her Grace and I agreed that could wait until the New Year. For the nonce, Leander enjoyed a degree of liberty most boys would envy.

Though he also, I suspected, endured a degree of boredom

unprecedented in his short life. "Have you written to your mama this week?"

"You asked me that yesterday. I write to Mama on Sundays because there's nothing else to do after supper on the Sabbath."

"I see."

"Mama writes back that I'm to be good, not to eat too many sweets, and to listen to you and Uncle Arthur, except Uncle Arthur isn't here."

"He will come home next year, or that's the plan. This toy chest is hard."

"It's wooden. Wood is hard."

I rapped my knuckles against the boy's crown. "Your head is hard. Would you like to make another trip to the stable with me?" A mountain of mail threatened to figuratively bury me at that suggestion.

"No, thank you, Uncle Julian. I'm reading now."

"You are no help whatsoever."

His gaze turned wary. "Help with what?"

I'd aimed a similar cautious, uncertain gaze on grouchy old Uncle Terrence countless times. "I was making a jest. Hoping you would help me avoid sorting all the mail and whatnot. You would rather be studious than abet my truancy."

He turned the page of his book. "Dragons breathe fire. I would like to breathe fire, but why doesn't the dragon get burned? Are dragons made of metal?"

"They are made of magic, and magic is impervious to flame."

Leander silently repeated the word. *Im-per-vious.* "I will be impervious to lemon drops. I will fill my tummy with them and never get a bellyache."

"A fine ambition. Well, if you have no further news to impart, I'll be on my way."

He shot a glance at the toy chest reserved for his various armies. "Will you come back tonight?"

"I will, and you can tell me what you've learned about dragons.

Perhaps Father Christmas will bring me one, seeing as I've been a good boy and all."

My humor was falling flat, and perhaps that's what I deserved for dodging carpet victories over the Corsican menace.

"You aren't a boy, Uncle Julian."

"True enough. I am a nephew, though, of sorts. My uncle Terrence will join us for Christmas, and he's something of a dragon in human form. Not very jolly, always seems to be finding fault." Though Aunt Bertha held perennial top honors among the Ancient and Distinguished Order of At-Large Critics.

"Was your uncle a soldier?"

An odd question, but then, Harry had been a soldier, and Leander measured all in his ambit by the lights of the father, of whom he had no memory.

"Yes, as a matter of fact, he was. Fought the Americans, among others."

"Maybe your uncle Terrence will play soldiers with me. I'm a nephew too."

"So you are, lad. So you are, but you might want to keep your dragon book handy in case Uncle Terrence isn't in a mood to play. He's not much given to merriment."

"Like you?"

I am not perishing cranky. "Yes, like me, at least lately. Uncle Terrence is coming to the Hall because he has nowhere else to go, and he is family, of a sort."

Leander returned to his book without firing further broadsides, and I left the nursery feeling like a dismal excuse for an uncle.

Leander was family *of a sort*, and he hadn't anywhere else to go. If I was lucky, the boy wouldn't pick up on the comparison, though lately, luck and I hadn't been keeping company much. Uncle Terrence at the figurative gate, flying footmen outside the library window, and now my nephew wasn't in charity with me.

I marched my not-cranky self to the study, sat at Arthur's grand desk, and pulled a stack of Arthur's important correspondence to the middle of the blotter. I had picked and shoveled my way through about half of it before I noticed a tray at my elbow. Toasted cheese sandwiches gone cold.

I picked one up and bit off a corner and reached for the next piece of mail.

The truth was, *I* hadn't anywhere else to go for Christmas, unless I wanted the solitary gloom of my London town house. Even in my cranky, grumpy, hungry, resentful state, I knew that was no solution for what ailed me.

CHAPTER TWO

At the bottom of the tower of mail, I found a letter addressed to me. Correspondence was a rarity in my life, in part because my years in uniform meant many of the fellows I might have written to were no longer extant. Many others would disdain any association with me whatsoever.

While I had served honorably, even dragging myself to Brussels for the fighting at Waterloo, military gossip painted me in a poor light. I had been taken captive by the French when I'd followed Harry from camp one night by the light of a quarter moon.

Like me, Harry had been a reconnaissance officer. Unlike me, he'd preferred gathering his intelligence in the towns and cities and working his way into relationships with Portuguese aristos and Spanish gentry. I'd thus been curious when Harry had violated several standing orders and quit camp without leave and without notice to me.

Curious, and more than a little worried.

I'd trailed him at a careful distance, hoping his objective was yet another romantic assignation, but an appallingly short distance from camp, he'd been picked up by a French patrol. Harry hadn't resisted, and thus I had felt duty-bound to fall in with whatever scheme he was hatching and make myself known to the same patrol.

I'd had other options, any one of which made more sense in hindsight. Create a distraction and trust Harry to take advantage of the disturbance. Maintain surveillance and report back to my superiors once I knew where Harry was being held. Offer myself in trade for Harry's freedom.

Instead, I'd reasoned that Harry and I could win free more easily together than either one of us could if taken prisoner alone, and with all the confidence of a new recruit strutting about the village green in his parade dress uniform, I'd embarked on a nightmare that had ended in Harry's death.

I still wasn't sure about the pertinent details of my own ordeal. Between deprivation and interrogation, my wits had gone begging, though the French commandant himself had informed me of Harry's demise. The ruddy blighter had been all dignified condolences at the time—I recalled that much very clearly—but commandant himself had subsequently denied knowledge of relevant particulars.

And yes, I had confronted him when the opportunity had arisen.

As Wellington had advanced into France, the enemy had abandoned the garrison where I'd been held, and I had been given the freedom to starve or freeze in the mountain wilderness. I had wandered for weeks in a state I can only describe as unhinged. I survived purely because I'd learned to live off the land, and spring came blessedly early. By the time I stumbled into a British military camp, Paris had been liberated, Napoleon had surrendered, and I—formerly presumed dead—was demoted from the status of officer fallen in the line of duty to suspected traitor.

Surely I had traded my brother's life for my freedom? Why else had I survived when Harry had not? Why else would my tale be so dodgy in the specifics? Why else had I been so slow to rejoin my regiment after my so-called *escape*?

And yet, with the Corsican vanquished and the Congress of Vienna looming, I had never faced a court-martial or even a board of inquiry. More puzzling to me still, when Napoleon had broken free of his island prison, the British military had welcomed me back for the Hundred Days. True, most seasoned officers had sold up or shipped out for Canada or the East, but still...

"I suppose one doesn't lightly accuse a ducal heir of treason," I murmured, slitting the seal on the lone piece of mail addressed to me personally. The wax was of a rose hue and lightly scented with gardenia.

My godmother, Lady Ophelia Oliphant, sent greetings and felicitations. She followed up with predictable platitudes and warned me that she'd arranged for a present for Leander, which would arrive in due course. In the event that she was unavoidably detained, I was to make the lad wait until Christmas Eve before conferring his gift upon him.

"Yes, my lady." Though I saw the order for what it was—a warning that she might take French leave over the holidays and ignore her invitation to visit at the Hall. Perhaps she'd had word that Uncle Terrence had grumbled his way onto the guest list. Her ladyship had a network of informants that Wellington would, and probably did, envy.

A scrap of paper fluttered from her ladyship's epistle, and my spirits rose. I recognized Hyperia's handwriting, which would ever be cause for joy. My beloved was discreetly corresponding with me, and that meant she was thinking of me.

My lord,

Dearest Healy is being a complete gudgeon. I will pry him loose from Town at the first opportunity, but the matter requires patience. More patience. Mind Mrs. G's toddies and remember to rest your eyes.

H.W.

· · ·

Healy was Hyperia's brother and thus her escort from Town. He was a gudgeon by nature, and he and I were not in greatest charity with each other. I would make sure the housekeeper put Healy in the rooms adjacent to wherever Uncle Terrence was housed.

"The matter requires patience," I muttered. "*More* patience."

I rubbed my tired eyes and rooted about mentally for some sense of satisfaction at having vanquished the epistolary dragon for the day. None came to hand, though I was slightly bilious, and my eyes stung.

"Ruddy coal smoke." I rose stiffly, intent on finding a sober footman who could grasp that I wanted peat rather than coal burned in the study henceforth.

My hand was on the door latch when the door flew open.

"Greetin's, guv! I brung the afternoon mail!" Atticus, my tiger and self-appointed aide-de-camp, grinned up at me. He was dark-haired, wiry, and struggling to conquer the written word. Good food was inspiring him to outgrow everything but his hat every other fortnight, and what he lacked in polish, he made up for in canny good sense—usually. The boy's age was a mystery and his patrimony equally shrouded in uncertainty.

What was very clear was that somebody—somebody who would pay a high price indeed—had allowed this mere child to overimbibe.

"Thank you for the mail," I said. "You will please go to the kitchen. You will tell Mrs. Gwinnett to ply you with hot tea and toast. You will swear off toddies for the rest of the week, and that is a direct order, Atticus."

He blinked at me, and his bibulous good cheer dissolved into confusion. "I ain't done nuffing wrong. Why you got to go all sniffy on me?"

"In future, you may give the mail to a footman, who will convey it abovestairs without tracking half the shire's mud onto the carpets."

Atticus glanced down at his exceedingly damp footwear. "Sorry. Snow on the lane." He burped dejectedly. "Feet are cold too."

I was angry not with the boy—he was a child, relatively new to service, and very new to a ducal household—but with the general laxness that had resulted in his inebriation and attendant breaches of protocol.

"Atticus, you are tipsy, a state of affairs a gentleman avoids in daylight hours. You have neglected to address me correctly when we've agreed that inside the Hall, proper decorum will prevail. I am not 'guv,' I am 'my lord' or 'your lordship' under this roof. You have abused Mrs. Henderson's carpets, and you have imperiled your health. I am not best pleased with you."

I was being a bit hard on the lad, but he needed to know that taking spirits irresponsibly had consequences.

"I ain't best pleased with you neither, your guvship. Lordship. Lord Guv. I like that."

My ire became laced with concern. "Atticus, how much have you had to drink?"

He burped again, and the fumes would have knocked my horse onto his handsome tail. "I do enjoy a toddy, guv, and nobody notices if you just help yourself to a sip here and a sip there. Goes down ever so kind. Best toddies in Merry Olde, Jamison says. He lets me have a sip of his too."

My father would have offered Atticus a full serving for his very own and allowed the lad to deal with the aftermath—the pounding head, body aches, fuzzy thinking, parched mouth, and profound remorse. I could not do that to the boy.

"I will overlook your various transgressions on this occasion, but your deportment requires amending. Moderation is imperative when it comes to Mrs. Gwinnett's holiday toddies, else next time you might come to real harm or give significant offense. A gentleman would not want that on his conscience, my boy."

Atticus shoved the woefully heavy mailbag at me. "I ain't a gentleman, 'case you forgot. I am a tiger." Enunciated with the unassailable dignity of the inebriate.

He spun about, righted himself on the doorjamb, and strutted off down the corridor, his little nose in the air. I closed the door after him, dumped the mail onto the desk blotter, and settled back onto Arthur's lumpy chair.

I had worked my way through about half the stack when a quiet tap on the door halted my progress.

"Come in."

The butler stepped inside and closed the door. "Vicar to see you, my lord. He said he hadn't an appointment, but he has joyous news and thought you should be the first to know."

Arthur had been sparing with advice, but he'd warned me about vicars bearing good news. After announcing that some parishioner's prize sow had safely presented the world with twelve new piglets, Mr. Humboldt would bend the conversation around to the need for a new roof over the nave, new hymnals, or a new bell.

Arthur had told him two years ago to give up on the bell. Backward we might be out in the shires, but we knew that divine services commenced at ten of the clock on the morning of the Sabbath, the same as they had for hundreds of years.

"Show him in," I said, moving aside the dozen epistles I had yet to read. "And send along the requisite tray, please. Did he walk the distance?"

"Afraid so, my lord."

"Give us twenty minutes and then have a sleigh brought around. I'll take him home myself."

Seeing Vicar safely back to his manse qualified as a good deed, and playing truant for the sake of a good deed counted as only half a truancy.

Arthur would doubtless have agreed with me on that point.

Vicar was still bouncing about on the seat of the sleigh beside me when I drew the horse up to the front door of the vicarage. After the jingling of the harness bells and Vicar's endless chatter, the ensuing silence came as a benediction to the ears.

The vicarage itself was spacious, some clergy being prone to large families, though our house of worship was a humble exponent of the species.

Gray granite construction, the foundation dating back to at least Norman times, and possibly the Viking days before that. The same stone used to encircle the oldest part of the graveyard, and more used for walkways. In winter, the whole was rather depressing, but in temperate weather, climbing roses, irises, and assorted other posies lent the churchyard a rustic charm.

The bell tower rose to a modest height, a gray sentinel against a lighter gray sky.

"All the way from London," Vicar was saying for the dozenth time. "And in time for Christmas! Come, my lord, you must see this splendid wonder for yourself!"

I had seen my share of church bells. As a boy, I'd sneaked up the tower along with Harry and played royal archer on market days. When I'd turned ten, the old bell had cracked and been retired. On reconnaissance in Spain, I'd climbed many a church tower for observation purposes, and once, I'd hidden in a bell tower for the duration of a freezing, spectacularly starry night.

Fear for one's life made keeping warm doubly difficult.

Vicar fairly leaped to the ground and held the gate for me. "Did you know, my lord, that this bell contains gold?"

Also silver, arsenic, lead, zinc, and tin, though the bulk of the metal was copper. "Does it really?" I secured the reins and climbed down more decorously.

"A mere dash, of course, but gold... In olden times, good souls would toss their gold and silver coins into the foundry as a church bell was made to sweeten the tone."

I'd heard the same from Mr. Mears himself, master founder at the Whitechapel Bell Foundry. For a sum certain, he'd included the appropriate tokens in this bell as well.

"What an interesting notion."

"Gold *and* silver. If we are to have only the tolling bell, we can be proud that it's of the best construction."

Mears had tried to talk me into a proper ring of bells, such as sizable establishments boasted, but that would have required a new and larger tower. Then too, change ringing was an art, and to my knowledge, nobody in our humble surrounds was acquainted with it.

"We haven't had a proper death knell for nearly twenty years," Vicar said, bustling up the walkway. "Vicar Winthrop was most distressed to retire from his post without having the bell replaced, but times have been challenging, have they not, my lord?"

For most of that twenty years, times had been bellicose, and Britain had the staggering debt to show for her martial enthusiasms.

"We hope for better days," I said, preceding Vicar into the church.

The bell sat upon a wooden trestle in the vestibule, looking like a great, drab bonnet. If Mears had cast it to agreed-upon specifications, our bell was a little over two-and-a-half feet across at the rim and weighed something less than a quarter ton.

"Isn't it beautiful?" Vicar said, beaming. "If only we knew who our benefactor was."

"That is a puzzle. We'll let subsequent generations rack their brains over it, shall we? I am more concerned with how we get the thing hung." Mears had explained to me the art and science involved, but executing same required carpenters and joiners expert in the craft.

"The fellows who delivered the bell said they will send us the bell-hanging crew for that miracle next week. One can hardly contain one's joy."

To see Humboldt in such transports was satisfying, but I hadn't procured the bell for him. I'd started the process nearly a year ago, when Arthur had muttered about being unable to ring a proper death knell upon our father's passing. Papa had been gone for some time, but this failure to uphold tradition had apparently bothered his successor.

And yet, in the greater order of needs and priorities, Arthur had been unable to justify the expense of a church bell. Not when tens of thousands of soldiers were returning from war to beg in the streets, and more thousands would never return at all and leave entire families destitute.

For their sakes, for the sake of all who would never have a proper funeral toll, I'd engaged Mears and company. By happenstance, my order had been completed in time for Yuletide. I had notified Vicar anonymously that a bell was in the offing, and he'd brought news of our impending good fortune straight to Caldicott Hall.

"I do believe," he said, tracing a reverent hand around the bell's shoulder, "this is the most perfect bell I ever did see. Mrs. Humboldt agrees."

"Well, it's our bell, and thus it must be a very fine bell indeed. You still have no idea whose largesse is responsible?"

"One suspects the duke, and it would be just like him to make such a magnanimous gesture when he's not on hand to hear our thanks, but I cannot be certain. Squire Pettigrew certainly has the means and is overdue for a display of beneficence, if I might say so without attracting any celestial lightning bolts. Lady Dorcas is devout and one to observe the niceties."

That I was not among the suspects should have pleased me. "The author of our good fortune wished to act anonymously. We must respect their preferences. We have the bell. Its peal will summon the faithful, celebrate their nuptials, and commend them to eternity's embrace. Life in the village will regain one gesture of the grace it enjoyed in former times."

"Just so, my lord, just so. Mrs. Humboldt would agree. Gift horses and so forth. I cannot wait to hear this bell. What do you suppose we should name it?"

Now that was going a bit too far. Bells had names, of course. Bells that hung in rounds and were rung in proper peals.

"Perhaps Mrs. Humboldt will have some ideas," I said. "I'd really rather not make the horse stand for too long in this weather, Vicar. I am overjoyed to see the bell has safely arrived and will look forward to the day when it's hung in its tower."

"Of course, my lord, of course. And may that day come soon. My thanks again for seeing me home. Are you sure you won't come to the vicarage for a cup of tea?"

Darkness was already encroaching, so early did the sun set in deep midwinter. "Thank you, no. The hour grows late, and I must be on my way." The *Report of the Committee for the Investigation of Wages for Masons, Apprentices, and Hod Carriers Engaged in the Construction of Enclosure Walls in the West Riding* waited for no man.

Arthur had declared that the art of proper leave-taking lay in knowing when to physically step away. Hovering turned parting into an endless exercise in good wishes and small talk. I took my brother's advice, replaced my hat upon my head, and left Humboldt beaming at the bell like a papa making the acquaintance of his newly hatched firstborn son.

I climbed into the sleigh, arranged the lap robe for maximum protection from the elements, and took up the reins.

"Walk on, Ladon."

The horse, only too happy to move in the direction of home, struck out on the lane that circled the green. He was an older specimen, one I'd drafted for teaching Atticus the rudiments of riding and driving. What Ladon lacked in elegance, he made up for in sturdiness and patience.

Once we cleared the arched bridge that marked the western entrance to the green, I let Ladon pick up the trot. I could have fallen asleep at the ribbons, and he would have seen me safely home, trusty soul that he was.

I wasn't asleep. I was annoyed.

The shape of a bell was simple, its parts from widest to narrowest being mouth, lip, waist, shoulder, and crown. The structure atop the whole, the part where the bell was secured to its headstock, was the canon. The canon was cast with the bell itself for the sake of greater strength. It provided one aspect of the bell founder's art where embellishment was permitted regardless of the pitch at which the bell was intended to ring.

I had specified that the canon embellishments on our bell were to resemble angels. The bell sitting in the church vestibule had boasted embellishments, but they'd been shaped like lilies.

Either the foremost bell founder in the realm had failed to follow directions, or he'd sent us the wrong ruddy bell.

If I called Mears's attention to his error, my attempt at anonymous generosity would degenerate into endless correspondence, talk in the churchyard, and an absence of joyous pealing on Christmas morning.

"So we have the wrong bell," I muttered as Ladon trotted between the Caldicott Hall gateposts. "Nobody will know." The sound of the bell was supposed to summon the faithful, chase away demons, and repel violent storms. Angels or lilies were immaterial to those jobs.

I handed Ladon off to the stable lads and faced the façade of my home, a dark shape looming against the coming winter night. My completed errand should have left me pleased with life and with myself. I was playing at being Father Christmas, though the timing of the bell's arrival was purely fortuitous.

"I asked for angels," I said to nobody in particular, my breath clouding before my half-frozen nose and chin. "A few little angels on the bell, and Mears even showed me sketches."

A voice in my head that sounded very like dear, departed Harry warned me that I was becoming Uncle Terrence well before I'd earned my curmudgeonly allotment of years.

But then, Harry was sporting about with his harp and wings. He wasn't inundated daily with the most soporific flood of correspondence ever to cross the desk of man. He wasn't missing his beloved to the depths of his soul. Harry wasn't facing weeks of Uncle Terrence's dubious company, nor was he regretting that he'd ever encouraged Arthur to travel.

As I made my way to the house's north portico, I chided myself for whining rather a lot for a fellow who had reasonable health, considerable wealth, and a loving family. A fellow whose country was more or less at peace. A fellow who was, for better or for worse, heir to a dukedom.

I was whining a very great lot indeed. Worse yet, my dolorous turn of thought could become a step on the road to the dangerous terrain known as melancholia.

I'd been captive to the blue devils for months both times when I'd mustered out. The stretch after Waterloo had been hellish. I'd been unable to concentrate on anything longer than a sonnet, uninterested in food, unable to sleep soundly. Overwhelmingly sad about everything and nothing, seeking solitude even when suffocatingly lonely.

Godmama had hauled me by the ear back into the literal sunlight, and a series of investigations since then had kept me preoccupied with other people's troubles. No investigations beckoned to me now, and for all I knew, I might never again involve myself with missing heirs, errant wives, or purloined pups.

Never again. An altogether gloomy thought.

"Please not at Yuletide," I muttered, though the black moods were notorious for coming and going on no discernible schedule. "I will brood and sulk and wander the night at length in the New Year if I must, but please no blue devils at Yuletide."

I let myself into the relative warmth of the Hall and had barely got my hat, coat, and scarf off when Her Grace came upon me.

"Waylaid by Vicar, were you? What was his great news? Let me guess. Mercy Holderness's nanny goat had triplets again."

"Unlikely at this time of year. Somebody has gifted St. Scholastica's with a new bell."

A footman lighting sconces—Young Jamison, in fact—stopped between candles. "A new bell, for our little church?"

Truly, discipline among the domestics was slipping. "A tolling bell. Lovely in its way. Not very large as these things go, but Vicar was in transports."

The duchess sent me a curious look. "What do you know of church bells, my lord?"

"A bit." Mears had spent the better part of a day lecturing, sketching, and waxing poetical about them. "I found myself in many a bell tower in Spain because they provide a good vantage point for reconnoitering unknown territory."

Her Grace's expression became carefully blank, as it did every time I mentioned my years in uniform.

"Well, that's just grand," Jamison said, moving on to the next sconce. "A new bell, and at Yuletide. Did Vicar say who'd done us this good turn?"

"An anonymous benefactor. Vicar claims not to know."

"Squire Petty-Grump, likely," Jamison said, replacing the glass over the flame. "Has a lot to atone for, you ask me. Didn't want us to plant him without a proper tolling."

"Now, Jamison," Her Grace said, "no disparaging the neighbors unless you want Father Christmas to bring you a lump of coal." She softened her reprimand with a smile and took a few steps up the corridor.

I was prepared to be less charitable with Jamison on the topic of encouraging Atticus to imbibe, but the duchess turned and addressed me again.

"Oh, Julian. More good news. I've had word that Aunt Bertha will also be joining us for the holidays. I'll put her in the Rose Suite, and it will be just like old times."

Her Grace swanned off after firing that salvo, and I nearly ran howling back out into the night.

"I'll warn the staff," Jamison muttered. "We've been spared the past few years—winters lately have been too blasted cold for much travel—but Mrs. G and Mrs. H will want to know."

"Raise the drawbridge, lower the portcullis, man the arrow slits, and bar the postern gate," I said. Uncle Terrible *and* Aunt Bother. "Jamison, I'll have a toddy in the study."

"In the study, my lord?"

I thought of the half pile of correspondence waiting for me there, soon to be joined by full piles and deluges and inundations. The masons and their apprentices and hod carriers ...

"Hang the correspondence. I will enjoy my toddy in my apartment, and in future, please let the staff know to heat the study exclusively with peat."

"Aye, my lord. Peat for the study, a toddy for your nerves. Just so."

He scampered off, likely to personally sample the spices blended with my restorative, and I did not begrudge him his tipple—this time. Aunt Bertha was a terror, plain and simple, and she was invading at the same time Uncle Terry would be underfoot.

The Battle of Nations would be a mere skirmish compared to the hostilities those two could engage in a weekday breakfast table.

"Make it a double," I called after Jamison, though in my present mood, I could have done justice to the whole pot.

CHAPTER THREE

Arthur's study was positioned in a corner of the Hall's first floor. The windows provided a fine view of the front drive and its lime alley and of the path that led to the stable and assorted other outbuildings. Another venerable stand of lime trees kept the working parts of the estate visually separate from the Hall's domestic splendor, and the blending of the park with the home wood gave the whole surrounds a peaceful sense of unity.

I loved those lime trees, the stately alley, the gently undulating hedgerow, the occasional specimens gracing the park or edging the wood. They took on a particularly luminous green when the foliage was bathed in sunshine. In autumn, they glowed a mellow gold before carpeting the grass in yellow leaves. Most had passed the four-century mark of their earthly span.

The trees were a sylvan reminder that winters came and went, centuries came and went, and so did visits from the family experts in peevishness and truculence.

As if to test the mettle of my conclusion, a sizable coach and four came trotting from the lime alley and rattled halfway around the circular drive. I did not recognize the equipage or the matched grays pulling it, nor was I expecting callers.

"Not yet," I said, setting aside the hungry masons of the West Riding. "Please don't let the hordes descend yet." Though neither Terrence nor Bertha could tolerate extravagance, and the coach rocking to a halt at the foot of the steps was splendid indeed.

To my immense relief, a fellow in a kilt emerged, followed by a lady in a green plaid cloak and a small boy. Somebody passed a trussed-up little bundle into the lady's arms, and my day became leavened with joy.

Two minutes later, I was surrounded by the noise, rumpus, and general mayhem occasioned by the return of any one of my sisters to the family seat.

"Jules, Jules, you are looking marvelous," Ginny said, alternately hugging me around the bundle of baby she carried and inspecting me with sororal thoroughness. "My brother has turned Viking on us, and they were such an interesting lot. Declan hasn't gone through his Viking phase yet, but I'm told it's unavoidable. Declan, make your bow to your Uncle Julian."

Declan, a dark-eyed copy of his strapping Scottish papa, flopped over at the waist. "Good day, Uncle Julian."

"Declan, welcome to Caldicott Hall. What an impressive set of lungs you have."

"Aye, he does," Lachlan, Earl of Kerrick, said. "Gets that from his mother, and just wait until you hear the wean. Puts banshees to shame." He was clearly proud of his little banshee and clearly in good health himself.

Kerrick was a throwback to the days when the Highlanders had been the tallest and brawniest men in Europe, part Viking, part Celt, and all fierceness. Ginny had met him at a cousin's wedding and promptly taken him captive. Declan had arrived a mere six months after the vows had been spoken, which my father had declared a fine example of upholding Caldicott family tradition.

"I look forward to making my niece's acquaintance," I said, "but might we move the introductions into the Hall?"

As I spoke, a second carriage drew up behind the first. This one was a humbler conveyance, doubtless housing the lady's maid, valet, and perhaps Declan's governess. In the usual course, those good souls would have been taken around to the side entrance, while the baggage piled on the roof and the boot would have been unloaded at the porte cochere.

A lone female passenger climbed down the steps, and my heart rose.

"Excuse me." I dodged around Declan and between Ginny and her spouse and took the latest visitor's hand in my own. "By God, you escaped. Never have I been so glad to see a familiar face."

Hyperia West looked a bit fatigued, but nearly as happy to see me as I was to see her.

"Jules." She treated me to a quick hug. "Ginny offered. Healy did not want to offend the earl by refusing the countess's generosity. At the first change, I graciously gave the nursemaid my seat in the traveling coach. Baby Orla in a taking can be quite the challenge to the ears."

I tucked Hyperia's hand around my arm. "I am never letting you out of my sight again. My delight in your presence is limitless, and my fondest hope has been granted." Wages in the West Riding, tippling staff, and a bell with the wrong canon design all faded to passing details.

To have Hyperia at my side put right every discontent, frustration, and woe, to a slightly unnerving extent.

"I've missed you too," she said as we joined Ginny's entourage climbing the steps to the terrace and passing into the Hall's drafty foyer. "Healy will follow soon. He promised. I am not sure what inspires him to tarry in Town when most of Society has removed to the shires, but he isn't frequenting the gaming hells that I know of."

"He had better not be." Wagering, drink, and rash accusations had nearly seen Healy West ruined. He was putting his finances to rights, but the process would take time.

I stood arm in arm with Hyperia as Her Grace welcomed Ginny, Kerrick, and the children to the Hall. My mother had been a beauty in her day, a stately redhead in an age where delicate blondes had been all the rage. She was beautiful still, though gold threaded her russet locks at the temple, and she needed spectacles when tending to her correspondence.

Watching her tear up at the sight of Ginny holding Orla, I was struck anew by the fact that Dorothea, Duchess of Waltham, was a *grandmama* many times over. While her three sons had produced no legitimate offspring, her four daughters were populating their respective nurseries with regular additions.

Mother and daughter embraced carefully around the baby, then the duchess drew back to peer more closely at Orla.

"She has Claudius's eyes," the duchess pronounced, referring to her late spouse. "Oh, she has his eyes to the life. She'll have the world wrapped around her little finger by her second birthday, see if she doesn't."

"Babies," Hyperia murmured. "They turn us into watering pots."

To my shock, Hyperia's eyes were shining too. "I thought you didn't care for babies?"

She professed a mortal fear of parturition, for which I had no argument. Women died in childbirth at about the same rate Wellington's men had died in battle, and those were bad odds. Hyperia and I were unofficially engaged—that was, we had more than an understanding and less than a public commitment—but we were taking our time with the whole business.

Of necessity.

"Do hush," Hyperia said, accepting my handkerchief and dabbing at her eyes. "I'm tired, and Christmas approaches, and I am so very glad to see you."

"I suspect you are in need of a toddy, but mind you go carefully. Mrs. Gwinnett is already in fine holiday form."

"Julian, might you take care of introductions in the nursery?" Mama asked. "I will see our adult guests settled."

I bowed over Hyperia's hand. "I will find you before supper. Depend upon it."

I left her in possession of both my handkerchief and my heart and snatched young Declan up for a piggyback ride.

"You have a cousin in the nursery," I said as the boy waved a grinning farewell to his parents. "His name is Leander, your late Uncle Harry's only begotten son." As best we could gather, anyway. "He's been looking very much forward to making your acquaintance."

Declan was no sprite. I'd put his height at just under four feet and his weight at about six stone. Robust for his age, but then, Kerrick topped my own six feet, two inches by at least an inch, and Ginny was tallish and sturdy as well.

By the time we reached the nursery suite, I was puffing a bit and happy to set the boy on his own two feet.

"Does Leander have a baby sister?" Declan asked.

"He has not been so blessed, to the best of my knowledge. Why?"

"Because Orla is loud and stinky, and she only says 'thank you' and 'shoe' and 'bye-bye' and baby words. She will stay with Mama and Papa at night, but if Leander had a baby sister, she might be in the nursery all night."

"No worries. You two fellows will have the nursery suite to yourselves, save for a few armies, some doting nursemaids, an occasional visit from myself or Her Grace, and frequent interruptions from the staff."

We reached the door to the playroom, where Leander spent much of his time. The footmen took the boy out to see the horses in the morning, the maids let him tag after them down to the kitchen, and I paid my avuncular visits.

Not an isolated life, but hardly the rollicking mischief Harry and I had got up to regularly.

"Why is your hair like that?" Declan asked.

"Like?"

"White at the ends, but blondish in the middle, and reddish near your head? Mama didn't say you'd have odd hair."

What had Ginny led him to expect? What sort of answer would she want me to give this innocently rude nephew?

I stuck to facts. "My hair turned white when I was taken prisoner by the French. I'm regaining my natural color gradually, or most of it. My locks were a shade darker than your papa's before I was captured." Except I hadn't been captured. I'd surrendered to the enemy without a fight, which was a violation of every military ethic in every army from every age.

"Mama says you'll marry Miss West."

"I hope to, eventually, but enough prevarication. Time to meet your cousin." Kerrick was at heart a shy man, despite trotting out a convincing rendition of the boisterous kilted laddie on public occasions. Declan appeared to have a bit of his father's retiring nature, with which I sympathized.

I rapped on the door, waited long enough for a boy to put away whatever forbidden toy he was playing with, and then proceeded into the warmth of the playroom.

"Leander Caldicott, you have a guest." I was in the process of changing Leander's name by deed poll, with the consent of his mother and Arthur's emphatic support. "Declan, greet your cousin."

The two boys eyed each other warily. Leander was shorter by two inches, though hardly diminutive for his age. He had Harry's brownish hair and a chin that could jut like Harry's too.

"I know all the battles," Leander said, chin much in evidence. "I have tons of armies."

"I know all the battles too," Declan said. "Let's do Bannockburn. You can be King Edward's men, and I'll be the Bruce."

"Bannock what?"

Both boys looked at me. "Bannockburn," I said. "A decisive battle in the fight to regain Scottish independence. Robert the Bruce prevailed with his smaller army over King Edward's larger forces.

Edward's army had been weakened by extended forced marches, and Robert chose his terrain and tactics shrewdly."

"I can show you," Declan said. "We need a castle and a marsh and a burn and some woods."

"Do I get any cavalry soldiers?" Leander asked.

"Hundreds and hundreds, but they can't save you because of the marsh, the woods, and the burn. You also have longbowmen, but they can't save you because once the battle is joined, you'd kill your own men as well as mine with your archers."

"You lose the battle," I said, "but Scotland eventually loses its independence as well, or most of it."

Declan scowled. "Not in a battle. Not in a fair fight. Papa says a parcel of merchants and nobles sold Scotland for a mess of pottage."

"And yet," I said, "Scotland kept her laws, her schools, and her church, didn't she? She also gained access to every British port in the world and is on her way to becoming a world-renowned shipbuilding center."

Leander apparently had no interest in the history lesson. He'd gone to a toy chest and begun setting boxes on the carpet.

"We do Bannockburn," he said, "and then Salamanca. I get to be Wellington, and you can be the French."

"What's Salamanca?"

Salamanca had been a bloodbath, but because casualties had been better than two-to-one in Wellington's favor, it was the sort of bloodbath characterized as a British victory. Madrid had been liberated (albeit temporarily) within weeks.

I left them to it, the nurserymaid embroidering a glove in the corner nearest the hearth. Boys played with soldiers. I certainly had, as did countless lads across the realm.

And yet, I didn't care to see the enthusiasm my nephews showed for reenacting death and violence. Didn't care for it at all. Leander had been playing with soldiers since he'd arrived at the Hall, and I'd reluctantly run through a few battles with him.

As I made my way to Hyperia's assigned apartment, I asked

myself why hadn't I read to him instead? Sketched with him? Taught him a verse or two?

With an effort that reminded me of carrying Declan up three flights of steps, I pushed the doubts and questions away, because they, too, could be symptomatic of a mind flirting with melancholia. Every answer could point in the direction of failure and inadequacy, and I had already spent far too much time staring into that abyss.

I rapped on Hyperia's door and found my beloved poking air into the fire. Her sitting room was chilly, doubtless owing to her unexpected arrival, and the fireplace opened on two sides—the bedroom and sitting room, both—which meant neither space was heated as effectively.

"I wasn't quite honest with you," Hyperia said, replacing the poker on the stand. "In fact, I might have fibbed."

My heart nigh stopped beating. "About?"

"Healy," she said. "He's up to something, Jules. Something he's trying to keep from me, and I had to get away from him, lest he involve me in some stupid scheme again."

"A scheme such as marrying you off for money?" He'd tried that once before, the varlet.

"I don't know, and I don't trust him."

"And he worries you."

She nodded, and when I took her into my arms, she came willingly, though I could feel the distraction in her.

"Then I am worried too, my dear. Tell me what you've observed," I said, "and we'll tackle the puzzle together."

I made the offer with a shameless sense of relief. I thrived on a good puzzle, and the daily conundrum of how to win the battle with Arthur's stultifying correspondence didn't qualify.

"I don't want to burden you," Hyperia said, slipping her arms about my waist.

"Please, dear lady. Burden me. If I cannot sink my teeth into a good investigation soon, I will lose what few wits I still claim."

She must have heard the sincerity of my plea, because she led me to the sofa and began an interesting recitation.

"My lady is napping," Kerrick said, pouring libation from a flask into a glass. "She does that a lot. What of yours?"

"The same." I'd left Hyperia snuggled up in bed, the most tempting picture imaginable on a chilly winter afternoon. "She's worried about her brother, who should join us in the next week or so."

"An occupational hazard of sisterhood. My wife frets about her brothers too." Kerrick lifted his glass in my direction. "To children who are through with the infernal teething and to the parents who survive it with them."

I saluted with my brandy. "Why would Ginny worry about me and Arthur?"

Kerrick settled onto the sofa before the library's largest hearth. For a big man, he moved quietly, and he also spoke quietly in the normal course.

"Arthur, for the obvious reasons and also because the poor lad doesn't have much enjoyment in life, save for, again, the obvious. To send him off frolicking with Banter was inspired."

I came down on the same sofa—the warmest perch in the whole room—a few feet away. "I thought so, too, at the time. Now... If Arthur has any sense, he won't come home, Kerrick. He'll find a comfortable little chateau whose previous owners expired at the hands of French Republicanism, and he'll set up housekeeping with Banter. We'll be lucky to see him for a few weeks in summer every five years."

"If you think His Grace of Waltham could stay away from his own patch that long, you're daft."

"The estate is lovely, I grant you, but the responsibilities that come with it, and with the title..."

Kerrick held his glass up to the light. "Aye, you feel like you can't breathe. Like a wanted man. Serve on this delegation, sit on that committee, call upon the occasional ambassador, and prance around at Court twice a year. When is a man allowed to take his son out for a wee hack or read a bit of poetry to his wife? You want my earldom? You may have it, provided I can keep the croft behind the lea rig, a good team, and my family."

"Do you mean that?"

"Some days, laddie, I do."

Arthur had no wife, and he and Banter would for the most part have to content themselves with the appearance of being good friends and neighbors. Banter's son was a cuckoo in another's nest, though being raised along with all the other nestlings at the Banter family seat. As for Arthur, he'd chosen me to serve as Leander's guardian simply because I planned to bide at the family seat in the duke's absence.

"How does His Grace manage, Kerrick? How does he get up every day and tilt at a pile of correspondence as voluminous as it is inane? How does he pretend to care about menus that offer far fancier delicacies than he prefers—year after year—and do the pretty with the legions of neighbors who all want to claim a close acquaintance with the ranking title?"

Kerrick sent me an unreadable glance. "Arthur was raised to be that duke, for one thing, and our Arthur is a plodder, for another. Unlike you, who enjoyed the challenge of learning new terrain and new dialects, Arthur is comforted by routine and predictability. He reserves all his adventurousness for the personal aspects of his life, or so Ginny has explained to me. Canny woman, my Ginny. Witness, she married me."

He finished his drink and rose to set the glass on the sideboard, then commenced inspecting the decanters.

"The amontillado is excellent," I said. "One of Harry's favorites."

"Sherry doesn't agree with me." Kerrick poured a serving of Armagnac into a clean glass. "This will do nicely. You are not to invoke the Ghost of Saint Harry to ruin your holiday. You did that last year, and your family was too timorous to interfere with that nonsense. You are fortunate that Orla's arrival kept me in the north, or I'd have sorted you out properly."

"I removed myself to London, the better to continue convalescing after my various ordeals." And once in London, I'd sunk into a misery so profound that fear for my own existence had burned down to a mere ember of honor.

Kerrick snorted and resumed his seat in the corner of the sofa. "Convalescence. Aye, of course. Tell it to your horse. You went off to brood and grieve. No shame in it, but Ginny fretted over you something abominable, and her dealing with childbed at the time. You're to be jolly this Yuletide."

"Or what?"

"Or I'll beat the English stuffing right out of you. Nothing like a good bout of fisticuffs to restore the humors."

"Said the man trying to space his children."

Kerrick sipped his drink. "Mind your tongue, though I do concede you have a point. Ginny wants more children, rather insistently. I've withstood temptation thus far because my countess is tired and cross much of the time, and we have years and years to grow our family. Besides, I have four younger brothers, and they're a healthy lot. The earldom won't go begging."

"The dukedom might." The brandy was working its dubious magic, as was too long a span of time without any man save Harry's ghost to confide in.

If Harry had been my companion, he would have been smoking a cheroot, despite Her Grace's prohibition against smoking in the library, and he would have been the one complaining about the burden of being a ducal heir.

"The dukedom is secure," Kerrick replied. "Miss Hyperia has plans for you, laddie. Depend upon it. Ginny agrees with me, as do her sisters. York is betting you'll hold out for a bit, but he's in the minority."

York was Kerrick's nickname for Meggie's husband, another earl, who hailed from Yorkshire rather than Scotland.

"You've placed bets?"

"Aye. We can't be moaning about our teething bairns all the time. I like your Miss Hyperia, by the way. She's sensible and noticing. Didn't let the dancing dandies turn her head, though, of course, they weren't wearing kilts. Much harder to resist a kilted laddie."

"You've clearly been at your flask the whole way down from Town."

"Laddie mine, I've been at my flask the whole way down from Scotland. Fatherhood imbues a man with fortitude of necessity. So what's your plan?"

Kerrick was not sozzled. He was coaxing me to believe we'd achieved a slightly tipsy sort of coziness, such as men frequently enjoyed at later hours and in exclusively masculine venues.

And bless him and his kilt, he was family, he was a good sort, and he was inviting me to enlist his aid. For form's sake, I stalled a bit. "Plan for what?"

"How will you go about being the Christmas duke? The job would be easier in Scotland. We don't make a great fuss over Christmas, as you do down here. We focus on the New Year, the proper celebration of which we take seriously. You lot turn Christmas into days and days of nonsense, and for that, a man needs a wee plan."

His diction was growing more Scottish, and outside the tall library windows, darkness encroached.

"I have a plan," realizing that I spoke the truth, only as I said the words. "I will be an anonymous Father Christmas."

"A ghost? We have enough of those already. My grandmother has been gone twenty years, and I still hear her voice threatening me with a lump of coal. She was half English." Said in tones that implied allowances must be made.

"I won't be a ghost, but I will put in train events without attribution."

"In secret, ye mean. Like a reiver, then."

"Like a stranger who passes through without anybody much noticing, until flowers bloom around the fountain the next spring." Holland bulbs Meggie had sent me, of all the whimsical notions. I'd planted them around a poor village's well in hopes somebody would water them, should they decide to grow and blossom in Spanish soil.

Also because the nuns in that village had been kind and generous in a time of war.

"Why the stealth?"

"Because a supposed drover on his way back to the hills had no business carrying Dutch bulbs in his kit. Those bulbs could have seen me killed, or worse, if I'd been taken by the Bonapartists."

Kerrick ran a hand through dark auburn hair. "No, lad. Not 'why creep about the booshes in Spain?' You're done with that. This is England, God help me. Why sneak about your own Hall at Yuletide?"

"You said I needed a plan, and I agree. The anonymous part has evolved organically."

He squinted at me. "Next, you'll be quoting Tacitus. Never could stand that sort of cleverness."

"No more spirits for you, Kerrick. We've supper to get through."

"And the night. The nights can be the worst. Little blighter slept most of the way down from Town—the rocking of the coach works a treat between changes—and she'll be in good form tonight. Tell me about your plan to steal Christmas."

I judged him sober enough to hold a confidence, only just, though few confidences should be safe from the intimacy of a healthy marriage.

"Last year," I began, "when I was in such low spirits, I decided that our dear departed deserved their death knells. Our village church hasn't had a bell since my childhood, and I took it upon myself to rectify the situation. Arranging to replace the cracked bell was one thing I could take off Arthur's endless list of charitable duties." At the time, I'd also reasoned that my own demise should be marked by the traditional tolling, for the comfort of what mourners I would have.

Even when profoundly morose, I'd assumed I would have a few, in deference to the family's standing if nothing else.

"A church bell matters," Kerrick said. "Cowbells matter too."

"You aren't fooling me, Kerrick. Orla is your second child, and Ginny intends that you have more. You are not foxed."

"Not yet," he said sanctimoniously. "The Scots are noted for their tenacity. And cowbells do matter."

"The church bell has arrived in the village, and Vicar Humboldt is determined that we should have it hung before Christmas. A crew will be on hand shortly to see it done, but I've kept my connection to the bell to myself."

"Without attribution," he said, enunciating each syllable. "One applauds your modesty."

"It isn't modesty. Somebody had to see to the matter, and I was in a position to do so. I've also found a good pony for my nephew. The boy will be presented with his steed on Christmas morning, again without attribution. The little equine will appear in a previously vacant stall, with a note on the halter declaring him the property of Leander Caldicott."

"Giving the lad the name, are ye?"

"He's Harry's son, and Arthur and I would not have it any other way for our nephew."

Kerrick finished his drink. "He's my nephew, too, mind, and cousin to my children. I'll enjoy another wee nip, I do believe. What else have you planned in the way of unattributed gifts?"

"That is my secret." My plan was far from complete and rather lacking in details. I'd enjoyed organizing the purchase of the bell, though, and enjoyed the Great Pony Search. "What is not secret is that Uncle Terrence and Aunt Bertha have recently been added to the guest list."

Kerrick ambled over to the sideboard and filled his flask from the decanter of Armagnac. "I knew we should have stayed in Scotland.

Both of the old besoms at once? Perhaps you could have Father Christmas anonymously kidnap me? A fine old holiday tradition in the Borders, kidnapping earls and such."

"Her Grace feels a sense of duty, and this is her home, and she is our holiday hostess. The guest list has been largely up to her."

"Shall I lend you one of my spare flasks?" Kerrick hadn't spilled a drop of the Armagnac.

"I have my own collection, thank you. You'd best go wake your wife if she's to have time to change for dinner."

"Good thought. We might be a bit late. Travel wears a body out."

"Orla is not yet a year old. Be strong, Kerrick, or you will get that bout of fisticuffs you mentioned so fondly."

"If so, you'll have to wait in line behind the duchess and Arthur. The Caldicotts don't mince words when it comes to the proper care of my countess. I've always liked that about them. You'd think there was some Scot not too far back on the family tree."

He sauntered off, kilt swinging, and left me to contemplate ghosts, plans, and possibilities.

CHAPTER FOUR

"I thought you should be told." Conrad Sigafoose, curate and local fixture since my childhood, regarded the large wooden box sitting in the wagon bed. "These fellows weren't keen on the delay, but your lordship deserved to be informed."

Some of my earliest ecclesiastical memories were of Mr. Sigafoose attempting to lead a children's choir in preparation for a Christmas pageant, while Harry attempted to lead the choir astray. Little Lord Harry would purposely sing off-key, tie Mabel Potts's braids in a knot, and make faces until Danny Bruderman burst out laughing.

Mr. Sigafoose had retaliated by assigning Harry a solo, and rehearsals had abruptly become more productive. Any deviation from strict decorum and, Harry had been warned, a children's duet for his naughty little lordship and the soprano of Mr. Sigafoose's choosing could be added to the program on short notice.

Over the years, Sigafoose had mellowed into a white-haired, genial, friend-at-large for all in the village. He offered spiritual comfort in the sickroom, a gentle voice from the pulpit, and rare dashes of subtle humor. He'd never married, and I had no idea if his unwed condition was due to lack of means or lack of a suitable parti.

The *fellows* Mr. Sigafoose had alluded to were four brawny specimens, collars turned up against the chill morning breeze. Their sallow complexions suggested they were London born and bred, as did their apparent unease in rural surrounds.

"May I see the bill of lading?" I asked.

Mr. Sigafoose passed me a single piece of paper. "Says paid in full, doesn't say by whom."

The bill of lading looked to be curiously in order, the letterhead recognizable as that of the Whitechapel Bell Foundry.

"Let's have a look at the goods." I hoisted myself into the wagon and appropriated a short, hooked crowbar sitting atop the wooden box. Some prying and yanking revealed a lot of chopped straw. Digging down, I found what appeared to be the canon of a sizable bell.

A canon with delicately wrought angels facing the compass points.

"We're not hauling that bell clear back to London without somebody in authority giving us the say-so," the largest of the four men said. "That's a proper tolling bell, bought and paid for, and we brung it here to Waltham village, exactly as directed. Don't nobody turn away a bell from the Whitechapel Bell Foundry without good reason."

He was tall, burly, and sporting at least a day's growth of dark beard, and yet, the pride he took in his association with a venerable business came through.

"Can you tell me who ordered this bell?" I asked, sliding the lid of the box back into place and banging it down with the crowbar.

"Some toff. Don't have a name. Youngish, but didn't look too long for this world, according to the foundrymen. Said they moved his order up on account of his health being not the best. Nobody canceled the order, so he must still be among the living, and here's his bell."

"There," I said, pointing across the green to the Goose and Gander, "is our local coaching inn, and they serve excellent fare. If you wouldn't mind availing yourselves of their hospitality, compliments of Caldicott Hall, I would appreciate an opportunity to consult Mr. Sigafoose regarding this lovely bell."

"Let's eat," said the smallest of the four, who had at least two inches of height on me and three stone of muscle. "Can't feel me ears, and I lost track of me toes twenty miles ago."

"Warm up," I said, "thaw out, fill your bellies, and sample the local ale. You won't get back to Town today even if you start off this instant. I do know that a bell was ordered for our humble house of worship, and the canon on this one fits the specifications described to me."

The four men looked to the driver, the oldest of the lot. "What of the horses and the bell?" he asked. "I don't like to leave a team standing in this bitter weather, and that bell cost a pretty penny."

Sigafoose beamed at them gently. "I can vouch for the safety of the bell in our churchyard. You good fellows can take the team over to the livery."

The driver nodded, and the little ballet of unhitching a team took place in less than a minute. Harness jingling in the breeze, the four equine behemoths were led around the green, their breath clouding white in the morning air.

"This is the right bell," I said to Sigafoose. "I spoke the truth when I said the bell's specifications had been described to me. The other bell has lilies atop it, while this one has angels."

"We've a spare bell, then?"

"I am not commissioning a second bell tower, sir." Somebody would suggest that a second tower could be constructed to house a dozen bells. Committees would be formed and prayers said. Complications would ensue of proportions only villages intent on good works were capable of, and I hadn't the fortitude for any of it.

Besides, we already had a perfectly functional tower awaiting its perfectly functional—if incorrect—bell.

"My lord was never one for telling tales," Sigafoose said, apropos of nothing I could divine. "But you know more than you are saying about this bell. It's not stolen, is it?"

"As far as I know, both bells boast of having a legitimate provenance. Both have apparently been paid for. Both delivered to our doorstep. Where is Mr. Humboldt?"

"Off regaling the bishop with tales of our good fortune. I have a suggestion."

"Now would be a good time to share it."

"I am responsible for services in Hop Bottom twice a month. Their church is larger than ours and also lacks a bell. Melted down for the war effort in the last century, or possibly the century before, war efforts being the Englishman's perennial burden."

Hop Bottom, named for the preferred local crop and the low-lying land where it thrived, was a few miles north of Waltham. Too small to have its own market, it nonetheless had its own house of worship.

"You are suggesting this bell be sent along to Hop Bottom?" I disliked the idea. *This* bell was *my* bell, with angels where angels were supposed to be, and I wanted *my* bell tolling for *my* funeral—or my nuptials, should that happy occasion befall me.

"Does my lord have another idea? Folk in Hop Bottom are as hardworking and pious as folk in Waltham. We don't need two bells, but if Mr. Humboldt sees that a second bell has arrived..."

"Right. Prayers and jubilation, committees and reports. I suppose I won't care which bell is rung at my funeral, will I?"

Sigafoose studied the leaden sky. "Has my lord's health taken a turn for the worse?"

"My health has slowly improved for the past six months."

"I see."

An entire book of sermons lay in those two words, little homilies about gratitude and deliverance, learned diatribes on generosity, and an exegesis or three on blessed are they who refrain from hoarding quarter-ton bells.

"Are you free today, Sigafoose?"

He fluffed his scarf, a sober navy wool article that made the Saxon blue of his eyes snap. "Mayhap I am. What does milord have in mind?"

"I can't very well show up in the Hop Bottom churchyard bearing bells from afar, can I? Somebody might think the bell was my idea when, in fact, we have no notion who is sending these bells down from Town. If we must give one back come spring, we can sort that out later."

"Back to whom?"

"Precisely. People intent on doing anonymous good deeds must reckon with the confusion their version of generosity can entail. I propose that we send our London friends along to Hop Bottom—it's on the way back to Town—and that you accompany them as the bell's ambassador. Get the thing unloaded, and when the crew comes along to hang Humboldt's bell, we'll have them toddle up to Hop Bottom and see to that one as well."

If they weren't already commissioned to do so.

"Then we are giving this second bell to Hop Bottom?"

"We're finding an orphaned bell a good home. Now, my own ears are getting a bit chilled. Need we debate further?"

Sigafoose studied the sky at some length. "I suppose not. What do we say to Vicar Humboldt?"

"That both villages have apparently been blessed with bells. *Gaudeamus igitur*, and all that." *Therefore, let us be happy*, though I was frankly puzzled by the appearance of two bells. "Please hire a closed conveyance and driver from the livery to get you to Hop Bottom and back at my expense, Sigafoose. I do not like the look of those clouds."

Too cold to snow, some might say, but I'd never known the weather to accommodate such lore.

"Very good, my lord. I will negotiate with the good fellows from the foundry, and we will consider the matter resolved. Expect a toast or two at the Boxing Day reception to whomsoever provideth the bells."

I was mentally accommodating myself to accepting the lily-bell in my home church and also accommodating myself to the thought of a restorative in the Goose's snug prior to facing the ride back to the Hall, when the sense of Sigafoose's words penetrated my mind.

"Boxing Day reception?" Mama had referred to a fete, and I'd been too preoccupied to take proper notice. Too much correspondence, not enough fresh air.

Sigafoose smiled, looking as benevolent as Father Christmas. "You needn't look so worried, my lord. The reception moved from the Hall to the local assembly rooms after the death of the old duke. Expecting a house of mourning to host revelry was thought inappropriate, and thus the tradition evolved in a new direction. I'm sure Her Grace will send along some good wishes and good food. Her Boxing Day baskets are the pride of the shire. His Grace was most generous last year as well, and he did put in an appearance."

That was a hint, and another homily.

"I will surely add the reception to my Boxing Day schedule, Sigafoose, and invite Her Grace to join me."

He patted my shoulder, the holy rogue. "Very good, my lord. Now, if you won't begrudge an old man a tot of fortification, I've a bell to deliver."

Off he went across the green—which was covered in white—while I thanked the celestial powers for a narrow escape. I'd forgotten all about the Boxing Day festivities, but standing around sipping punch for half an hour could hardly be considered onerous. In years past, the reception had transpired at the Hall, an occasion of yet still more feasting, imbibing, song, and dance.

As a child, I'd thoroughly enjoyed the whole business, but I was no longer a child, and my perspective had matured accordingly. The entire village had tromped up to the Hall, the ballroom had been decorated as befit the season, and squire, duke, diker, and drover had enjoyed hours of merriment under the same roof.

The noise had been abominable, the punchbowl bottomless, and my subsequent bellyaches legendary.

A reception in the assembly rooms suited me quite well, thank you very much, and I would not blame the duchess if she sent me forth on that occasion as her designated emissary.

Perhaps I'd inveigle Kerrick, Laird of Many Flasks, into accompanying me.

A light snow was falling by the time I trotted Atlas back to the Hall, and my spirits were falling too. My grand gesture, my great anonymous benevolence to the village and surrounds, would toll in Hop Bottom forevermore.

Not quite the fate I'd had in mind for my bell, but Sigafoose had been right too: The neighbors to the immediate north were as deserving of a bell as the neighbors closer to the Hall's gates.

I was silently lecturing myself along those lines when I swung down from a cold saddle, suffered the predictable, painful shock to my feet and ankles, and handed Atlas's reins to a groom.

"We've company, my lord."

The news was conveyed in less-than-cheery tones. "Company?"

"Aye, and you might want to take your time returning to the Hall."

I hid from no man. "Who is gracing us with their presence, Peters?"

He glanced over his shoulder while Atlas waited patiently, snowflakes dotting his dark mane. "Two aunties. The older lads call them Bother and Crosspatch, but I don't think those are their proper names."

"Two aunties?" *But Her Grace invited only the one.* Or only the one had invited herself. "Aunt Bertha and Aunt Crosby?"

"That's not what the lads call 'em."

"I appreciate the warning."

"Come along, horse, and there's a bucket of oats in it for ye."

Atlas trundled off, and I considered my options. The snow meant business, the estate was devoid of hiding places suitable for the occasion, and Hyperia would be attempting to handle the invaders all on her lonesome. She was equal to the task, of course, but I was the nominal host at the Hall, and duty called.

My first mistake lay in not changing out of my riding boots when I went to greet my guests. My second was in failing to comb my damp hair. My third was in my militarily correct posture. The list grew from there.

"This is not a parade inspection, young man," Aunt Bertha said when I'd bowed over her hand. "You might have done us the courtesy of changing out of those wet boots, though. Tracking snow on your mother's carpets is the behavior of a heedless boy."

How Atticus would howl if he'd heard me scolded thusly. Aunt Bertha was shortish, roundish, and unpleasantish, though never more rude than her age and station entitled her to be.

"Wet hair will see you afflicted with an ague," Aunt Crosby said. She was tall and slender, and perhaps more pale than I recalled her being. When properly addressed, she was Lady Thomas Caldicott. What she lacked in vigor she made up for in vigilance. No lapse, transgression, or shortcoming ever went unremarked in her presence. That she'd married jovial Uncle Tommie, who'd appeared to be headed for permanent bachelorhood, went under the heading of Family Puzzles That Had Best Remain Unsolved.

In the years since Uncle Tommie had gone to his reward, Aunt Crosby had become a yet still more severe judge of human nature. To say she was universally disliked was an overstatement, only just. She and Bertha got along well enough in a bickering and sniffing sort of way, and Aunt Crosby had a devoted lady's maid by the name of Winters.

"I appreciate your concern for my health," I said, bowing over Aunt Crosby's hand. "I assume Miss West has sent for a tray?"

Hyperia slipped her arm through mine. "Of course, and I've offered to put Aunt Crosby in Lord Thomas's old suite."

Which a platoon of maids would be dusting and scrubbing apace, while footmen got a roaring blaze going, cleaned every sconce in the apartment, and hung the mattress over the balcony for a quick beating.

"I'd rather my quarters were less drafty," Aunt Crosby said. "High ceilings are fine for keeping cool in summer, but grossly impractical in the colder months."

Aunt Crosby always stayed in Uncle Tommie's old apartment. Always. My mother had once offered her a change of scene to the Rose Suite, thinking to spare Aunt Crosby a longer traipse to the main staircase.

The resulting silence had made Lower Canada in January seem toasty by comparison.

"Will the Rose Suite do?" Hyperia asked sweetly.

"I suppose I can manage there as well as anywhere."

Hyperia herself had been put in the Rose Suite, which meant the rooms were clean and warm and the bed laid with fresh sheets.

"If you'll excuse me," Hyperia said, "I'll have a word with the housekeeper." She deserted her post with a kiss to my cheek and a pair of curtseys, one for each auntie.

"You'd best marry her," Aunt Bertha said, sinking into a wing chair beside the fire. Hyperia had put the ladies in the family parlor, doubtless because the fire was kept lit in here, whereas the formal parlor would have been chilly in the extreme. "She won't wait about forever."

"Perhaps she's not keen on marrying you?" Aunt Crosby took the second wing chair. "One hears a great deal of unpleasant talk about your military career, sir. Have you frightened off the only lady who'll have you?"

Happy Christmas to you too. "Miss West and I esteem each other greatly and have an understanding as to the possibility of a shared future. How was the journey down from Town?"

"'Understanding,'" Aunt Bertha said with a snort. "In my day, we signed betrothal contracts. None of this mincing about beneath the kissing boughs."

"I noted several of those," Aunt Crosby muttered. "Encouraging licentiousness at the Hall, are we? Not all traditions deserve undying loyalty, my lord."

I poked up the fire for something to do, and also because neither auntie had suggested I take a seat. I was torn between gentlemanly manners, which required me to wait for the permission of the ladies before getting off my cold, itching feet, and the ridiculousness of a grown man, host at the familial ducal establishment, shifting about like a small boy waiting to be acknowledged.

I ceased fussing with the fire and took a corner of the sofa. "The kissing boughs are decorative," I said, "and the staff would mutiny if we denied them the holiday touches."

"Now that is the sad truth." Aunt Bertha was clearly prepared to launch into a discourse on disloyal staff, laziness, and knowing one's place. The tea tray spared me that harangue.

Though, of course, the tea could have been hotter and was too strong for such a robust blend.

"The blend is His Grace's choice," I said. "I enjoy it." I enjoyed Mrs. Gwinnett's meadow tea more.

"Please recall," Aunt Crosby said, "that Arthur is off gallivanting on the Continent with his dear friend. You will kindly instruct the kitchen that in future I'd like a pot of gunpowder on my trays."

She was being contrary, which she did exceedingly well. Aunt Crosby had ever been a devotee of strong China black. The stronger, the better.

"Of course, Aunt. Have you any other instructions for the kitchen?" Any other excuses to send me poking my nose belowstairs where my nose had no business being?

"I'll convey them through Dorothea. Where is your mother, Julian?"

If Mama had any sense—she had loads—she was halfway to

London. Aunt Bertha and Uncle Terrence acted as a check and balance on each other. Each was careful to let the other be the most rude in a given conversation, to be the most critical. They competed, but they also attempted to goad one another past the bounds of civility, and with occasional success.

Aunt Crosby's unannounced presence shifted the battle lines. Terrence would not take on both aunties, which meant he might ally with them. That notion made a seasoned officer tremble in his wet boots.

"Her Grace was intent on visiting Mrs. Swinburne," I said. "Her cottage lies between here and the village, and the duchess might well have gone on foot."

"In this weather?" Aunt Bertha sent a baleful glance at the windows. "Ah, youth."

The duchess was a good twenty years Bertha's junior, though only a few years younger than Aunt Crosby. Despite his own mature years, Tommie had taken a wife in her second Season, with the result that Aunt Crosby would likely spend far longer widowed than wed.

Which seemed to bother her not at all.

"Mama enjoys great good health." Nobody had poured me a cup of tea, and I wasn't about to ask for one. "And Mrs. Swinburne is dear to her."

"Fraternizing," Aunt Bertha said, sipping primly. "Just because a housekeeper earns her pension doesn't mean she's family all of a sudden. Mark me on this."

Mrs. Swinburne *was* family. She'd swatted my little bottom when I'd stolen pies from the kitchen window and kissed my bruises better when Harry had got the better of our earliest brawls. When I returned from France the first time, she had enfolded me in a hug that had conveyed joy, relief, and love. My second homecoming had presaged the same welcome—from her.

She was getting on, and a grandmother several times over, though her extant progeny all lived in Philadelphia.

"What do you hear from Arthur?" Aunt Crosby asked, finishing her cup of too-strong, not-hot-enough tea. "He disdains to write to his aunts, and we live in hope that he is equally negligent toward Terrence."

"Arthur is enjoying his travels. Banter is an art enthusiast, though they are both men of the land at heart. French roses, German beer, Austrian hops... His Grace has started sending me cuttings and seeds by the week."

"Tommie was like that," Bertha observed. "Harry too. Curious to the bone. Perhaps that's what got Lord Harry killed."

I poured myself a cup of tea rather than take that bait. *My* curiosity, my following Harry from camp by dark of night, might well have been why Harry had perished, but a pair of nosy old busybodies couldn't be trusted with such a confidence.

The tea, with a dash of honey and a drop of cream, was just right.

"You'd best send some footmen to retrieve Dorothea," Aunt Crosby observed. "She's at that age where one's declining powers are still coming as a surprise, and this snow is serious."

"Do you suppose the snow will prevent Terrence from joining us?" Bertha seemed pleased by the prospect, the way a bettor was pleased when the pugilist he backed landed a stout blow.

"Delay," Aunt Crosby said. "Not deter. Terrence will join us."

A look passed between the ladies that suggested plots and schemes I wasn't to know about, which was fine with me. My job at that moment was to keep them company until Hyperia informed me that she'd moved her own effects from the Rose Suite.

I wished she might join me in my apartment. We'd spent the occasional night cuddling and kissing, but such was the dreary state of my manly humors that I could offer her no real passion of the body. Not yet, maybe not ever.

I chased those thoughts off lest the aunties sniff out their presence by virtue of diabolical powers of materteral divination.

"There's Dorothea," Aunt Crosby said, going to the window. "What can she be thinking, trudging about in this snow? She'll catch her death. Illness at the holidays is the height of inconsideration."

Aunt Bertha joined her. "She's looking spry enough. For now. Be wretchedly bad timing if she came down with something at Yuletide, but she's not as young as she used to be."

Who is? "More tea, ladies?"

They returned to their perches by the fire. "You haven't told us the local news," Aunt Bertha said. "If we're to have the advantage of Terrence, you must tell us all the latest local gossip and tattle. Terrence hates to be late to the party."

At that point, I'd have welcomed Uncle Terrible simply because he'd distract the aunties from their interrogation of me.

"We have a new bell for the church," I said. "An anonymous benefactor has remedied a long-standing oversight. The crew should be along to hang the bell in the next week or so. Vicar Humboldt is in transports."

"A new bell?" Cleary, Aunt Crosby found this news less than riveting. "Arthur finally bestirred himself to see to it, then. One knows when a church has no bell. One is reminded every Sunday."

"And at every funeral," Aunt Bertha noted piously.

"And every wedding," I said, and earned two beady-eyed appraisals for my cheek.

"We live in hope," Aunt Bertha murmured, "that nuptials are in the offing. *You* aren't getting any younger, and Arthur has no proper heirs. Somebody had best do his duty and soon."

The rising tide of melancholia threatened to slosh into my little holiday boat. I was Arthur's *proper heir,* at least legally. True, I wasn't the old duke's progeny, but by law I was a legitimate Caldicott scion, and I loved the Hall dearly.

Her Grace had never told me who my father was, and I hadn't asked. She and I did not enjoy that sort of relationship and had only recently progressed from civil to cordial dealings.

"Regarding the ducal succession, we must trust to divine providence," I said, which was balderdash. I trusted to divine providence only as a last resort, when planning, hard work, and faithful allies had all been exhausted.

"Trusting to divine providence is for clergymen on Sundays and fools at their leisure," Aunt Crosby said. "Your Mr. Humboldt is a bit of both."

Now she was insulting a man of God, and Bertha looked ready to bring up the rear. Fortunately for their immortal souls and my patience, Kerrick strode into the room without knocking.

"Keeping all the best company to yourself, Julian? Not the done thing. Hello, darling aunties. Give a lonely laddie a kiss in greeting and tell me the best recipes for quieting teething babies."

Bless you, bless you, bless you and your kilted blather. He entertained them for the next quarter hour, at which time Hyperia arrived and offered to show the ladies to their respective rooms. I gallantly tendered my escort to Aunt Crosby, but she waved me off, saying she had questions for Hyperia.

The ladies left, Kerrick offered me his flask, and I partook.

"That's tea, you fraud." Good, strong tea too.

"Aye. Could not be kissing the aunties with whisky on my breath. Married men learn these things. I really don't know why you dread the elders so."

"Not all elders. I am very fond of my godmother. The duchess is dear to me. Uncle Tommie was a scamp but good company. These women, though..."

"They are a warning to us. The curtain will come down. Be careful what we make of our own final acts. We will have many young critics and no encores."

And that was why I not only liked Kerrick, but also respected him. He could play the charmer in plaid, though he'd served in uniform for two bloody years, seen human nature at its best and worst, and looked the world squarely in the eye.

"I had not thought of the aunties as admonitory tales," I said. "I suppose they are. If you will excuse me, I am off to change my boots."

"You'd best brush your hair while you're at it, my lord. A married man learns to tend to such details."

I threw his flask at him and left him laughing in the toasty parlor.

CHAPTER FIVE

I changed into dry socks and my Hessians, loose, comfortable, tasseled half boots that would not do for riding, but kept my feet dry in the out of doors. When I had rendered myself presentable, I tapped on the door of the duchess's apartment and waited until she granted me permission to enter.

"Your Grace." I did not bow, but neither did I presume I was welcome. My mother and I had come far in terms of a thawing in relations, but we were not easy companions. I myself wasn't entirely sure why or when we'd grown awkward with each other.

In my early childhood, Her Grace had been unfashionably involved with her children, and not only her daughters. She'd been the queen of a hundred picnics, our first dancing master, and first to delight in our lopsided drawings and rhyming couplets.

That had changed as I'd matured and as I'd gained a subtler understanding of legitimacy and my own lack of it, but the duchess had also put some distance between us. She'd recently explained that my godmother, grieving her own young son, had swept into my life, and kindness had dictated that Godmama be allowed to intrude.

That explanation fit with my recollections, but not with my

instincts, and thus I remained somewhat wary in dealing with Her Grace.

"Julian, I did not invite her." The duchess paced before a roaring fire, her hems whipping about her boots. "Not this time. I have included her on many previous occasions, but this Christmas... She can be overbearing on her good days. I'm sorry."

"You had no idea Aunt Crosby was coming?"

"Of course not. She casts a pall of gloom over all in her ambit, and the holidays are no time for that sort of behavior. We put up with her twice a year as it is, and we must welcome her whenever she chooses to visit, but I deserved some notice. Tommie's apartment hasn't been aired since Michaelmas."

I left the topic of gloomy holiday moods alone and wondered, not for the first time, why Her Grace was so unnerved by Aunt Crosby's particular brand of vinegar. Perhaps the ladies were too close in age, perhaps Aunt Crosby had been the more conventionally pretty younger woman. The roots of discord were old and well entrenched.

"Hyperia put Aunt Crosby in the Rose Suite. Aunt claimed Uncle Tommie's apartment would be too drafty."

Her Grace fetched up against the mantel, tapping a nail on its polished oak surface. "Those rooms face north, and the ceilings are majestically high. Tommie never let anybody quite forget that he was the son of a duke." Said with a twinge of asperity, by a woman who was seldom allowed to forget she was a duchess.

"The Rose Suite was clean, warm, and ready for a guest. Hyperia will make do wherever we put her."

Mama shook a finger at me. "See that you don't put her in your bed, young man. You and she take risks, spending so much time together. If you aren't to marry her, Julian, then you should keep your distance."

"And if she doesn't want to marry me?"

The duchess resumed pacing, her heels beating a tattoo on the Axminster carpet. Green silk graced the walls of her sitting room, and the furniture was upholstered in burgundy velvet. The carpet incorporated both hues in a pattern of rioting flowers and greenery, and fresh camellias added a dash of pink on the escritoire.

A lovely room, and a refuge from the wintry landscape steadily turning a more uniform white beyond the windows.

"Why wouldn't any sensible woman want to marry a ducal heir, Julian?"

Precisely because she was sensible. "Hyperia has a fear of childbed, and we would be expected to secure the succession, or at least give it a good try." I wasn't *capable* of doing my part at the moment, but marriage was for life, and I wanted children irrespective of the title.

"So space your offspring, hire excellent midwives, and see that Hyperia gets the best of care. No woman looks forward to bringing forth her children 'in sorrow,' but the business is bearable or the race would expire."

In a good number of cases, *the woman or her child expired.* My mother, who'd given birth seven times, had to know that.

Clearly, the duchess was flustered by Aunt Crosby's ambush. Time to change the subject. "Leaving aside matrimonial topics—"

"For now."

"Leaving them *aside,* I want you to feel free to pop up to Town and do some last-minute shopping. Conspire with Godmama to buy out the shops, enjoy an oratorio or a pageant, and leave the aunties to kick their heels here until Christmas."

My mother sent me an annoyed look. "I am Hyperia West's chaperone. Until her brother deigns to join us, I cannot abandon my post."

"The aunties are both here, and they will serve for the sake of appearances."

My mother's expression underwent a progression of shifts, from irritated, to blank, to intrigued, to pleased, then irritated again.

"If I nipped up to Town, those two old schemers would desert the regiment and leave you here with Hyperia, causing tongues to wag. They will not chase me out of my own home at Yuletide. I will make that very plain to them and be equally clear that as hostess, I have decided the menus, the seating arrangements, the guest lists, and sundry other details those two will think to meddle with."

Well, isn't this jolly? I now had a third warring faction at Caldicott Hall: the aunties, Uncle Terrence, and Her Grace. All had allies and enemies among the staff, and all were wily and tenacious in social battles.

"Your Grace…" *Please don't make the holidays any more difficult. Don't make my holidays any more difficult.*

"You cannot expect me to take this insult quietly, Julian. They think because Arthur isn't on hand that they can pull nonsense like this. They have insulted you as well, presuming on the hospitality of the Hall at a time of year when you cannot in good faith stuff them back into their coach and commend them to the elements."

I was abruptly tired and vastly unamused. I hadn't the heart for a cheerful Yuletide season, but my wits would assuredly not survive weeks of acrimony.

"Your—Mama, might we not consider that Bertha is getting on and could well have forgotten to send you the requisite letter asking to include Aunt Crosby in her invitation? Might she have misplaced it, or drafted it and never ordered her lady's maid to copy and send it? Must we attribute the worst motives even to family?"

The duchess tossed herself into the chair behind her escritoire and took up the family seal from her wax jack. "You are being reasonable. You were always the most reasonable of my boys. Arthur can be a stickler, in his way, and prodigiously stubborn. Harry was given to outrageousness, while you… Oh, very well. I shall try to be gracious. I have spent a lifetime learning the art of appearing gracious. But, Julian, I warn you, if those women push me too far, I will not answer for the consequences."

"All I ask is that you try. Hyperia will try as well, and so shall I. How is Mrs. Swinburne?"

The duchess sighed, and a lot of the fight went out of her. "Lonely. Harry is lost to us. We know that, and we grieve his absence, but poor Mrs. Swinburne… Her children are thriving, her grandchildren are thriving, but they are thriving on the other side of a wide and dangerous ocean. Every year, she grows more certain she will never see them again."

Mama set aside her seal and rose. "You are right, Julian. I have no business being cross. Does the kitchen know we have an unexpected guest?"

"I'm sure Hyperia made them aware."

"Please thank her for me. You ought to marry her, Julian."

"One grasps the merits of your suggestion." I withdrew rather than invite another harangue. The relevant question was not who *ought* to do what, but what Hyperia *wanted* to do with her life. She had allowed me an understanding—private, mutually acceptable intentions to pursue courtship and matrimony—but she had not given me her hand in marriage.

Yet.

I went in search of my beloved to thank her for dealing with the Attack of the Aunties, and I found her in a surprisingly agreeable location.

"I developed the habit of coming here over the summer," Hyperia said. "The southern exposure was wonderful for reading in the morning. Do you mind?"

She'd chosen Harry's old rooms, which still bore his stamp. Harry's ledgers and journals marched along the shelves behind his desk. Harry's favorite landscape of the Hall hung over the mantel. The colors—blue and maroon with gilt and cream accents—were his favorites. The hassock and reading chair by the balcony windows conjured his ghost, lounging with day-old London newspapers or frowning at some bill he'd yet to pay.

Harry's cavalry sword, which deserved to be conspicuously displayed in the library or first formal parlor, hung casually from the curtain rod, half hidden by the blue velvet drapes.

"Why these rooms?" I asked. "I don't mind, but it's a curious choice."

Hyperia studied the landscape, which depicted the Hall in autumn. The lime alley was a blaze of gold, the sky over the front portico a cerulean blue, and the house itself radiated dignified contentment.

Would that its occupants did as well.

"The duchess agreed that Harry's apartment should be made available for visiting family. He's been gone two years, and this wing is much handier to the kitchen and public rooms than the guest wing is."

The sitting room was cold, but a hearty fire was chasing the chill away. I assumed another blaze was heating the bedroom.

"The duchess agreed," I said, "but then, she did not give the order to have Harry's things boxed up. The spirit is willing, but the heart hesitates." Though as to that, Harry's journals and ledgers were only so many bound volumes. To the casual observer, they might have been novels, biographies, or plays.

"What's bothering you, Jules? Besides Aunt Crosspatch inserting herself onto the guest list, Harry's ghost, and Her Grace's dramatics?"

I took Hyperia's hand. "How did you know? Mama was in a proper taking. I reminded her that Bertha might simply have forgotten to send along a note warning us of Crosby's intent to visit. The letter might have gone astray, and Crosby is a grouch, but she's generally a mannerly grouch."

"And Her Grace listened to you." A conclusion, not a question. "I hope you noticed that."

I looped my arms around Hyperia's shoulders and drew her near. She came into my embrace willingly, and for a moment, I simply held her. When she was close, I was less inclined to fret and fume. I could think. I could sort emotion from facts.

"I love you," I said. "The next few weeks will be busy and challenging, but I want you to know that I am glad you are here. I hope we can make some sweet and lasting memories, despite the ill will simmering among the elders."

"So do I. They'll sort themselves out, Jules. They've been bickering and sniping for years."

I led Hyperia to the sofa, and we sat side by side, hips touching. She fit against me perfectly, and should we ever marry, I promised myself I would never take the pleasure of her casual affection for granted.

"May I ask for your help with something, Perry?"

She took my hand, and I looped an arm around her shoulders. "You never ask for my help."

"I never have to, because you give it almost before I know I need it, but in this instance, I am not investigating a puzzle. I need a different sort of help."

"Name it."

A small knot of worry eased. I did not deserve such loyalty, but I knew enough to treasure it. "My spirits have dipped," I said, dodging the blunter truth. "The darkness, the cold, the greater awareness of those no longer present... My last memories of my father in any sort of health were of him at Yuletide. He had a capacity for silliness that I lack, and I miss it."

I was digressing, or stalling.

"Harry is gone too," Hyperia said, "and I've appropriated his rooms. I can move, Jules, but the housekeeper allowed as this was the simplest solution, and I do like these rooms. They are comfortable and unpretentious."

As my apartment was. "You should stay here," I said. "I like the notion of you nearby, and the housekeeper was right that the simplest solution makes the most sense. Harry wouldn't begrudge you his old rooms."

For Hyperia to occupy these rooms, this sofa, Harry's bedchamber was tangible evidence that Harry's place as my closest confidant, the person who knew me best in the world, had been superseded by Hyperia, though Harry would never be replaced in my heart. As much a friend as a brother, as much irritant as inspiration.

"He would not begrudge me these rooms," Hyperia said, stroking my knuckles, "but you miss him terribly."

"Some times more than others. He was like Papa about Yuletide. The pair of them were self-appointed Lords of Misrule, every year, without fail. They would lurk under the kissing boughs and spike the ladies' punch, and sing loudly enough to be heard in the village—at all hours—using lyrics for the old carols that would shock Vicar to his toes."

"Naughty lyrics."

"And hilarious. Arthur and I are cut from more sober cloth." I was still dithering, still gathering my courage. I kissed Hyperia's knuckles and plunged onward. "I am daunted, frankly, by the prospect of presiding over the Hall's holiday festivities."

"You are daunted, and your spirits are dipping," Hyperia said carefully. "Tell me how I can help, Jules."

"If I threaten to make a bonfire of Arthur's correspondence, don't indulge me. He asked little enough of me, ever, and a daily pile of letters and invoices and reports ought not to be a challenge. That said, I cannot seem to get ahead of the Royal Mail, and Arthur assured me winter is when the correspondence slows down."

"Do you need an amanuensis?"

"Arthur's clerks serve well enough in that capacity. What I expect I need is a distraction, and thus I have planned a few acts of anonymous generosity. The first was replacing the church bell, though it seems somebody else had the same idea. I've found a pony for Leander. The beast is admittedly big for him. Good bone, wonderful eye. Better too big than outgrowing your pony in a year or two, or so I reasoned."

Hyperia was staring hard at the fire, my hand in hers apparently all but forgotten.

"Perry, am I being ridiculous? I've kept the pony at the livery, and even Mr. Blentlinger doesn't know for whom he's boarding the creature."

"Oh, Jules." She rose up and settled in my lap, her arms about my neck. "You are so sweet. Leander will know the pony is from you, but go ahead and be shy. I love that you would be so generous, and the church has needed a new bell for years. Just your luck that somebody else would think to remedy the situation when you decide to see to it. Tell me more."

Another knot of worry loosened, though I had a few more in reserve. "Mama was saying that Mrs. Swinburne longs to see her family in Philadelphia, and as I think on it, Mrs. Swinburne has her pension and the use of the cottage, but that doesn't mean she has the funds for a comfortable passage, much less to establish herself for any length of time in Philadelphia."

"She won't want to be a burden on her daughter," Hyperia said. "You're right about that. She won't want to crowd the household or strain the budget. She'll want to go as somebody with something to contribute, though you do realize, Jules, we might never get her back?"

Hyperia made the most perfect lapful. When she settled against me, her head on my shoulder, the sense of rightness surpassed even perfection and wafted into the realm of the divinely ordained.

"Mrs. S put Caldicott Hall first for more than forty years, Perry. She came here as a scullery maid and served loyally and well. We owe her the choice, and I intend to see that she gets it."

"Anonymously."

"A bearer bank draft is anonymous." Having turned my mind to the matter, a bearer bank draft seemed almost too easy.

"I like it, Jules. I like the generosity and the discretion. If Mrs. S wants to keep her good fortune to herself, or send the money to her family, you give her that latitude by making the gift without fanfare."

"But she shouldn't be without her family..." I fell silent, because Hyperia was right. Swinnie should make whatever choices suited her. She might move to Philadelphia, make an extended visit there, or set the money aside for her progeny. That was none of my business.

"This is my plan—to spread some quiet holiday cheer, to occupy myself with improving Yuletide for a few others, so I fret less about low spirits or blue moods. It's not much of a plan, so I am consulting you before I get too attached to it."

Hyperia kissed my cheek. "It's a good plan, Jules. Throw yourself into it, and I will help any way I can. You like puzzles, and these Father Christmas projects will require some puzzling over. The time of year is dreary—no getting around that—but we can distract ourselves from the dreariness. I do like this plan exceedingly."

My heart felt lighter for having her encouragement, and then another thought struck that raised my spirits considerably.

"I have something to show you," I said, rising with Hyperia in my arms.

"Jules, I can walk."

"I'd have to set you on your feet if you walked, and I don't want to let you go." We passed into the bedroom, and with Hyperia's help, I got the door to the dressing closet opened.

"We need some light," I said, setting my burden down reluctantly. "Stay here. I won't be a moment."

I found a carrying candle and lit the sconces in the dressing closet. Hyperia's effects—dresses, capes, shawls, dressing gowns—hung in shadowed folds on pegs along the outside wall. A wardrobe filled half the wall opposite the door. I turned my attention to the fourth wall.

"Somebody might have repaired it," I said, moving aside hatboxes and boots. "But one can hope."

I felt around the wainscoting, found the familiar groove between two unprepossessing panels of oak, and tugged. The panel swung open, and a musty breeze issued forth. When I pushed against the boards standing two feet beyond the wainscoting, I was greeted with the scents of lavender and cedar.

"What's through there?" Hyperia asked, hunkering down to peer into the gloom. "Is that another dressing closet?"

"That, my dear, is the finest view of my own dressing closet you will ever see. Harry and I found this little opening, which might have been left over from the days of priest holes or servant passages. We kept it to ourselves, and as far as I know, not even the footmen know of it."

"How interesting." Hyperia sat back on her heels. "Jules, I do believe we will enjoy a very Happy Christmas indeed."

We kissed in celebration of that notion and in celebration of nothing in particular, save the joy of anticipated closeness shared with a dear and precious companion.

Supper was an ordeal.

Four courses of excellent food were served with Aunt Bertha's signature *sauce du malheur et misère* poured over every topic of conversation.

The lovely cream of potato soup occasioned a lament about spices losing all their potency when improperly stored. The duchess asked for a second serving in response.

Mrs. Gwinnett's artichokes au gratin on toast was pronounced too rich. Her Grace made it a point to eat every bite of her serving.

The roast, done to a turn, was assessed as overcooked. Mama went dangerously silent.

By the time the raspberry fool was brought out—a public school treat for fidgety boys, according to Aunt Bertha—Ginny and Kerrick had exhausted the topic of Scottish holiday traditions, and I had exhausted my patience. Hyperia had gamely complimented each dish, but even Aunt Crosby seemed exasperated with Bertha's carping.

Mama rose when Aunt Bertha had consumed only three bites of

her dessert—finding fault at length did occupy the mouth—and smiled brightly around the table.

"Ladies, shall we leave the gentlemen to enjoy their port? Bertha might not care for her sweet, but I vow I could not eat another bite of Mrs. G's delightful fare."

Hyperia smothered a smile. Ginny looked relieved. Kerrick and I busied ourselves holding chairs and offering our elbows to the ladies. Mama marched ahead unescorted, while I took the curiously quiet pair of beldames down the corridor, and Kerrick escorted Hyperia and Ginny.

"If Bertha does not moderate her capacity for unprovoked odium," I said as Kerrick and I gained the privacy of the dining room, "I will take up fasting."

"Ye cannot fast, laddie. You're too skinny as it is. Ye might consider developing a chronic case of the wind. Cabbage will serve, along with beans. Too bad peaches aren't in season. I can make a positively foul wind out of a quarter bushel of peaches."

"Flatulence wouldn't deter those two."

Kerrick wandered to the sideboard, picked up the entire serving bowl of raspberry fool, and brought it to his seat.

"If you want some, Jules, you'd best speak now. Raspberry fool is just cranachan without the oats and whisky, which I can partially remedy." He produced a flask and liberally doused the fruit and cream with same.

"That is not tea."

"How perceptive my lord is, but then, we heard you were the noticing sort." Kerrick took up his spoon and closed his eyes. "For what I am about to receive, seeing as I have been such a good little laddie, I am grateful. Amen."

I opened the cupboard on the left end of the sideboard and took out a couple of decanters. "I will not last another month of suppers like this one, Kerrick. I mean it. Arthur's correspondence has daunted my spirits, Bertha's carping delivers another blow to my mood, and

Uncle Terrence has yet to stick his oar in. I wanted Yuletide at the Hall to be..."

Kerrick looked up from his devouring. "Aye?"

I wanted my holidays to be sweet, quiet, and pleasant. Not grouchy, trying, and disappointing. "Peaceful," I said. "I wanted this season to pass peacefully."

"No sense of fun, that's your trouble. You've a teething baby, two bored little boys, fretful elders, and exhausted new parents on hand. I grant you, Hyperia seems disinclined to cause trouble, but I'd keep an eye on Her Grace. You'll not get peaceful with this lot, Jules, but then, peace can be boring."

No, it could not. Not to me.

I set the decanters on the table within Kerrick's reach. "I'm going for a walk. Excuse the rudeness, but I'd rather enjoy some fresh air than watch you fortify yourself for the mandatory half hour around the teapot."

"It's worse than that." He scraped together a bite of whisky cream and fruit. "Ginny will plead fatigue, and she is knackered, so I will smile and send her off to bed. Miss Hyperia and the duchess will follow in her wake, and I'll be alone and defenseless before two of the most tiresome old trouts ever to cheat at whist."

"Do they cheat?"

"I will accuse them of it when they pick my pockets." He took the last bite, set the bowl aside, and patted his flat tummy. "I suspect they have been playing together so long, they don't need to cheat. They can convey an entire hand and a strategy with a glance. Ye bletherin' gods of war and destruction, I am a tired mon."

Also a dear man. "Tell you what, Kerrick. You do the duty this evening, and I will spell you tomorrow night. If we both get some respite, we'll hold up better."

"Now you're thinking like a parent. On your way, then, though a puny little Englishman like you is daft to wander out of doors on a night like this. Six inches of new snow and a ring around the moon."

"But the wind has died down, and the stars will be magnificent."

The special quiet that came with new-fallen snow would be even more glorious.

"Mind you don't get lost among the drifts." Kerrick rose, straightened his sporran, and squared his shoulders.

"I know my way around this property." I had made up my mind to complete a certain errand before going to bed, lest I lose my resolve in the midst of a mountain of reports and letters.

I stopped by the estate office to collect a document, then bundled up in gloves lined with lamb's-wool, old boots, a thick cape, and two scarves. I hadn't far to go, but Kerrick was right. The night was bitter, dangerously so if the wind picked back up.

I also had to be careful to avoid the usual paths and instead stuck to hedgerows and shadows. To use the old senses—the instinct for terrain beneath fresh snow, the knack of sticking to the lea of the drifts and the natural windbreaks, did restore a measure of my good cheer.

The stars were breathtaking, as only they could be on a clear night in deep midwinter. When I'd gone some distance from the Hall, I stood for a moment and let the quiet envelope me. On a night like this, the new church bell would be heard for miles, and that was a comforting thought. I marched onward, pleased to be out in the elements, pleased to have an objective other than enduring Aunt Bertha's incessant bile.

My destination was a tidy cottage along a meandering little burn. The water moved mostly beneath ice, a brittle, determined trickle, though the surface was still broken in places by rocks and bracken. As cold as the air had become, by morning, that sound would be silenced until the next sunny day.

I paused to reconnoiter and closed my eyes the better to consult the senses of hearing and smell. A slight tang of peat smoke hung in the air, which was the equivalent of the all's well. A visual inspection of the little dwelling gave the same result. No lights, no movement, save for wisps of smoke rising in moonlight made brilliant by the blanket of snow.

Far away, a dog barked. I sent up a prayer the beast would find shelter soon and stole across the open ground to admit myself to a darkened kitchen. The fire had been banked, though the hearthstones still radiated warmth, and the kitchen itself smelled of baking bread.

Mrs. Swinburne's cottage was a solid, even gracious structure of six rooms. The lower floor consisted of a half-sunken kitchen at the back and a dining parlor and sitting room at ground level. The first floor, I had reason to know, boasted two bedrooms and another parlor, with accommodations for a maid beneath the eaves.

As pension cottages went, it was lavish, but then, Swinnie's loyalty had been unstinting. Still, I was confident she would rather have had more modest accommodations and much greater proximity to her family. I made my way upstairs—the third stair creaked—and found the informal parlor where Swinnie likely wrote letters by the dozen to her family in Philadelphia.

A desk—one could not call it an escritoire—sat in the moonbeams that streamed through the window. With a sense of suppressed glee, I crossed the room and extracted a document from the pocket of my cape.

Let Swinnie travel to see her loved ones come spring and decide for herself whether to bide in Merry Olde or Merry New. I unfolded the document—a generous bank draft, if I did say so my humble self—and looked over the desk for the perfect place to...

The blotter already held a document, and that document, when I peered at it by moonlight, revealed itself to be a bank draft made out to bearer. The sum was the same as I'd filled out mere hours earlier on my own bank draft, though the two documents differed in one detail: This one, the one written by an anonymous benefactor, had three words scrawled in the lower left corner.

Other than that, and the account numbers in the upper right corner, the drafts were the same. What a coincidence.

CHAPTER SIX

I held the two documents and wrestled with an odd mix of emotions. Astonishment, certainly. Somebody had seen Swinnie's loneliness and been moved to take the same steps I'd taken to address it.

The exact same steps, right down to the sum conveyed, the date upon which it was conveyed, and the bank from which it was issued.

I was also resentful. A bearer draft bore no features that identified to the recipient from whose account the funds would be drawn. Swinnie would simply present the draft to, in this case, Wentworth's bank, receive her funds, and go on her way a wealthier lady.

And I was puzzled. What to do with the bank draft in my left hand, for one thing, and who was Swinnie's benefactor, for another? Her Grace had not mentioned leaving Swinnie an anonymous gift, and Arthur would have told me if the funds had come from estate accounts.

I crept down the steps and avoided the third stair, tucked my bank draft back into my pocket, and let myself out into the painfully cold night air.

Killing cold, the sergeants had called weather like this. The shifts on picket duty had been cut in half, and still, men had lost toes and earned medical leave as a result.

More gloomy thoughts circled as I traveled back to the manor. Perhaps Squire Pettigrew had been offended that the Caldicotts would not see a loyal retainer safely into the arms of her family? He'd be generous out of an urge to make the ranking title look parsimonious, though I could not ascribe to Pettigrew the magnitude of largesse I'd found sitting on Swinnie's blotter.

What to do with the sum still in my figurative and literal pocket? I was pondering that conundrum when I noticed a shadow moving along the privet hedge that flanked the walk between the house and the path to the stable.

Somebody was bending low, trying to keep out of sight, but the moonlight and natural stillness made the task difficult. A third factor —the tendency for sound to carry across a fresh blanket of snow— meant I heard footfalls and muttering, even from fifteen yards away.

"Halt," I said, "and show yourself."

The figure bent behind the hedge and ceased moving.

I was unarmed, but in my present mood, I was disinclined to deal leniently with attempted housebreaking. The footmen, maids, and stable boys were free to come and go as they pleased once their duties were attended to, and folk from the village were welcome in Mrs. Gwinnett's kitchen at any reasonable hour.

Which left... "Uncle Terrence, what are you doing impersonating a thief when my own dear mother has invited you to enjoy the hospitality of the Hall?"

He straightened slowly, a moonrise of scarves, mufflers, and put-upon dignity. "That you, Julian? Fine night for a stroll, isn't it? Saw you coming across the park, had no idea who you were, and assumed you were up to no good, eh? I see your hair still ain't right. Pity that. Might have recognized you if you were back to normal. Still, you have hair, no matter it's the wrong color. Comes a time when you'll be grateful for any hair at all."

I would never be back to normal, if normal was the man I'd been before buying my colors. "None of which explains why you were skulking like a rat among the hedges."

A tall rat, skinny but for a slight paunch. Uncle wore his white hair long and queued back in the old-fashioned style, though he was quite thin on top.

He strode past me, making straight for the entrance to the back hallway. "Fine way to greet your uncle, young man. I wasn't skulking, though you appeared to be. You think a frail old fellow should simply allow himself to be set upon by a footpad?"

"How many footpads frequent Caldicott land?"

"Only takes one, and you're all swaddled in dark wool. That's how footpads dress."

I had not missed Uncle Terrence, but there was something back-wardly comforting about his unchanging hubris.

"Sensible people wear wool in weather like this, and I note that you yourself are styled a la footpad, if dark wool is the defining trait. Why not walk in the front door, Terrence? You have been invited, and you are expected."

He paused at the back door, hand on the latch, his posture worthy of Mrs. Siddons in a tragic role. "You'll ruin everything."

"What scheme have I threatened by taking a brief constitutional beneath a spectacular night sky?"

He let himself into the relative warmth of the Hall. We were in the lower reaches, which were cozy indeed, and redolent of the supper roast and damp wool.

"I was *trying* to arrange my arrival as a surprise. Trying to add a bit of spontaneous good cheer to tomorrow's breakfast. Here is long-lost Uncle Terrence, braving the elements to join those in need of company, strolling into the breakfast parlor as if he's just come down from his bedchamber instead of all the way from London. Making an entrance, you know? I'm not David Garrick, of course, but I do enjoy causing a bit of a splash."

He was not David Garrick or Sarah Siddons—he was a poor liar. "You were up to something."

"Such an untrusting nature, Julian. So many who served in uniform returned with suspicious attitudes. I don't suppose you might offer a guest newly arrived from the bitter snows a tray? A toddy? Anything? I understand you are playing the host in Arthur's absence. One would never know it from your present behavior."

Take your lying, old, reprobate self up to the family parlor, use the bell-pull, and run the poor night footman off his feet. To say that would be ill-natured, and in point of fact, I wasn't playing the host.

I was the host. "Her Grace has put you in the Gentian Suite," I said, information I knew only because Hyperia had passed it along. "If you can find your way to the family parlor, you can warm up there, and I'll send a footman to light the fires in your apartment."

Terrence unwound a scarf from his neck and stuffed gloves into the pockets of his greatcoat. "And sustenance?"

"I will alert the kitchen and have a pot of tea and some comestibles sent to you in the family parlor. You might well find Kerrick and the ladies lingering over their scandal broth. I'll join you in a moment."

"I don't want to find Kerrick and the ladies, my boy. I want to make my entrance at breakfast tomorrow."

"Then you can wait in the formal parlor, which is colder than the ninth circle of Hades, and unless I mistake the matter, you would have me believe you just crossed the tundra on foot, holes in both boots, trudging uphill into a headwind the entire time, while enormous wolves howled for your blood."

"No need to be sarcastic." He passed me his cloak and sauntered up the shadowed passage. "Come along to the family parlor when you've seen to the tray."

That degree of disrespect would never do. "Terrence."

He paused and half turned. "Hmm?"

"I am not the duke. I am the family disgrace, according to many, and I earned my suspicious attitude in a very hard school. You are here at my sufferance. Watch your step."

He let me have the last word—this time. I took off my outer garments and wished myself back in Spain. I'd spent my winters not at Wellington's headquarters, but out in the countryside. I'd been cold and hungry and very often thirsty, but the solitude and quiet had suited me.

Trading barbs with Uncle Terrence did not suit me, and I was abruptly tired of the day, the season, and the role I was trying—without much success—to fulfill.

"My lord?" Winters, Aunt Crosby's lady's maid, had emerged from the servants' hall. She, too, carried a cloak, and her features had the carefully composed quality of one who finds his lordship in a part of the house where he ought not to be.

Her looks had not changed in all the years I'd known her. She was spare, gray-haired, and blessed with a perfect complexion. Harry had once told me she was a lady fallen on hard times, but whether that was his surmise or reliable intelligence, I did not know.

"Miss Winters, good evening. I thought to take a peek at the stars, and I found Uncle Terrence coming in from the stable."

"The stable?" Winters allowed the merest hint of puzzlement into her tone. "I grant you the stars are magnificent tonight, and I went out for a few minutes myself to enjoy the quiet, but Mr. Tuttleby isn't one for stretching his legs unnecessarily."

Precisely. "He has taken himself up to the family parlor, and I am charged with conveying the need for a pot and tray to the kitchen."

"I'll have a word with the undercook, my lord. You'd best join Mr. Tuttleby and the ladies." Her smile was mostly in her eyes, though I suspected she well knew I'd rather have gone right back outside and admired the stars until spring.

Instead, I went to the family parlor, and to blazes with changing my boots and brushing my hair. I had questions to put to Uncle Terrence before he had time to fabricate any fairy tales about his reasons for stealing about the grounds under cover of darkness.

~

"Do you believe him?" I asked Hyperia as I escorted her up to her apartment. "A post chaise to the village and then a hired cart from the livery?"

"A hired post chaise is expensive," Hyperia said. "Every mile adds to the cost, so yes, Uncle Terrence might have taken a post chaise down from Town, though he was vague as to the reasons for that extravagance. Even Town gents are occasionally found on the stage coaches."

Particularly unmarried fellows racketing about at their leisure. "I will ask questions in the village, though as cold as it is, my guess is nobody saw what conveyance he arrived in."

Hyperia stopped outside her door. "Does it matter?"

Oddly enough, it did—to me. Having solved a half-dozen vexatious puzzles for polite society, my ability to ignore lies, inconsistencies, and discordant facts had all but disappeared. I had put myself on reconnaissance, the same orders I'd been given in Spain, though my terrain now was manor houses and villages rather than mountains and plains.

"I will explain," I said. "Invite me to bide with you for a moment."

Hyperia glanced up and down the deserted corridor, then bussed my cheek. "Bide with me for a moment, Julian. The day has been long, and your company is an antidote to every ill."

I unlatched the door and used my carrying candle to light a candelabrum on the mantel and two sconces in the bedroom. When I rejoined Hyperia in the parlor, she was tucked into a corner of the sofa, her slippers off, her feet up on a hassock. I loved the look of her at her leisure and loved that my company was any sort of boon to her.

"Join me," she said, patting the cushion beside her. "What do you care if Uncle Terrence arrived from some gambling bacchanal masquerading as a shooting party? He's independent and of age."

I took Hyperia's hand for the simple pleasure of touching her. "I decided to favor Mrs. Swinburne with enough coin to relocate to Philadelphia if that's what she wants to do."

"And I applaud your generosity."

"My attempted generosity. I sought to act swiftly, before I had a chance to doubt myself, and thus I made my way to her cottage after supper. I hoped to leave a bearer bank draft where she was likely to find it in the morning. Somebody apparently had the same idea, right down to the amount on the draft. I found the document on Swinnie's blotter. Her benefactor added three words: 'Do enjoy Philadelphia.'"

Hyperia scowled at her stockinged feet. "The same, Jules?"

"Different accounts, and that little memo was lacking on mine, but the same amount, the same date, the same bank as I use."

"Did you memorize the other account number?"

"I did, not on purpose, but Quinn Wentworth wouldn't tell me who owned that account if I put him on the rack and tickled him with goose feathers."

"Interesting image. Whoever this rogue Father Christmas is, he apparently had the same motive you did—to give Mrs. Swinburne a nudge toward rejoining her family. That suggests somebody local."

I looped an arm around Hyperia's shoulders, grateful in my bones for her willingness to discuss what was surely an odd coincidence.

A second odd coincidence, if the church bell counted as the first. "I thought perhaps Her Grace might be responsible. Wentworth handles her finances, and she is concerned that Swinnie is lonely."

"And the duchess is generous," Hyperia said. "She's very loyal to her charities. Will you ask her?"

"I have another theory."

Hyperia curled up, such that her head was on my shoulder, and her knee rested against my thigh. "Do tell."

"I know Mama's handwriting, and the D in 'Do enjoy Philadelphia' was not her style. Her given name is Dorothea, and she adds a little flourish to her capital D's. We can't rule her out entirely, but the handwriting tends to exonerate her. Uncle Terrence was sweet on Swinnie at one point, though I don't think anything happened."

"So what if something happened? Consenting adults and all that, and Mrs. Swinburne is a widow."

I hoped that someday Hyperia and I would be consenting adults. "Uncle Terrence might have waved off his post chaise in the village and walked the remaining distance—it's less than a mile on the bridle path—the better to slip a bank draft onto Mrs. Swinburne's desk blotter. He claimed he sought to make an entrance at breakfast. He, in fact, may have hoped to obscure the hour and means of his arrival."

Hyperia studied her toes. "You have a point, Jules. A cart from the livery stable might not have presumed to pull up to the front door, but they should have taken a guest of the Hall around to the porte cochere rather than leave him to slog in from the stable. Or maybe they did drop Uncle Terrence at the porte cochere, and he waited until he had the privacy necessary to sneak over to Mrs. Swinburne's cottage."

"No tracks on the drive. I checked. Terrence came either by the hedgerows or in a humble conveyance."

Caldicott Hall, like many rural manors, sat a short distance from the estate village. As was the custom, a grand formal front drive curved through the park and around a central fountain before delivering guests to the Hall's southern façade.

From the stable, though, narrower bridle paths also led to the village, to neighboring estates, and along most of the local bodies of water. One could also take a fairly direct lane from the home farm to the village, and that byway—lined by trees and frequented by local traffic—would have been the preferred route for the livery stable cart.

"You could ask Terrence what he's about," Hyperia said, stifling a yawn.

"I tried that. Got a lot of blustering and insults, which is what made me think Terrence is hiding something. If the opportunity arises, you should ask him."

Hyperia sat up, let her feet fall to the floor, and stretched. "Ask him if he's playing Father Christmas to lonely retired housekeepers? The gift was apparently anonymous, Jules. You are piqued because twice now your own attempts at generosity have been foiled."

I rose and offered her my hand. "You are right, in part. I found a home for my bell, and I will find a home for my bank draft. I don't suppose you know of a deserving charity that could use a hundred pounds?"

"*A hundred pounds?* That's more than some people earn in a lifetime."

"Terrence could afford it. Her Grace could." I certainly could, and other people—say, our dear curate—could earn that sum in a year or two.

"I could afford to be that generous as well," Hyperia said, "and so could the aunties, but still... Maybe Terrence and Mrs. Swinburne did have an affair. That is a lot of money."

"Ask about that, then. How smitten was he, and does he keep in touch enough to know her situation now? Two coincidences this close together smack of an intrigue."

Also, vaguely, of an insult. In my first attempt at the role of host of Caldicott Hall, somebody was assuming responsibility for gestures that were mine to make. Perhaps this somebody sought to be helpful, but I did not feel aided. I felt frustrated and incompetent, surplus to requirements, just as I'd felt when I'd mustered out after the Corsican's first abdication.

Hyperia hugged me. "Let it go, Jules. So you are not the only kind and generous denizen of the shire. That ought to be pleasant news, though I know you will fret all the same. I'm off to bed, and when the boys and I kidnap you tomorrow, try to act surprised."

"I am surprised. Kidnap me for what?"

"You'll have to wait and see. I thought I'd take Declan, Leander, and Atticus for an outing, unless the snow starts up again. Say you will join us."

Hyperia was nothing if not brave. I could not claim as much courage, but I was loyal. "I will join you."

"You won't plead mountains of correspondence or ledgers or a meeting with the steward?"

Well, drat the luck. "I am meeting with the land steward at three of the clock, the house steward at four." By which time, I ought to have subdued the day's mail.

"We'll be back at the Hall by then. Dream of me." She kissed me on the mouth and stepped back before I could get into the proper spirit of the undertaking.

"Always ambushing me," I said.

Hyperia brushed my hair away from my forehead. "Are you complaining? You could ambush me back."

Lovely thought. "I have your permission to ambush you?" The question wasn't as frivolous as it might have seemed. "I will exercise utmost discretion."

She patted my lapel. "I would rather not be accosted under the kissing boughs, Jules. A bit of seasonal silliness is acceptable, but the Hall is awash in mistletoe."

All of which, now that I thought about it, Hyperia had avoided— as had I.

"No public silliness. My nature rebels at the very thought." Some of my nature did. "Yes or no, Perry? Are we to skirmish as equals, or do I defer to your timing on all occasions?"

She worried a nail. "Yes, as equals, bearing in mind that Healy is supposed to be underfoot soon."

A qualified yes was still a yes. "We'll consign your brother to sleeping in the dairy." When I bowed over Hyperia's hand—a different kind of silliness—I kissed her knuckles with lingering warmth, then her cheek, then her brow.

We were only informally engaged, true, but if my ambushes went well enough, by the end of the Yuletide festivities, that might change for the vastly better.

Nonetheless, as I drifted to sleep, I was not pondering how best

to woo my intended. I was instead stuck on the notion that two coincidences were two too many. Had the same person funded the bell
and Swinnie's travels, and if so, why now, when I had been intent on
the same ends?

And what was I to do with the hundred pounds that Swinnie no
longer needed?

CHAPTER SEVEN

Theodoric Pettigrew was a grouch and a miser. He'd been infamous for his penny-pinching even in my boyhood, though it was said he'd applied a lavish hand to his daughter's settlements. She, for reasons a gentleman did not speculate on, had declined to visit at Pettigrew Manor since marrying her East Anglian baronet.

One did not *like* Pettigrew. He would have been appalled at the very thought of such neighborly presumption. One tolerated him to a greater or lesser degree, and I, oddly enough, fell into the greater category.

When I'd come home from the war the second time, Pettigrew had made it a point to shake my hand in the churchyard. He had looked me in the eye and offered unexpected consolation.

"You made it home, boy. Many did not. Endure for their sakes, if not for your mother's."

He hadn't spoken to me in the intervening year, but his admonition had been timely and helpful. I hadn't the right to throw my life away, not in despair, pique, shame, or for any other reason.

I had needed the reminder.

Seeing Pettigrew climb down from his ancient sleigh in the livery stable yard and totter into the barn, I silently thanked him for his wisdom. I left Atlas dozing at a hitching rack in the sun, though the air was positively frigid.

"Come to see the gift horse?" Mr. Blentlinger asked, touching a finger to a wool cap. Blentlinger was bald, skinny, and had the honed musculature of a former jockey. He'd ridden over fences—long, grueling, dangerous races—and always seemed to be slightly hunched forward, as if some part of his awareness remained ever in the saddle.

"Gift pony," I replied, "and yes. You still have no idea who left him here?" That had taken a bit of work, leading the creature in the small hours along the shadows and wrangling gates without alerting the livery's night watch.

"Beast is in great good health," Blentlinger said, bustling up the barn aisle. "I don't like to turn the ponies out with the horses. Too much squabbling, don't you know, and the horses often get the worst of it. Now that we have another pony, your little friend is a happier fellow."

"Is somebody else to receive a first mount for Christmas?" We stopped before a stall with a short rope lattice across the door at pony-chest height. Two winter-shaggy equines shared the space, both munching hay from the manger along the outside wall. The window had been closed, doubtless to keep in some warmth, a testament to just how bitter the day was.

"I thought maybe your lordship had had a change of heart," Blentlinger said.

The larger of the two animals—*my* pony—came over to sniff Blentlinger's hand and earned a thorough scratch behind the ears for his good manners. He was a sturdy bay and tall enough that Leander would be able to ride him for several years. The other specimen was dapple gray with a cream mane and tail and was of a more delicate build.

Fancier, one might say.

Further along the aisle, I could hear Pettigrew in discussion with a groom, the topic some recipe for a foot poultice to draw an abscess.

"The little one is quite pretty," I said, offering a gloved hand for the bay to sniff. "Is he for a girl?"

Blentlinger straightened to the extent he ever stood completely erect. "That 'un's bound for the Hall, too, my lord. Came with a note, tied to the tail rather than the mane, but much like the other beast."

Well, of course. *Three* coincidences. "Might I see the note?"

"Aye. Come along."

I was in Blentlinger's stable, and whether a visitor was a lordship or a groom, Blentlinger was king here. I came along to what passed for his office, a stall made over into a human space by virtue of solid walls and a door. The window had glass, and a potbellied stove standing on a bed of bricks made the place blessedly warm.

Blentlinger passed over a vellum card pierced through one corner and trailing a red ribbon.

I am to be delivered to Caldicott Hall on Christmas Eve and given to young Leander for naming on Christmas Day.

The capital D in *Day* appeared the same as the letter D that had been written in *Do enjoy Philadelphia.* Tidy, legible, with only a hint of a flourish at the bottom. The hand appeared neither masculine nor feminine and might have been learned anywhere from a dame school to a select academy or from tutors or governesses.

"When did he arrive?"

"Two nights ago. Afore this wretched cold settled in. M'wife says we're for it all week."

"Nobody saw the pony delivered?" I knew the answer, but I had to ask.

"Darts night, my lord. We saw the bottom of many a tankard. To be honest, we didn't notice him until morning. Good thing they get along."

Somebody had known when darts night was, which again weighed in favor of a local hand. "What's Pettigrew doing here?"

"Has a mare tending to thrush. MacNeil is a proper scientist when it comes to feet, and even the squire listens to him."

Plausible. When it came to Atlas's welfare, I was fussier than a biddy hen with one chick. "I favor apple cider vinegar, myself."

"The very thing, but squire says the smell puts the mare off, so she won't hold still for soaking. A lady of particulars, and he do set great store by her. Was his daughter's horse. What shall we do with the bay, my lord? Or shall we bring two ponies up to the Hall on Christmas Eve?"

Three coincidences. Two ponies. A partridge and a pear tree were doubtless to cross my path at any moment.

"Bring both, I suppose. That's what their anonymous benefactors directed." Leander did not need two ponies, for pity's sake. A guest pony would be one more equine who needed exercise, hay, oats, and pasture, and I well knew that Leander would choose the fancy little gray over the bay, if the decision was left to him.

My bay pony would make a fine—a very fine—guest pony.

Blentlinger opened the door of the stove, tossed in a square of peat, and rose. "We'll take them both along, then. Was there anything else, my lord?"

Horses didn't stop making manure just because the local courtesy lord dropped by for his daily dose of coincidence—rather like the Royal Mail and the mound of correspondence I'd left sitting on Arthur's desk.

"As a matter of fact, yes. Did anybody from your stable take a guest by cart up to the Hall last evening?"

Blentlinger rubbed his chin. "Wouldn't know, sir. I was home with me missus stringing together pine roping. Wasn't no money in the pot this morning, but I don't begrudge the lads the after-hours fares. The Hall is barely a hop, skip, and a jump. Wouldn't have been but tuppence."

"Might you inquire as to fares last evening—fares to the Hall?"

"I can ask. I'd best see how Squire and MacNeil are getting on, if your lordship will excuse me. MacNeil saves all his manners for the horses, and we know how the squire is."

We parted in the stable yard, where I collected Atlas and swung into an exceedingly cold saddle. The sensation—unique in all the world—reminded me of winters in Spain, which for all its sun also boasted a lot of high, cold mountains.

And then there were the Pyrenees, which had tried to finish the job of killing me that the French had started.

Don't think of that. The voice was Harry's, and his advice was sound. Two years ago, I'd spent Christmas as a prisoner of the French. One year ago, I'd been a prisoner of melancholia, guilt, shame, ill health, and overwrought nerves.

This year, I was losing a battle of generosity with an unseen opponent, and the weapons of choice were bells, bank drafts, and ponies.

An improvement, of course. Though, as I turned Atlas in the direction of the Hall and the morning mail, I was unhappy to find myself in any sort of contest at all.

"Miss West, good day." I rose from behind Arthur's desk, very much on my best behavior because three small boys—the sternest judges of adult male deportment to roam the earth—had crowded into the office with her.

"My lord, we have come to kidnap you. Resistance is futile. Boys, seize him!"

Leander had me by one wrist and Declan by the other in the next instant. Atticus, older, of the servant class, and quite particular about who touched whom and how, hung back.

"Where are you taking me, you brigands?" I put up a minor struggle while Declan made growling noises and Leander trod on the toe of my boot. "I won't go without a fight."

"Will too," Atticus called. "We're going ice-skating, and Miss says you're good at it."

"Ice-skating is not on my calendar." I was only half teasing. While the morning mail had been light, the contents were mostly reports, which required *reading* and *replies*. Both.

"Ice-skating is on your calendar this minute," Hyperia said, sashaying out the door. "Don't worry, so is picnicking. We have the basket all packed."

"And a rope," Atticus said, closing the study door as I was towed into the corridor. "In case the ice is too thin to hold you. Miss says we must always bring a rope."

The relatively high quality of Atticus's diction suggested he participated in this outing willingly. He'd be dropping aitches and blaspheming if he were at all uncomfortable.

After a stop to bundle up in several layers of good English foot-pad-quality wool, we trooped across the back terrace and headed for the trout pond. The outing should have been a lovely break from office drudgery, but the worst challenge my weakened eyes faced—the very, very worst—was bright sunshine on fresh snow.

I had my spectacles on and pulled my hat brim down, but as I descended into the garden, a thousand tiny hammers slammed away in my eyeballs. The pain would subside, eventually, but the residual sensitivity would linger.

My captors had run ahead, Atticus demonstrating the proper way to slide down the stair railing and nearly landing on his backside on the snow. Declan gave it a try, while Leander pointed and laughed.

"Jules? Were you truly willing to be kidnapped?" Hyperia asked, linking her arm through mine. "Despite the cold, it's a beautiful day."

My eyes throbbed, my mind was stuffed with reports, and my heart harbored resentment against a fetching little dappled pony.

"Any day when I can behold my beloved is gorgeous. How did you convince Atticus to play truant from his duties?"

"He hasn't many duties at the moment, thanks to the snow. The stable is quiet when nobody goes visiting or to market, and Mrs. Gwinnett has the holiday preparations down to a well-rehearsed parade drill. What did you learn at the livery stable?"

A snowball fight commenced, as of course it must. Every boy for himself, and none of them blessed with good enough aim to be much of a threat.

"Blentlinger was home last night. He will make inquiries among his grooms, but I could not be very specific, lest—here they come."

The lads had taken it into their heads to gang up on me, and from close range, I was pelted with three snowballs at once.

"Villains!" I bellowed. "Halt in the king's name!"

They scampered off to the trout pond, shrieking with glee.

"Harry and I would go after Papa the same way," I said, brushing at my sleeves, chest, and thighs. "Papa got even."

"Washed your little faces with snow?"

"Thoroughly, and made sure we got it in our hair and down our backs." What had Arthur made of that nonsense? Had Papa missed our foolishness when we'd grown older and more dignified?

"You can't be too rough with them, Jules. These are boys without brothers. Bring them along slowly in the manly art of horseplay."

"Interesting observation. I miss Arthur." I had not meant to say that. In fact, I hadn't even properly thought it, for all I'd spoken the absolute truth.

"I wish I could say I miss Healy, but I'm merely worried about him. What could be keeping him in Town?"

We arrived at the trout pond, which some obliging footmen—doubtless between snowball fights—had scraped clean of snow on the shallower half. Any adult who fell through the ice should have been able to stand up in that end of the pond.

"Perhaps Healy is loath to risk being kidnapped," I said. "Town is quiet over the holidays, while the shires perk up a bit socially. Why isn't Healy at the family seat?"

"Good question. The picnic basket and skates are in the gazebo. Jules, is something wrong?"

She knew me better than I knew myself. "Mr. Blentlinger is to deliver two ponies to the Hall on Christmas Eve, both for Leander."

"Two?"

"Somebody procured a dainty dapple gray for him. He'll outgrow the pony in a year, two at most, but it's a very fine beast."

"Finer than yours?"

"Arguably. That's not the point. Who is doing this, Hyperia, and why?"

We tromped up into the gazebo while I silently lectured myself about the stupidity of indulging in unjustified low spirits and the ridiculousness of a grown man pouting because somebody else had been generous.

Absolute nonsense, and yet...

"Two bells, two bank drafts, two ponies," Hyperia muttered, taking a seat on a bench along the side of the gazebo facing the pond. "Odd, I grant you. Have you more good deeds planned?"

"I do now. Let's find our skates."

We sorted through a box full of skates, got them strapped on little feet and on our own. The boys clomped down the steps and awkwardly across the snow.

"You lot wait here," I said. "Where is the rope?"

Hyperia hefted a stout length of hemp. "Be careful, Julian."

"Be careful," Declan mimicked. "You might fall and break your bum."

"Don't say bum," Leander countered, shoving his cousin. "It isn't polite."

"What should I say? Don't break your ruddy arse?"

Hyperia pretended to admire the view of the Hall, while Atticus looked equally horrified and fascinated.

"Language, gentlemen," I snapped, more forcefully than I'd meant to.

"Well, he's a flatus-faced Scot," Leander muttered.

"And you're a—"

Hyperia put her hand over Declan's mouth. "His lordship will strike out across the ice. This could be a dangerous moment."

She exaggerated, of course. As cold as it had been, as still as the pond was, the ice ought to hold me, Atlas, and Beowulf, Arthur's grand gelding.

I started off on a circuit near the bank, and the skill came back to me instantly. Harry and I had skated almost as much as we'd gone fishing and climbed trees, and this pond had been our favorite patch for winter fun.

A few moments later, I was executing a pirouette in the center of the pond, then on one skate *a la arabesque* in a curving line back to the bank. I stopped with a sidewise scrape of blades over ice and bowed.

"Miss West, if you'd care to join me?"

"I want to do that," Atticus said. "What you just did. That spinning thing."

Declan returned fire immediately. "You'll get dizzy and fall on your—"

"One watches a fixed spot while whirling around," I said. "One does not get dizzy, though it takes practice. Miss West, I am at your service."

Hyperia and I had skated together previously, just as we'd ridden horseback together, danced, and even on one memorable occasion, fenced. Any excuse to hold her hand was cause for joy, and we were soon cutting a dash *en promenade*.

"Who is my next partner?" Hyperia asked when I returned her to the bank.

We introduced the boys to the rudiments of skating, each child starting off holding two adult hands, then one, then wobbling carefully on his own and sometimes coming to grief.

"They'll have bruises," Hyperia said as the activity shifted to emptying the picnic basket.

"They had fun, and bruises are sometimes part of it." I passed her a cheese tart, the boys having chosen to eat sitting on a wool blanket spread over the ice. Hyperia and I enjoyed the relatively civilized comfort of the gazebo.

"You are not having fun." She took a bite of tart and passed it back. "Perhaps you need a toddy."

That way lay ruin. "Sorry. I am prone to the blue devils this time of year."

"Why?" Hyperia asked, fishing a cinnamon biscuit out of the basket. "Why now?"

"Because it's cold and dark?" Very cold and very dark, some years, but Hyperia's question—*why now?*—caught my attention. "Because I miss loved ones more at the holidays?"

She passed me a biscuit, though I wasn't done with my cheese tart. "When did it start, Jules? How old were you when you took the holidays into dislike?"

I thought back as the boys, now skateless, went running and sliding across the ice. "I wasn't keen on Christmas even before I went to Oxford." Sixteen and full of myself. As a scholar, I was the equal of most, but as a man of the world, I'd had much to learn. Harry had done what he could to educate me, but some things a fellow had to sort out for himself.

"Have you always disliked Yuletide?"

I didn't dislike the holidays, exactly. I dreaded them and endured with a sort of bewildered wistfulness most years.

"When I was very young, I looked forward to the whole business. From Stirring Up Sunday to Twelfth Night. As an adult, I don't see how anybody can sustain a sense of celebration for five straight weeks. The Scots probably have the right of it. A roast at Christmas, a couple days of merriment over the New Year's bonfires, and onward we march."

Sensible and far less subject to the judgmental eye of any religious authority.

"Tell me your first Christmas memory, Jules."

My eyes still hurt, but I wanted to watch the boys. The center of the pond might not be as safe as the parts the footmen had scraped clean, and little boys had a positive instinct for getting into mischief. The game now was for one boy to run as fast he could, then collapse onto the ice and slide into the other two fellows, who tried to stay on their feet when impacted by a human cannonball.

The result, every time, was a heap of laughing, yelling boys on the ice, then an argument over whose turn it was to slide next.

"I was given my first pony at Christmas," I said slowly. "I'd been in the saddle enough to have a decent seat, but I rode one of Arthur's old castoffs or one of the docile little mares kept to pull the trap. I loved them all and was happy just to have a mount."

"But then you had your very own steed."

"Gilgamesh, hero of a thousand epics. Gray, fat, but surprisingly game over a fence. He lived to be eight-and-twenty. Took a nap out in the paddock one day and simply did not wake up. I had theoretically embarked on early manhood at that point, but I sat beside him and cried like an orphan. The grooms left me to it, and then I helped bury him where he lay."

The memory should have been sad—would Leander one day cry for his first pony?—but instead provided an odd comfort. The grief had been crushing at the time, the true end of my childhood and the loss of a friend who'd shared many of childhood's best hours with me.

In the intervening years, I'd shed most of that grief and kept the memories. I could get through another Yuletide too.

"Tell me about the day you met your Gilgamesh," Hyperia said, "and eat that cheese tart. Being held hostage by brigands is hungry work."

I kissed her cheek and finished my tart, then told her about one of the most joyous days of my life.

My mood was better for having spent time with Hyperia and for having recounted some happy boyhood memories of the holidays.

The Christmas morning I'd first beheld Gilgamesh peering at me placidly with wisps of hay adorning his forelock, I had been the happiest lad in creation. That had been the finest Christmas ever.

The next year, Mama had organized a scavenger hunt, boys against the girls, and the competition had gone on for days. Harry took a notion to leave our sisters false clues in his best imitation of Her Grace's handwriting, the ladies retaliated in kind, and we boys fell for it. Mama's hints became increasingly arcane—and in verse too —and the terrain covered by the hunt expanded to include the entire Hall.

Another delightful Christmas, though I recalled Aunt Crosby muttering endlessly that year about *why must children run everywhere* and *why can't they play out of doors if they must be so* loud.

I was capable of enjoying the holidays. I'd just misplaced the knack somewhere along the way, and what had been misplaced could be found.

Despite throbbing eyes, I tackled the climb to the summit of Mount Morning Mail with renewed vigor and, for the first time, subdued the lot before the midday meal. Partly in deference to my vision, and partly out of improved spirits, I skimmed the reports and dashed off replies noteworthy for their brevity.

Excellent work. Carry on, and I will look forward to next month's totals.

"Julian, might I have a moment of your time?"

My mother had probably knocked, but I'd been so engrossed in shirking my duty that I hadn't heard her.

"Your Grace." I started to rise, but she waved me back into my seat.

"Must we be so formal even when private?" She sank into a wing chair by the hearth, and I took the one opposite her.

"Of course not, and yes, you can have all the moments of my time you like. The correspondence has been subdued for the nonce."

Her Grace stuffed a pillow at her back. "One sometimes wonders if the invention of the written word was a good thing. Maybe we were better off when we had to express ourselves to one another directly. No dispatches from the battlefield. No pigeons just trying to get safely home despite the weight of a message about their necks."

"You are feeling fanciful."

"My besetting sin as a young lady was too much imagination. I have come to ask a favor."

Never in my entire life had my mother asked a favor of me. She had recently *ordered* me to join her at a house party, where I had been tasked with finding some missing letters, but a favor? We were breaking new and encouraging ground—I hoped.

"Ask. If it is within my power to give, it's yours."

"Does it feel grand to say that?"

She was in a fanciful, contrary mood. "Not grand, honorable." Then too, all my attempts to be magnanimous thus far had been foiled by the anonymous benefactor.

"I'd like to invite Theodoric Pettigrew to join us for Christmas and as much of the Twelve Days as he pleases to spare us."

Of all the unlikely requests... "Certainly, but might I ask why?" We had oodles of room, and one more curmudgeon in the collection couldn't be that much more of a bother.

"His daughter has written to me. She's approaching another lying-in, and her holidays will be subdued, or she would invite her papa to East Anglia. He doesn't accept her invitations, says he cannot abandon his acres at the darkest time of year, and she worries about him."

And Pettigrew, whatever his faults, doubtless worried about his daughter. "Will he accept your invitation?"

"No, but he might accept yours. He was a soldier, and you aren't the duke, and I'm sure you'll think of some way to appeal to his vanity."

"Pettigrew is dignified, not vain." Also gruff, grouchy, and miserly.

"Invite him in person, Julian. Don't just send a scribbled note. Use your imagination and be gracious."

I could not lie to Pettigrew, nor would he be susceptible to flattery. Mama had handed me a puzzle, and I did enjoy puzzles in the normal course. I gathered my courage in one hand and my improved spirits in the other and put a question to my mother.

"I will be the soul of diplomacy, and in return perhaps you might answer a question for me: When did I come to dislike the Yuletide?" If I could figure out the when, I might gain greater insight into the why and thus into how to remedy the situation.

Her Grace rearranged the pillow at her back in the same manner I'd seen Aunt Crosby fuss. "Dislike Yuletide?"

"Or Yuletide dislikes me. The blue devils are trying to take up residence where all should be merry and bright. This has become an annual misery, predating my time in uniform and even my time at university. I don't care for it."

Her Grace nodded. "When all around you are in high spirits, your own doldrums are a special penance. One sympathizes, but I would have to give the matter some thought and consult a diary or two. You have never indulged in willful unpleasantness, Julian, but you are given to seriousness, sometimes excessively so."

Did I get that from my father—my biological father? Claudius, Duke of Waltham, had been conscious of his rank, but not prone to undue gravity. He'd been downright silly on many occasions.

The moment was unusual, in that Her Grace and I were private, and she had just asked me for a favor—for two favors, in truth. I was not only to entice Pettigrew to join the household for a visit, I was to endure his dour company among our rogues gallery of elders.

Instead of a scavenger hunt, we could hold a contest for best holiday grouch honors.

Except that I might win.

"I have wonderful memories of the holidays in childhood," I said. "The day I met Gilgamesh, skating with Harry on the trout pond, sitting on Papa's lap when we took the sleigh to divine services, that glorious scavenger hunt you organized..."

"Your father wrote half the clues," the duchess replied. "He declared the whole notion ingenious and tried to take control of it, but as he was the neutral referee of record, I scotched that notion."

My father... Except the duke hadn't been my father. *Ask her.*
"Your Grace..."

"I thought we had agreed that formality need not constrain us in private, *my lord.*"

"Very well, then. I have a somewhat delicate question to put to you."

She waved a hand. "What you and Miss West get up to *discreetly* is not my business. You know I think the two of you would suit. You already are *suiting*, or do I miss my guess?"

Did the duchess know about that little passage between dressing closets? Not the question of the moment.

"I have been wondering lately about—"

A tap sounded on the door, followed by Hyperia poking her head into the room. "Luncheon is—excuse me. I wasn't aware you had company, Jules. In any case, you two, time to eat. If you leave me and Kerrick to contend with the elders alone, we will run all the way to Scotland before suppertime. Ginny was up half the night and is pleading a nap. Please do not desert me in my hour of need."

She drew the door closed, and the duchess was on her feet. "Such a dear person, your Miss West. Doesn't miss much either. What was it you wanted to ask me?"

Ask her. Except then we'd be late for luncheon, because I needed more than a name. I needed an explanation for that name, context, a recounting of how matters stood between the parties now, assuming my father was extant, though he probably wasn't.

"The query will keep for another time," I said, holding the door for Her Grace. "Nothing of any moment, and we must not leave Kerrick and Hyperia to manage without reinforcements."

"Perish the thought. Will you ride over to call on old Pettigrew today?"

I didn't want to. The sun was as bright as ever, and I had for once pulled even in the race to deal with Arthur's mail.

I offered Her Grace my arm as we moved down the chilly corridor. "Tomorrow won't do?"

"Mrs. Swinburne was very certain we're in for more snow before the end of the week. She was in great high spirits this morning. Trudged to the manor in this weather and asked for a word with me. She's all of a sudden making plans to travel in the spring. I don't suppose you know anything about that?"

I knew a bit too much about that and not enough. "Who doesn't long to see some of the world? I assume she's setting a course for Philadelphia?"

"Directly, and hasn't said if it's a visit or a remove. I doubt we'll see her again, Julian."

"We will be loyal correspondents, then, and wish her the best."

"I will miss her. She was a staunch ally. Stood with me even against your father. He wanted to have a shooting party right here at the Hall, and between us we convinced him otherwise. Swinnie threatened to give notice, and the matter was decided for the distaff."

Your father. "You need not fear the near occasion of any shooting parties, at least not while I'm in residence."

She paused outside the breakfast parlor. "Gunfire bothers you?"

"Not as badly as it used to, but yes. I expect it always will."

My mother hugged me, and I was glad I hadn't opened the awkward topic of my paternity. Her Grace and I hadn't been on hugging terms. We'd exchanged embraces since I'd sold my commission, but with a few notable exceptions, those had been mostly gestures.

This was a mama hugging her son. "If I haven't said it before, Julian, I am saying it now: I am grateful every day, to the depths of my soul, that you came home to us."

She preceded me into the breakfast parlor, from whence emanated warmth and the smell of a cloved ham.

I lingered in the corridor for a moment, grateful to the depths of my own soul. I might not know who my father was, but I was damned sure who had brought me into this world and had loved me every day since.

CHAPTER EIGHT

"A sleigh handles differently from a wheeled conveyance," I said, taking up the reins. "For one thing, the sleigh often has no springs."

"Bouncier?" Atticus asked, climbing in beside me and piling the lap robe over his bony knees.

"Depends on the snow. A sleigh can also be quieter—no jouncing and squeaking, though bells on the harness are common. One generally shares the lap robe, Atticus."

"One shoulda brought an extra. It's bleedin' cold."

"Language, young man." I gave Ladon the office to walk on. "In the stable, you can use colorful vocabulary for your own amusement and the entertainment of the grooms. You are not in the stable."

He sighed mightily. "I'm not in the house. You said manners are for the manor. Make up your mind, guv."

The complaint was valid. Atticus, as my tiger and sometimes general factotum, occupied an odd position. He was inside staff when I bided anywhere but the Hall, though at the Hall, he was attached to the stable unless the head gardener, housekeeper, butler, or sundry other domestic authorities had need of him.

"Fair point," I said. "I should have been more clear. Knowing how to express oneself often comes down to the company one keeps rather than the location one occupies."

"Declan knows all about that. About expressin' hisself. He knows the Gaelic, and he's learning Latin. Leander will know the Latin too, and French."

"Declan knows nothing about how to drive a sleigh." I handed the reins over, and Atticus sat up straighter. I then whisked the lap robe off his knees and spread it over both of us.

"That's cheatin', guv."

"Mind the horse. He has a harder job with a sleigh, because the vehicle is more likely to slip all over the place. The solution if you get into a slide is often a slight, temporary increase in speed rather than a decrease. Ladon will understand that, and his natural tendency to sluggishness will ensure that he slows down when the going is safer."

Generally within six paces or less. The old boy was getting on, and his temperament had been notably placid for his entire, shaggy life.

"Can I ask him to trot?"

"Not yet. In weather this cold, he'll need a little extra time to get his joints limbered up. How are you coming with your reading?"

I put the question to Atticus in part to distract him from the task of driving. Yes, I wanted him to pay attention to the horse, the snowy lane, and any potential hazards, but he was staring at Ladon's hindquarters with a focus excessive for the task at hand.

"Miss Hyperia has been busy lately. Miss says Lady Kerrick needs some respite, and Leander and Declan need supervision. I do some readin' betimes. The newspapers predominantly."

The last word was spoken carefully. A new addition to the word hoard for my trusty little dragon. "Declan and Leander are years your junior and haven't your inherent common sense."

"So what does it mean?" Atticus guided the sleigh around the sweeping curve of the drive and between the lime trees half clad in snow. "Flatus-face? Is that dog-Latin?"

"It's pure rudeness. A flatus is a fart. Using that sort of language around Miss West was gauche in the extreme."

"Gauche is rude?"

"Gauche is ignorance and rudeness rolled together. From the French for left-handed or awkward."

"So it counts as both a French word and an English word?"

That mattered because when Atticus could navigate passably in both French and English, I would begin educating him in the use of weapons. As he rattled through his French vocabulary—*merci, de rien, bonjour, bon nuit, bon chance,* and so forth—I pondered the larger conundrum.

What was I *doing* putting notions of French and firearms into the head of a lad who'd very likely spend much of his life mucking stalls and grooming muddy equines?

In the alternative, what was I *doing,* consigning such a bright, canny young fellow to a life of mud and manure, when he was capable of learning foreign languages and would enjoy the process? There was honor and art in tending to horses—great honor and great art, for some—also danger and drudgery.

The third declension had never kicked anybody in the face with an iron-shod hoof. French pronouns weren't known for biting off fingers.

"Can we trot now, guv?" Atticus asked after steering Ladon through the gateposts. "The longer we're out in the cold, the more likely we are to get an ague."

"Who told you that?"

"Aunt Crosby. She said I wasn't to call her Lady Thomas, because that was formal address, and this was a family gathering."

But you are not family. I would have expected Aunt Crosby to keep that fact squarely in mind. "Was Leander underfoot at the time?" He was family, albeit on the wrong side of the blanket.

"Leander and I were playing patience, waiting for Declan to finish setting up the Battle of Connor."

"He does Irish battles too?"

"Edward Bruce was Robert's brother, so it was a Scottish victory. Edward became high king and won lots of battles."

"Edward lasted less than three years as king before he was defeated and killed. You may ease Ladon into a trot."

"Declan knows all about battles. Ladon, trot on!"

Ladon plodded ahead at the same steady trudge.

"Ask nicely twice, then dangle the whip where he can see it."

Ladon picked up his pace at the sound of my voice, or perhaps his horsey vocabulary included the word *whip*.

"Declan seems to know Scottish victories," I observed, "which is a very different thing from knowing Scottish history. You will note his battles all date from centuries ago."

"How many centuries?"

"Roughly five."

"Five hundred years?"

"More or less. More recently, Scotland has had a bit of a rougher go, at least from the Scottish perspective." I did not say that Scotland had been defeated repeatedly by her English neighbors and all attempts at rebellion savagely suppressed. "We'll soon come to the bridge. A bridge covered with snow and ice will sound and feel different to Ladon than the bare wood variety. You don't change how you're driving. Eyes up, hands soft, and—"

"And nose froze."

"—and steady as she goes. Pettigrew's is less than a mile beyond the village."

"Why call on him? Jamison says he's a grouchy old besom, and we already have a whole broom closet full of those."

"Her Grace asked me to invite him to join us at the Hall. Jamison should mind his tongue."

"He should mind his toddies," Atticus said. "They go down so easy but come at a price."

That insight qualified as a victory on the road to adulthood if anything did. "Eyes up. The bridge is no reason to pull on the reins or to hold your breath."

Ladon trundled onto the bridge, a plain plank affair over a glori-
fied ditch that years of storms and snowmelts had turned into a year-
round stream running a good six feet below. The horse stopped dead
in the middle, the sleigh rocking forward awkwardly.

"He don't like it," Atticus said, a thread of nervousness in his
words. "Ladon, walk on."

The horse's head came up, and he pawed at the snowy planks,
which had the effect of sliding the sleigh back a foot.

"Don't touch the whip," I said quietly. "Give him a moment to
find his bearings."

"This bridge ain't got no rails, guv."

"You remain calm, and he will remain calm."

Another pawing, followed by an attempt to sniff the ground, but
the check rein, intended to prevent grazing in harness, also prevented
Ladon from indulging his natural curiosity.

He instead took a step back, which canted the sleigh at an angle.

"I could get out and lead 'im," Atticus said. "Ladon, walk on." He
clucked to the horse, to no avail.

Two more steps back and the runner of the sleigh would be
sticking out over open air. The vehicle was small, which was fortunate, given how narrow the bridge was.

"Ladon," I called. "Walk on, you silly beast."

The pawing stopped, then resumed, along with another step
back.

"Give me the reins," I said, taking them from Atticus's grip. "Out
you go. Stroll up to his head, pat him, then saunter along in the direction we're to travel. Don't grab his reins or otherwise try to control
him. Talk to him so he knows you're on the move."

Atticus scrambled down. "Ladon, you picked a rotten time to be
contrary. It's just a stupid old bridge with some stupid old snow on it,
and we're only going a mile beyond the village." He patted the horse's
shoulder and gave him a scratch on the neck.

"Now walk the rest of the way across the bridge," I said, "not a
care in the world, then wait for us a few yards up the lane."

Atticus got himself to safety, and all the while, Ladon watched the boy. That same boy had fed Ladon countless treats, had groomed him by the hour, and spent more hours on his back. That boy was a generally benevolent quantity in a large and dodgy world.

"Ladon, walk on," I said, putting the slightest vibration on the reins.

He sighed and plodded forward. We paused to pick up Atticus and were soon trotting on our way. The whole business had been a two-minute delay on a mundane errand in the middle of a quiet afternoon, but the image of Atticus being dumped over the side of the sleigh, plunging through thin ice into frigid water...

Not to be borne. Not to be remotely imagined. The boy had guarded my honor and my welfare as fiercely as Cerberus had ever guarded Hades's front door. He mattered to me.

The thought stuck with me all the way to Pettigrew's front door.

I owed Atticus more than a life being ordered about from one taskmaster to another, a life beyond muck carts and *merci*. What that life would look like, I did not know, and perhaps it wasn't entirely for me to say, but the debt had to be honored.

Had to be.

"Lord Julian." Pettigrew eyed me up and down. "What brings you to my door?" Pettigrew had answered that door himself.

I'd sent Atticus around to the kitchen, and Ladon was enjoying some hay and a bucket of water with the chill taken off. A penny-pincher Pettigrew might be, but he hired only competent grooms.

"I come as an emissary of Her Grace," I said, feeling foolish standing on the stoop. "I needn't trouble you for tea, only for a moment of your time."

He stepped back, and I was reminded of myself when I'd slunk off to London the previous year. My town house had been my covert, and I'd holed up there, prepared to die of regret, resentment, and sadness. Like Pettigrew, I'd let my appearance go—his white hair stuck out on one side, as if he'd not brushed it upon rising—and he'd swaddled himself in a lavender shawl that I suspected had once belonged to his daughter.

His jacket was unbuttoned down half its length, and a fingerless glove peeked out of a pocket. For all his dishevelment, his appearance still had a leonine quality, a fierceness that harked back to handsomer, more vigorous days.

"Fire is lit in the study," he said, shuffling from the foyer. "Close the door lest you let out all the heat."

What little heat there was. I could see my breath despite closing the door. I did not remove my coat, nor did he ask me to. I followed him down a corridor characterized by dinginess. Dingy carpet, dingy paintings, dingy windows. How could he stand to live in this gloom, like a rat scurrying around beneath porches and sheds?

"Damned cold," he said, waving me into a cramped cave of a room redolent of coal smoke. The space was marginally warmer, also cluttered with books, ledgers, newspapers, and pamphlets. A desk sat by the window, equally strewn with documents, the lot topped by a fiddle and bow.

A decanter at low ebb sat on the mantel, along with a glass half empty. Was I the only man not drinking his way through the holidays?

"What has Dorothea put you up to, young man?"

I had taken time to consider strategy, and thus I half dissembled with my reply. "Her Grace is challenged by the presence of Aunt Bertha, Aunt Crosby, and Uncle Terrence at the Hall. They will bide with us through the holidays and possibly beyond."

"Guests." Pettigrew spat the word. "Freeloaders, though that lot is well-fixed enough they don't have to rely on charity."

"We consider them all family." Crosby was family by marriage, as was Bertha at some vague remove, while Terrence was not family, but as good as.

"Heard you also acquired a relation in the nursery. Young lad, Lord Harry's get."

"You hear correctly. Leander is a son Harry acknowledged in writing. Harry intended to marry the boy's mother but was called back to Spain before the ceremony could be scheduled."

Pettigrew barked, which I gathered was as close to an expression of humor as he was capable of. "He dodged off, did our Lord Harry. He was a great one for dodging off. Came by it honestly. Can't blame him entirely. You'll do right by the lad?"

Why was that any of Pettigrew's concern? "We have legally bestowed the Caldicott name upon him, and he will be raised with every advantage we can give him."

Pettigrew's rheumy gaze wandered the room, coming to rest on the violin on his desk. "But some advantages he will never enjoy, even if Waltham were to ascend to the throne itself. All you can do is stand by the boy when the insults start. The term 'polite society' is often a fine example of irony."

"How is your mare?" I asked, rather than belabor Society's many shortcomings or Leander's illegitimacy.

"Mare? She's pigheaded, if you're asking after Una. She's coming around nonetheless. If we give her an apple mash when we soak her foot, it hides the scent of the vinegar. How did you know she had the thrush?"

"I was in the livery stable when you consulted MacNeil. Blentlinger explained your errand." The coal smoke fumes were giving me a headache and bothering my eyes. The chimney needed cleaning, clearly, as did the whole house.

"Did you notice the ponies?" Pettigrew pushed some papers around on his desk. "A dapple gray and a bay? MacNeil didn't know what they were about, taking up a stall and going through stacks of hay. Very few livery customers have need of a pony. Which one is for the boy?"

Both, and what business was this of his? "How do you know either one is intended as a gift for Leander?"

Pettigrew located a pipe, the stem much bitten. "Because the little beasts were being pampered. Both of them brushed to a high shine, not a burr in the mane or a knot in the tail. 'Bound for the Hall,' I said to myself. One or both. I know the look of a Christmas pony."

Because he'd favored his daughter with one, or because he'd procured such a pony himself for the orphan at the Hall? I could not see Pettigrew exercising such largesse toward a boy he'd only spotted a time or two in the churchyard, but Pettigrew had doted on his only child.

And she had been half orphaned from a young age. Interesting. "If you had to choose one of the two ponies for a small boy, which one would you give him?"

Pettigrew rummaged further, opening and closing desk drawers, then peering into the depths of a cabinet. When neither location yielded what he sought, he tore off a page of newspaper and twisted it into a slender spill.

"The tobacco is on the mantel," I said.

"So it is." He crossed the room and pinched out enough to fill the bowl of his pipe, then used a nail from his pocket—the one not sporting a fingerless glove—to arrange the tobacco to his liking. "Most would say the dapple gray is the prettier of the two, and that's true, but pretty isn't everything. Told my Mandy that over and over. Pretty fades. Pretty can lack bottom. Pretty isn't brains or heart or common sense. Women think men set too much store by pretty, but the ladies idolize it."

Quite a diatribe, but then, pipe-smoking seemed to lend itself to philosophy. "You wouldn't favor the dapple gray?"

"I'm sure the gray is a fine beast, but he's small. The boy will outgrow him in a year—you Caldicotts run to height—and then you're left with a creature very few can ride. Your gray will be able to pull a market cart driven by a child, and little else. Go with the bay, if you must choose. Not as flashy, but the better bargain."

Precisely. "Uncle Terrence would argue for the gray. A boy would cut a dash on an elegant gray."

"Terrence Tuttleby? That braying sot cares only for fashion and fribbling. What he doesn't know about horseflesh could fill the Channel at springtide."

Pettigrew's observation was interesting for its vehemence. Most of his grumbling was of the chronic, casual variety. Mention of Uncle Terrence had provoked true scorn.

"Terrence would argue that a man's mount *is* a fashionable statement."

"Tutt-Tutt would argue whether a flea can hop farther than a fairy can leap, and he has probably lost that very wager more than once. Your mother must have been in a very charitable mood when she invited him to bide at the Hall."

"She has also invited Aunt Crosby and Aunt Bertha, and they are already in residence."

Pettigrew looked up from filling his pipe. "That is a recipe for misrule right there. Tuttleby will harangue the ladies without ceasing about that time Spring Breeze fell at the St. Leger twenty yards shy of the finish line. Tutt-Tutt Twaddle-By will reminisce the ladies daft in a sennight."

"Mrs. Gwinnett's toddies aren't helping."

Pettigrew passed me his makeshift spill. "Old knees..."

I hunkered to light the paper from the flames on the hearth, then handed it back, a little torch amid the gloom. Pettigrew tended to his pipe and tossed the spill onto the andirons.

"Her Grace means well," he said, taking a puff. "Mrs. Gwinnett means well, and her toddies are legendary." Pettigrew began to pace. "Legendary, not to overstate the matter."

"Uncle Terrence is rather fond of those toddies."

"Uncle Tiresome. I suppose Dorothea gets dragged into making up the fourth for whist, poor thing. Hardly seems fair. She attempts to be kind to an old reprobate and ends up having to partner him while he tries to cheat—clumsily, I might add."

If only we had another reprobate... "The holidays are very busy for Her Grace. You are right about that. She tries to do too much. I am inundated with estate business in Waltham's absence, and the aunties aren't all that patient with me to begin with."

"Tuttleby uses up all the patience they have. I suppose the neighborly thing to do is lend a hand." He sucked on his pipe and released a surprisingly fragrant cloud. Vanilla and cherries.

"Lend a hand? We wouldn't want to impose, but Her Grace is hoping you'll at least call from time to time. The aunties would appreciate it, and so would I."

"I can do better than call for a spot of tea, young man. I can *pay a visit.*"

I adopted a conflicted expression—hopeful, but duty-bound to demur. "That would be asking too much. An occasional respite from Uncle Terrence's monologues would gain you the undying gratitude of both aunties, the duchess, and my humble self." To say nothing of Hyperia, Kerrick, Ginny, and the entire toddy-swilling staff.

"Nonsense. Terrence Tuttleby has made a career out of imposing on his betters, and both Lady Thomas and Bertha Higgins deserve reinforcements. If Tutt-Tutt wants to reminisce about his stupid horse races, I'll recount every day of my crossing to Canada back in '83. We wet the sails to catch the wind, and the damned things froze overnight. Never seen the temperature drop that quickly and hope to die without repeating that experience. Nearly sank in the North Atlantic for our cleverness."

I had heard that tale at least half a dozen times. "You're sure a short visit wouldn't be too great an imposition?"

"Never more certain in my long and distinguished life, young man. Tell Her Grace to expect me tomorrow afternoon, but don't tell Tutt-Tutt or the ladies. I want to see the look on his face when I remind him that Spring Breeze never ran in the St. Leger. He fell in the Oaks. Saw it myself. Shouldn't have run 'em in the mud like that, but the stewards weren't about to disappoint the crowd."

"The Oaks?"

"I'd bet Una on it, and I set great store by that old mare."

"No wagers, please. That would be taking unfair advantage, what with the toddies."

Pettigrew blew another cloud. "Penny wagers, then. For the principle of the thing. Miss Bertha would agree with me."

Miss Bertha? Well, well, well. "We'll expect you tomorrow, then, and thank you for giving Mama a day to tidy up another guest room. Very thoughtful of you."

"Ladies." Pettigrew growled the word. "As delicate as Toledo steel, and they do like to keep us on our toes."

"I go on my way a happier man for knowing we'll have fair odds at the whist table tomorrow night. Until we meet again, Pettigrew."

He saw me to the door, and when I left, he was muttering about the Oaks, and the St. Leger, and Tutt-Tutt-Twaddle-By. The mutter sounded a bit gleeful to my ears, but then, what did I know? I had either just finessed a delicate negotiation or sealed my holiday doom.

Perhaps both.

CHAPTER NINE

"Drop me by the bridle path," I said as Atticus squirmed on the bench beside me. "I have an errand to run."

"You want *me* to take old Ladon back to the stable?"

"For a quarter mile on a mostly straight lane, in the direction of home, yes. I think we can trust Ladon not to turn up contrary." He might trot a smidgen more briskly without my weight in the sleigh, but that would be the extent of his mischievous tendencies.

Atticus sat up straighter. "Where you going?"

"To pay a call on Mrs. Swinburne. I'll walk back to the Hall."

"Ruin your boots, then, guv. Don't make no difference to me."

"I'll go by the bridle path, and they aren't my best pair." Even as I spoke, I knew what Atticus was thinking. He had only the one pair of boots. Newish, and they fit him well. He treasured them as only a boy expected to go shoeless for much of the year could.

While I had three pairs of riding boots, a dress pair of Hessians, a casual pair, two pairs of half boots, my old cavalry boots, and my favorite pair. Utterly disreputable and divinely comfy.

"Tell Mrs. Swinburne thanks for the biscuits." Atticus maneuvered Ladon to a halt and made the beast stand while I climbed down.

"What biscuits?"

"She sends 'em over on Mondays. Shortbread biscuits. Cinnamon mostly, though in summer lemon and orange were frequent. When I die, I'm not going to heaven unless Saint Peter promises me some of Mrs. Swinburne's biscuits for all of eternity. She can make them look like little biscuit wreaths and biscuit stars, according to Jamison."

"I'd forgotten about her stars. Mind you don't prose on about them too loudly around Mrs. Gwinnett."

"It's Mrs. Gwinnett's recipe, so she don't mind. Ladon, walk on."

Ladon responded with his version of alacrity.

I headed up the bridle path and then cut along a stone wall until I came to the hedgerow. My eyes reproached me for spending so much time in the bright sunshine, but the mission—the neighborly call on Pettigrew—had been successful. I was entitled to a bit of investigating, even if my detour meant Arthur's afternoon mail sat for another half hour.

Mrs. Swinburne had loomed as a majestic authority over my childhood. With every passing year, she now seemed to shrink. She would never be elfin, but I towered over her, and her hair, once coal-black, was snow-white.

She hugged me on sight, though I knew that at the Hall, she would have been more circumspect.

"To see you does a body good, my lord. Tell Mrs. Gwinnett to make your portions larger. You are too thin by half."

"I do justice to her cooking on every possible occasion, Swinnie. I bring thanks from young Atticus for your biscuits. He is your devoted admirer, along with the entire junior staff."

"I have to pass the time somehow, and baking warms up the house. Come sit with me." She slipped her arm through mine and escorted me down the short hallway to her guest parlor. I was pleased to see the fire burning merrily and a substantial pile of peat squares stacked in the brass bucket by the hearth.

Beyond the parlor windows, Caldicott Hall sat on its slight rise, looking austere and dignified. Without spring greenery or summer flowers, the Hall was a staid piece of neoclassical architecture. Abundant swaths of pine swagging gave the place a welcoming air. Red ribbons threaded through the wreaths hung in every other window added another dash of cheer.

"Do you miss it?" I asked, standing by the window. "The hum and bustle at the Hall?"

"I did at first." She settled onto a tufted blue sofa and took some knitting from a wicker workbasket. "Now I wonder how I managed all I used to do in a day. The young people look in on me from time to time. They mostly want tea and sympathy, but I listen to their troubles and commiserate with their woes. I could never do that as housekeeper."

"Her Grace tells me you are thinking of traveling in the spring."

The needles clicked steadily, the soft periwinkle wool forming half a closely woven triangular shawl. The color was nearly the same shade Pettigrew had been wearing, though this shawl would be warmer than the rag the squire favored.

"I am not thinking of traveling in the spring, my lord, I am determined upon it. Some kind soul has provided the means. While I'm still spry enough to make the journey, I most certainly shall. I wrote to my Daphne this morning, and unless she tells me to stay put, wild seahorses will not stop me from flying to her side."

Swinnie, bastion of domestic rectitude, was tearing up. I produced my handkerchief and took the place beside her on the sofa.

"You miss her."

Swinnie put aside her knitting and took my offering. "Miss her? My heart breaks with longing, my lord. I haven't even laid eyes on the two youngest, and Bradley was just a babe in arms when they sailed. My own grandchildren and they won't know me, I'm growing so old and feeble."

"Older, I grant you. We all grow older, but feeble? Don't be ridiculous." A year ago, I'd been truly feeble. Winded at the thought of climbing a set of stairs. I'd had to gather my energies just to rise from my bed to use the chamber pot, and consuming more than tea or toast had been beyond me.

Please let me not fall into that state ever again.

"Well, not feeble, then." Swinnie dabbed at her eyes. "But one day I will be feeble, and when that day comes, I want my Daphne nearby."

"Have you any idea whose generosity has made this dream come true?"

She studied me with the sort of scrutiny recruits faced at parade inspection. "I assumed you were behind it, my lord. It's the sort of thing you'd do, sneaking about in the dead of night when sensible souls are all abed."

Amazing, how she could accuse me while complimenting me. Truly, those grandchildren would be better off with her on hand.

"I am innocent of the generosity you attribute to me, but I hope you will let me know if additional means would make your journey more comfortable."

She tossed my handkerchief back to me. "Additional means? Perish the notion. I'm rich as a nabob, thanks to whoever is playing Father Christmas. I won't be a burden to my Daphne, and that matters to me a great deal."

"It truly was not me, Swinnie, but it should have been. I have no idea who your benefactor is."

"Might it be the duchess?" Swinnie asked, taking up her knitting again. "She's ever so kind, and she knows how a mother misses her children."

"Her Grace has not claimed responsibility, and she seemed surprised to hear of your good fortune."

"I was certainly surprised. Cousin Philomena won't believe me when I write to her."

I mentally dug through neighborhood history. "Your cousin kept house for Squire Pettigrew and went to East Anglia with Miss Mandy when she married the baronet."

"Cousin is still keeping house for Miss Mandy. Two children already and a third on the way. I hoped the squire would visit his daughter for the holidays, but Mrs. Gwinnett says he didn't want to be underfoot if the baby came early."

Or he didn't want a new arrival competing for Mandy's attention. Perhaps the old fellow was simply unwilling to risk travel in winter. I was about to comment to that effect when another piece of stray local history crossed my mind.

"Mandy's mother died in childbirth, didn't she?"

"Mrs. Pettigrew lived for a few weeks, though the fevers got her in the end. Squire was never the same, but Miss Mandy has wanted for nothing, despite what people say about her papa. The baronet dotes on her, too, according to Cousin."

"The squire has apparently disdained to hire another house-keeper. I called on him just now, and his dwelling is less than spotless."

"I do hear things." Mrs. Swinburne paused to switch rows on her knitting. "Young Jamison took some biscuits and currant bread to Pettigrew's, and he claims the house needs only bats and a ghost to qualify for one of Mrs. Radcliffe's novels. Such a shame. It's a fine old place."

Young Jamison—when sober—was an accurate observer. "A thorough dusting is long overdue, and the footmen have neglected the windows inside and out. I doubt the chimneys have been cleaned since Miss Mandy spoke her vows, and that's plain foolishness. The whole place is sad."

"Pettigrew doesn't want to hire new staff. His footmen recall Queen Anne's coronation fondly, and his cook worked for Noah on the Ark. She's a dear, but not at all in Mrs. Gwinnett's league. Never was, if I might be honest."

"Nobody is in Mrs. Gwinnett's league, and I would say that to Carême himself."

"Now who is exaggerating?"

"Certainly not me. Swinnie, you truly have no idea who is funding your travels?"

She clicked through a quarter of a row. "I do complain sometimes to Cousin in my letters. I tell her how I miss my Daphne and long to see the children. Cousin might have mentioned something to Mandy, and Mandy does write to her father regularly."

"You think Pettigrew might be your benefactor?" Pettigrew, who had taken specific notice of the ponies in the livery stable. Pettigrew, who well knew that our church steeple had been without a bell for years.

"If the squire had that much money to spend on a widow who misses her family," Swinnie said, pushing her stitches along her needle, "why not hire some young footmen to take that house in hand?"

Valid question. "Because that would offend the old footmen?"

"Hardly. They would boss the youngsters without mercy, my lord. That's how it works. If you do find out that Pettigrew has turned up generous, please let me know. I'd like to thank him."

If not Pettigrew, then who else had the means to give away such a large sum? Too many of the gentry were rich in acres and poor in cash. And yet, Pettigrew was a miser and a grouch.

Or circumstances had turned him miserly and grouchy. I spoke before common sense could stop me. "You could thank Pettigrew by organizing a thorough cleaning of his house, Swinnie. Nobody can see as much done by maids and footmen, or see it done as well, as you when you take a notion to clean."

Her needles went still. "One cleans like that in spring, my lord, when a house can be properly aired." Despite her demurral, her eyes had taken on a particular gleam.

"If the young people on staff at the Hall have time to maunder on about their broken hearts and lost wagers, they have time to spare you a day of cleaning at Pettigrew's."

"We'd need two days at least. He'll never allow it."

"He won't know a thing about it. As of tomorrow, he'll bide at the

Hall for the holidays. Do your worst, Swinnie. Vinegar and newspapers for the windows, fresh sachets on the bedposts, brushes up every flue. Beeswax and lemon oil on the wainscoting, and every carpet beaten within an inch of its wool."

The longer I spoke, the more the gleam in Swinnie's eyes turned to a fire of determination.

"If that man made it possible for me to be with my Daphne—and I'm not saying he did and also not saying he didn't—then I will personally scrub his floors with my own signature lavender wax."

I rose, half dismayed at the mischief I was suggesting and half amazed at my own daring. "And you will swear everybody to secrecy, lest Pettigrew not appreciate the gesture."

"I will counsel discretion for the sake of the squire's pride, but secrecy and young footmen are not close companions."

She truly knew her infantry. "I leave the details to you, then, and will be thoroughly surprised when Squire's windows sparkle on Christmas morning."

"They will sparkle by this time next week, or my name isn't Helen Marie Swinburne." She got to her feet with the energy that had characterized her throughout my youth. "I will need supplies from the Hall, and you will please alert your dear mother to this scheme, my lord, lest she think half her staff has joined the Royal Navy."

"Her Grace will applaud your generous spirit, as I do."

"Flatterer." She hugged me again at the door and adjusted my purple plaid scarf so my ears were covered.

I doubtless looked ridiculous swaddled like that, but I made my way back to the Hall a bit lighter of heart for having instigated a good turn for a neighbor and a little project for a woman who knew how to keep thirty female inside staff organized and occupied.

And as to that, Pettigrew might well have been Mrs. Swinburne's benefactor. That did not prove he'd purchased the church bell or bought the dapple gray pony.

Puzzling, the whole business. Damned puzzling.

The afternoon mail was as voluminous as it was dull. I dealt with the simple matters—pay this, thank you for that, a polite explanation that His Grace was traveling for the other—and plowed onward to the reports and estate matters.

A tap on the door made me glance at the clock.

Ye gods and dancing elves. Despite approaching darkness, I still had two hours before the dressing bell rang in anticipation of the evening meal.

"Enter."

"I come bearing gifts," Hyperia said, slipping around the door and closing it with her hip. "Tea and biscuits to spoil your supper." She set the tray on my desk, right on top of my carefully sorted piles of mail.

"Mrs. Swinburne herself has admonished me to eat more. Are these her biscuits?" Little shortbread rounds dusted with cinnamon.

"They are. The stars are all gone, but Mrs. Gwinnett saved back some of these. I brought gunpowder. I hope that suits?"

Hyperia sat opposite the desk. I didn't want the expanse of wood, blotter, and mail between us, so I came around and took the chair beside her.

"Any excuse to set aside the great debate between rutabagas and mangel-wurzels suits. Did you know it's becoming popular to breed Norfolk ewes to Southdown rams? The progeny lack their mamas' horns, but they mature early and make good mutton. Crossing that progeny with Cheviots or merinos might result in good-quality wool as well. Please say you find the topic fascinating, because I am only halfway through the report, and I never want to see another sheep again in all my born days."

Hyperia passed me a cup of steaming tea with two biscuits tucked onto the saucer. "Jules, are you well?"

"Well enough. I am not Arthur, though. God in heaven, I am not Arthur. I tell you, Perry, the man is a dear brother and a conscientious steward of the family holdings, and he is also a living saint. Mangel-wurzels and rutabagas, for pity's sake, and nobody can plant anything until a decree goes out from the Hall as to how many acres of which are most desirable."

She patted my arm. "Spring is some months off. You have time to deliberate."

My darling was mocking me, and I mostly deserved it. I dunked my biscuit into my tea and consoled myself with the buttery sweetness.

"How does Mrs. G or Mrs. S turn sugar green?" I asked. "Atticus was most impressed."

"Spinach, I suppose. Mash it up, and it will turn everything, including your fingers, green. I'm told you persuaded Squire Petti-grew to join us. Her Grace is in alt."

"Her Grace was sworn to secrecy. Pettigrew wants to make an entrance, exactly like Uncle Terrence did, and I am inclined to abet Pettigrew. He honestly did not take much convincing to join us."

The tea was hot and sweet—I often drank it plain, but Hyperia had doctored mine with honey—and the biscuits were luscious. As rich as everyday shortbread, but sweeter and lighter.

"You don't sound happy to add him to our collection of grouches, Jules. He's all alone in that musty old pile of his, and winter came early this year."

To those shut up in musty old piles, winter probably came early every year. "Mrs. Swinburne thinks Pettigrew might be financing her travels."

Hyperia took her time selecting a biscuit from those on the tray. "What does it matter who paid the shot, Jules? She's delighted to go, and we are delighted that she's happy."

Had *Hyperia* arranged for Mrs. Swinburne's reunion with her daughter? "Perry, dearest..."

She dunked her biscuit and held it dripping over her tea. "What?" A little cross, a little defensive.

Rather than make a blunt accusation, I kissed her.

"I love you," I said, which was absolutely true. "You were kind to bring me the tray, and a respite with you from rutabagas and rutting sheep is a dream come true."

"You are ambushing me."

"I am expressing my gratitude to you. Mrs. Swinburne is certainly grateful to whoever is funding her remove to Philadelphia."

Hyperia bit off half her biscuit. "Jules, let it go. Somebody had the same kind idea you did, and that is simply coincidence."

"The same somebody arranged the business with the dapple gray pony."

"Why does any of it matter? Are you simply in want of an investigation? Aren't the mysteries of root vegetables and sheep breeding enough to keep your curiosity in good form?"

I took another biscuit from my saucer and considered the question. Why was I fixated on the fact that my little holiday schemes had been thwarted by another? The point had never been to take credit for the gestures.

The point had been to alleviate hardship, to rectify an oversight. Or that had been part of the point.

"Arthur has done a spectacular job executing the duties attendant to the title," I said. "He stayed at the Hall and contended with rutabagas and rents, MPs and cabinet ministers. He did all this while Harry and I were off playing soldier."

Hyperia set down her tea cup. "You were not *playing* anything."

"At times, we were. Harry especially had a flare for enjoying the job, a bit too much for my comfort. In any case, Arthur often had the harder task. I see that now. Not more dangerous, but the risks Harry and I took on were risks we chose. Arthur never chose to be the duke."

"Very well, Arthur is a good fellow. We knew that. What does it have to do with your church bell or the ponies?"

"Arthur is a good fellow, and I want him to find his duchy in better shape when he returns than it was in when he left it. I want to pay my debt to him, Perry, a debt I wasn't even aware I had until well after I mustered out. The reports alone... They blind me every bit as much as excessive sunshine does. Arthur has been reading them for years, taking them seriously, *recalling* them."

Hyperia looked puzzled. "Arthur would say you owe him nothing. That you served your country in your way, and he served in his. Both matter, and both were done to the best of your respective abilities."

How to explain to her that getting Harry killed and myself captured by the French was by no means a best effort? The opposite, in fact.

"You ask why the bell, pony, and Mrs. Swinburne's bank draft matter. They matter because those gifts were to be my contribution above and beyond the call of duty. My efforts to do more than the required minimum at the job Arthur left me."

Hyperia poured me more tea. "You are a good brother, Jules. Also ridiculous. Arthur had years to order the village another bell. He wasn't concerned about it."

Maybe because he hadn't faced death at such close range as I had, not yet. Maybe because a church bell was a luxury compared to developing sheep that were equally valuable for their mutton and wool.

"Or he was concerned, but simply lacked the hours in the day to tend to the church bell too. In any case, I want to do more than hold the reins here at the Hall. I want to move at least a few matters forward. Picking out a pony for Leander was another job Arthur would take seriously if he were here, so I took it seriously too."

"And you adore Mrs. Swinburne."

"Somebody else apparently esteems her just as highly, but in Arthur's books, she was very comfortably retired, and for him to meddle in any regard would have been disrespectful. I saw her situation differently. She was pining and lonely, which is no condition to be in later in life."

Or earlier in life. At any time of life, and especially not at the holidays.

"Drink your tea, Jules."

I complied, the tea being less sweet for having been topped up, but still hot, and Hyperia wasn't scolding me. She was reminding me not to neglect food and drink.

"I don't like secrets, Perry, and that's also part of why these coincidences trouble me. I get on better when I have a puzzle to solve, though I usually grumble all the while, and this Father-Christmas-by-Stealth situation is a puzzle."

"It is that," she said, finishing her tea. "And how we will manage Squire Pettigrew, the aunties, and Uncle Terrence is another puzzle. I vow Bertha would criticize Saint Peter because his halo wasn't bright enough. At the very least, she shows me the sort of elder I do not want to be."

"You are nothing like her, dearest Perry. Now tell me why you really sought me out among the rutabagas."

My darling looked at her hands, and lovely hands they were too. "I have a favor to ask."

"As long as it doesn't involve breeding sheep…"

"I still haven't heard from Healy, Jules. Might we send a pigeon to Town and have somebody look in on him?"

"You fear he's developed an ague?"

My teasing earned me a scowl. "People do, especially foolish people who neglect themselves at the coldest time of year. London reeks of coal smoke in winter, and Healy barely socializes anymore."

Socializing for a fashionable bachelor was an expensive undertaking, and Healy West was trying to exercise economies.

"Whom shall I ask to look in on him, Perry?" The town house was minimally staffed, what with His Grace out of the country and the remaining family ruralizing, but through the butler, I could get word overnight to just about any London household.

"Fashionable Society has gone to the shires for the holidays," Hyperia said, getting up to pace. "Where is Lady Ophelia?"

I rose as well, sensing the conversation had finally arrived at the subject of greatest concern to Hyperia now that I was through with the afternoon's quotient of bleating and whining.

"Godmama is in Hampshire, I believe, or that's where she claimed she was off to when last we corresponded. Would you like me to nip up to Town and drag Healy back with me?"

To my shock, Hyperia tucked herself against me. "What if Healy is in a sponging house, Jules? They'd charge him a fortune just to send word to me."

Healy West, owner of considerable acreage and a pedigree that went back centuries, would have to have been a very great fool indeed to land himself in a sponging house. That was the last stop before debtors' prison, a diabolical combination of jail and rooms to let, where every glass of water and blanket added astronomically to the debtor's tally.

"He's not in a sponging house," I said, stroking Hyperia's back. "He has funds."

"He *had* funds. He doesn't discuss his finances with me, and he's been very secretive lately."

The mail would reach Himalayan heights if I abandoned my post. The elders would be aghast that I'd jaunt off on little notice, and I had every confidence that in my absence Mrs. Gwinnett's toddies would result in Caldicott Hall's first winter bacchanal.

"I'll leave in the morning," I said, kissing Hyperia's cheek. "You can make my excuses to Pettigrew for not welcoming him properly. The press of ducal business, an urgent matter with the solicitors. Make up any Banbury tale you please, and I will have Healy down here by the end of the week."

She let me have her weight. "Thank you, Jules. I didn't want to ask, but I no longer know my brother as well as I once did. He's still my brother."

We held each other, and a frisson of some vague desperation threaded through me. May the day never come when Hyperia feared to share her burdens with me. May the time never arrive when I was so consumed with duty and debts that I neglected to honor this sweet, kind, fierce lady.

She fortified me, with her esteem and her affection, with her pragmatism and pride.

I had not lied to her: I wanted to know who our at-large anonymous benefactor was, because so far, their generosity had thwarted my efforts to serve with distinction in Arthur's stead. I had also been truthful when I'd admitted that puzzles had become nigh irresistible to me, and a vexing investigation would alleviate my creeping case of the dismals.

I had not, though, admitted to Hyperia that I hoped, if I was a good enough steward at the Hall, and a clever enough investigator, that perhaps I could be forgiven for being just the extra, illegitimate spare who'd bungled so badly in uniform.

CHAPTER TEN

As Arthur's traveling coach lumbered northward, I put all thoughts of correspondence aside and hoped some kindly elf would burn the lot of it before I returned to the Hall.

"Whyn't you bring Atlas, guv?" Atticus occupied the opposite bench, while I sat facing the horses.

"Because fairness to my mount dictates that he be brought up to Town in reasonable stages, which might have us leaving just as he's arriving. This is a lightning raid."

"On what?"

"Old Londontowne. Stop eyeing the hamper, lad. We will eat after the second change." We'd be in London after four changes, if all went according to plan. I'd made this journey dozens of times and knew every inn and crossroads along the way. John Coachman typically changed teams every ten or twelve miles, but bad going would shorten that interval to eight miles or so.

The number of changes didn't affect the length of the journey in the usual course. Hostlers experienced at the job could swap out tired horses for fresh equines in less than a minute. The condition of the roads, by contrast, could result in progress so limited that walking to London would have been the faster alternative.

Fortunately, the same cold snap stinging noses and fingers meant the roads were frozen into rigid washboards. A well-sprung coach could keep moving under such conditions, and now that we were en route, I was eager to reach our destination.

"What are we raiding in Old Londontowne?" Atticus asked, swinging a heel against the bench.

"If anybody asks, we are retrieving Healy West so he can join the merriment at the Hall."

"What merriment, guv? You being ironical?"

"Give it a week or so. The merriment has started among the staff. Pettigrew will swell the ranks of guests today, and the punchbowl will be set up in the foyer on Sunday. By tradition, we decorate inside the Hall the day after."

"If you hung any more kissin' boughs inside the Hall, we wouldn't see the rafters. What decorating is left to do?"

"Cloved oranges, wreaths, ribbons. The pine swagging must wait until Christmas Day, but Mama is following the recent fashion for decorating conifers with candles and trinkets. She has small trees set up in the servants' hall and the music room. The whole business is quite lovely."

So lovely that last year I'd slunk off to London rather than endure another impromptu chorus of "God Rest Ye Merry, Gentlemen" from the footmen. Everywhere I'd turned, I'd seen giggles beneath kissing boughs, bright red ribbons wrapped around banisters, silver bells hung on door latches, wreaths, punchbowls...

So much gaiety, and I hadn't had the heart for any of it. Part of me still didn't, hence this respite in London afforded me some guilty relief.

"What if we can't find Healy West?" Atticus thumped the bench with one heel after the other in alternation.

"He's a sizable specimen. Why would he be hard to locate?"

"Because he don't want to spend his holly-days listening to a bunch of old besoms carp at each other." Atticus struck a pose, nose in the air, hand at his throat. "'Not to be critical, but everything at the Hall is soooo intolerably duuurty. Young people today don't know how to dust, or curtsey, or bow, or breathe. Such a pity!'"

He had Aunt Bertha to the life, the little rotter. "That is rude, Atticus."

"What's rude is bellyachin' all the time. Aunt Crosspatch isn't so bad, but that other 'un... Even when she says thank you, Aunt Bother is somehow saying you disappoint her. She puts me in mind of the matrons at the poorhouse. Always scolding a lad, and sounding nice while they did it."

Aunt Bertha was in good form indeed if Aunt Crosby benefited by comparison. "You can recall the matrons?"

"Aye. One of 'em wasn't so bad. Mrs. Hipple used to pass me an extra piece of bread sometimes, and she'd put butter on it too. I still love me some fresh bread with butter. Mrs. Hipple found me the post at Makepeace House. Last I saw of her, she was warning me to say please and thank you, not speak unless spoken to, and say my prayers every night. Always had us prayin', the matrons did. Grateful for this and grateful for that. I woulda been grateful to have a pillow for me poor knees, we did so much prayin'."

I made a mental note of the name Hipple because Atticus's antecedents could at some point bear investigating. He was an orphan cast upon the charity of the parish, and because that had been a London parish, the chances of ever learning his story were minuscule. Even a single name, though, might illuminate a few facts.

"Young Jamison was glad to come up to Town with us," Atticus went on. "Said he needed a repairing lease for his health. The undercook gets him beneath the mistletoe and don't let him go."

The undercook was Mrs. Gwinnett's niece, a fetching armful of about twelve stone, and all of it jolly. A junior footmen could face worse fates.

"I can assure you, Atticus, the repairing lease was necessitated by an excess of toddies rather than an abundance of holiday affection."

"You ain't seen 'em go at it, guv." The boy sounded utterly bewildered.

"Avert your eyes and ignore the spectacle." Life in an army camp had involved a great deal of averting the eyes and ignoring spectacles, another reason why I'd preferred to wander the countryside on my own.

The coach rolled on, the passing miles giving me an opportunity to ponder. I let my thoughts wander from church bells to besoms, from the poorhouse to the sponging house. Because we passed within a few streets of the West address, I asked John Coachman to drop me on its doorstep and take Atticus on to Caldicott House.

We'd made good time and were thus arriving in London in the early afternoon. The darkness in the sky—dense coal smoke—made the hour seem later and gave the day a sinister cast. In the country-side, the sun might be shining, but here in the metropolis, all was reeking winter gloom.

The knocker was off the Wests' front door, but I banged my fist stoutly several times anyway. I had run tame in this house as a boy, just as Hyperia had been a frequent visitor in the Caldicott dwellings. Healy, too, though he was enough my junior that we'd not been in the same forms.

Nobody answered my knock. I took myself in a full circuit around the house. The walkways, save at the front, had not been swept or shoveled. Smoke curled from only a single chimney, and a peek into the mews showed no evidence of West's horse in residence.

Odd.

I returned to the front of the house and made my way to the area steps, which descended from a side walkway to the level of the kitchen. When I rapped on this door, it was opened by a young woman in two shawls, a full-length apron. and mobcap.

"He ain't—isn't—here if you're looking for Mr. West. Sorry."

She attempted to close the door, but I'd already wedged my boot into the opening. "I am looking for Mr. West indeed. Might I come in?"

"Wouldn't be proper. Mrs. Helms ain't—isn't—here either."

The young woman should not have told me that. I'd put her age at about sixteen, and her rosy complexion suggested a rural girlhood. New to Town and wary, but not yet wise.

"I am Lord Julian Caldicott, a friend of the family. Miss West is visiting at Caldicott Hall for the holidays, and she asked me to fetch her sewing basket while I was in Town. I won't be but a minute." I offered my best harmless-fellow smile, though Hyperia had asked no such thing of me.

I wanted to look around the house, for several reasons.

The maid stepped back, and I passed into a surprisingly cold kitchen. A weak fire smoldered on the enormous cooking hearth. No heat came from the oven. No scents of food preparation hung in the air.

"You're here alone?"

"I'm not supposed to say. I think you'd best leave, my lord."

More proof that she'd been newly hired and from the shires. London lords did not take orders from scullery maids.

"I'll just be a moment." I brushed past her and mounted the stairs that led to the ground floor.

She remained at the bottom of the steps, clearly torn between the need to keep an eye on an intruder and the need to keep herself safe.

"Mind you take only the sewing basket!" she called after me.

Her wages would be at the very bottom of what the agencies demanded, if she was receiving wages at all. She would not be able to afford coach fare back to her village, and she likely hadn't a friend in the entire city.

What in blazes was Healy West up to?

The rest of the house was deserted and frigid. Draperies were drawn over every window. Dust was accumulating on even the railing of the stairs that led up to the first floor. Either Healy West was not in residence, or he'd taken to selling his best boots, half his clean shirts, half his morning coats... His jewelry box was similarly half emptied, and his bed had been stripped.

One was normally escorted to a sponging house in the clothes on one's back, though for a sum certain, somebody might have been dispatched to gather up Healy's effects.

And yet, no furniture or carpets had been sold, no paintings taken off the walls for permanent "cleaning." The pianoforte remained in the music room. I made a brief pass through Hyperia's apartment—I had business there too—and of course came across no sewing basket.

I returned to the kitchen and found the maid huddled in a blanket near the desultory fire. I stirred up the coals and looked around for kindling to toss on the embers.

"Wherever Miss West's workbasket is, it's not where she told me to look. Wait here."

I went out into the garden and broke a dead oak sapling into eighteen-inch lengths. I gathered up sticks and dead leaves and returned to the kitchen.

When the fire was making a bit more of an effort, I took an empty metal bucket to the back of the pantries where the coal hole emptied and found barely enough fuel to fill a scoop.

Not good. Not good at all. I brought what coal I'd found back to the kitchen.

The maid gathered her blanket more tightly around her at the sight of me. "Coalman won't bring no more unless he's paid."

"You aren't staying here."

"I ain't got nowhere else to go, and I've been hired here proper. I'm to stay. I will get wages for biding where I was hired. Cook said."

A thread of hysteria ran through the girl's obstinance.

"Let me put it another way." I rummaged until I found the tea drawer and a small crock that held some crystalized honey. "You will freeze to death if you stay here much longer. I am offering you the hospitality of Caldicott House, and I will send around one of our maids to fetch you. She can vouch for your safety beneath a ducal roof."

"You're a *duke*?"

Dukes were not, strictly speaking, "my lords." More proof of her recent arrival to London. "I am the brother of a duke." The kettle held some water, probably melted snow, and I swung it over the growing blaze. "The duke himself would be addressed as Your Grace. When did you last eat?"

"Day before yesterday. Scraps from market."

My next objective was to find a mug. "I beg your pardon?"

"I go to Haymarket, and when a vendor packs up for the day, they sometimes leave scraps behind—a dirty carrot or two, some parsnips. I'm not particular, but I'm also not very fast. The street boys let me have some carrots, though. Probably felt sorry for me."

The notion disgusted her, clearly.

"It's worse than that. They were earning your trust so that when you were truly starving, you'd go with them to the nice landlady who needed a scullery maid for her busy, warm kitchen. What they would not have told you was that the lady was an abbess, and your duties would not be in the kitchen."

The girl put a hand over her mouth, eyes round. "I told me uncle London was wicked. Aunt told him, too, but he wouldn't listen. 'Wages are better,' he said. 'You'll catch the eye of a handsome man,' he said. 'You're a hard worker, and you'll get on fine in Town.' Uncle is a fool."

Uncle was no more foolish than half the yeomanry in the land. Peace had brought the opposite of prosperity, and times were hard in the countryside. What the tenant farmers did not realize was that times were unimaginably worse in the slums and always would be.

I found a clean mug and filled a tea strainer with a portion of China black. When the kettle had whistled for a minute, I poured boiling water over the leaves and set the tea on the hearth near the maid.

While she held the steaming mug in two red hands, I poured a dash of hot water into the honey pot and swirled it around.

"Give it another minute," I said, "and you can sweeten your tea. Do you know where Healy West has gone?"

"No, sir. He gave the senior servants holiday leave, but I don't think he gave them their packets before he sent them off. I was to take in the mail and such, but mostly I've been shivering."

Healy must have decamped the instant Hyperia had stepped into Kerrick's traveling coach.

"Did you see him go?"

She breathed in the steam from the steeping tea. "Aye. He simply walked up the street and turned the corner."

"No luggage? Not a satchel or valise?"

"He packed one. I think one of the footmen took it someplace before they left Town."

West would not bide at his club and leave a servant behind to starve and freeze. I was nearly sure of that.

"What was Mr. West wearing when he left?"

The girl removed the strainer from the mug and set it on the hearth, then poured a portion of the honey water into her tea.

"Don't gulp it," I said. "Your tummy will rebel if you've been missing meals." Spoken from experience.

She sipped silently, and I was reminded of Atticus, repeatedly exhorted to be grateful for a life of hardship and hunger.

"Mr. West was wearing his fancy coat, sir, the one with three capes. Fancy boots, all shiny. Come clear up to his knees. He has gloves lined with lamb's-wool, and he were wearing a black scarf. Perishin' cold, it was, and he jaunted off like he was going to see his tailor."

"When?"

"Right after Miss West went with that countess in the big coach."

This was bad news. Hyperia would expect me to find Healy West, and he had days' head start on me. "What's your name, miss?"

"I'm Clark. Hannah Clark, from Dunking Cross in Hampshire. This tea is ever so wonderful."

"You are free to wait here, Miss Clark, until I can send a maid for you. Caldicott House is only a few streets away. In the alternative, you may finish your tea, and I will escort you myself to Caldicott

House, where you will be welcome to spend the holidays with what staff remains."

She was young, afraid, and far from home. She ought not to trust me.

"You ain't an abbess," she said, hands wrapped around her mug.

"I'm not Father Christmas either." That had been proven three times over. "I intend to find Healy West and get some answers from him. He might simply have returned to the family seat for a few days before joining his sister at Caldicott Hall. He might be visiting friends, but he left you to make shift under trying conditions, and that worries me."

"Worried me something powerful. I suppose I'll go with you. You ain't looked at me wrong since you stuck your boot in the door."

Some things were the same, town, village, or country. "Collect your things. What you can't carry, we can always retrieve for you later."

She finished her tea and rose. "I can carry me things. Give me a minute." She disappeared down a dim corridor, leaving me to tidy up and to lecture myself about displays of temper before servants.

She returned a moment later, the blanket now formed into a knotted bundle of pathetically small portions. "I'm only borrowing the blanket, sir. I promise that."

"You're borrowing a decent cloak, too, and a bonnet, scarf, and gloves, Miss Clark. Let's be on our way, shall we?"

I made no effort to relieve her of her possessions, concluding she'd rather keep hold of them herself, what little she had. As we traveled the distance to Caldicott House, I listed more reasons why Healy might have abandoned house and staff and absented himself from his home.

None of my excuses—for that's what they were—held any merit. A friend falling ill would not summon his chums to catch his malaise. If Healy had been set upon by footpads, he'd not have packed half his belongings before trundling off for a gratuitous pummeling. If Healy had nipped off to look in at the family seat, he'd had no need to keep that journey a secret from his sister.

"Watch out what you wish for," I muttered as we approached Caldicott House.

"Beg pardon, sir?"

"Nothing of any moment." I'd bemoaned a lack of substantive investigations to occupy me, and now I'd found a true puzzle. Hyperia would be wild with worry, and I was not a little concerned myself. By the time I found Healy, Arthur's mail would be stacked to the heavens, and Aunt Bertha would likely have inspired the entire staff to give notice.

Happy Christmas.

"This is Caldicott House," I said as we approached a staid three-story façade. "I will introduce you in the kitchen. The circumstances are unusual, and you are not responsible for them."

She looked at me blankly, poor thing.

As it happened, I did not have an opportunity to shock the Caldicott House staff by intruding belowstairs with a scullery maid in tow. We were greeted at the door by the butler, who exhorted me to take myself to the cozy study and await a tray with all the trimmings.

"And Atticus?" I asked.

"Being stuffed with biscuits in the kitchen. He is delighted with the cinnamon shortbread. I will see to Miss Clark, my lord."

He padded off, Miss Clark sending me a dubious look and scuttling after him.

I followed orders and made for the study, ready for both warmth and sustenance. What I found was Healy West, cuffs turned back, boots up on Arthur's desk, and newspapers strewn about the blotter.

"Get your rubbishing feet off His Grace's desk." I advanced into the room, which was cozy indeed.

West stared at me over the Society pages. "Julian. What are *you* doing here?"

I shoved his boots aside and might have planted him a facer except that he was seated and I was standing, and even brawling must be conducted according to certain rules. Then too, if the fates were kind and Hyperia generous, Healy West might one day become my brother-by-marriage.

Assuming he lived to see the sunset.

"I am here by right of familial ownership of this dwelling," I retorted. "What in blazes are you doing here?"

He rose and sidled away from the desk. "Didn't think you'd mind."

"You didn't think I'd find out. Hyperia has been worried about you, fearing you've been taken up by the blacklegs or tipstaffs. She envisioned you shivering with a lung fever in some sponging house, unwilling to spend even the blunt necessary to contact her for help."

West made a production out of organizing the newspaper—*Arthur's* newspaper. "Hyperia has a vivid imagination."

"She is the soul of good sense and sororal devotion. You, by contrast, are a mooching trespasser."

He paused in his rattling of pages. "Mooching, I grant you, but trespasser? I've been a guest in this house."

"You've been a caller, on very rare and distant occasions. What the hell do you think you're doing, idling about like some remittance man who must keep out of sight of his uncle?"

Healy West had no title, but his pedigree was venerable enough to be far, far above reproach. For many generations, the family had prospered, but Healy's parents had died before acquainting him with the finer points of preserving inherited wealth. The Corn Laws would keep him afloat for a time, but his best hope lay in patience, prudence, and sound investments.

In addition, of course, to some of the economies I'd suggested when I'd thwarted the blackmailer draining what coins remained in Healy's coffers.

"It's not my uncle begrudging me a spare groat," he said, laying the newspaper beside the blotter. The blotter itself held several pages of writing in various stages of drying. "Nobody warns a fellow that the tailor who's always so glad to suggest the latest fashions turns into a bloodhound come December. The vultures were circling, and without Hyperia in residence, I knew what I was in for."

"So you left some girl just in from the shires to turn the duns away from your door while you bolted to the nearest ducal residence?"

West had the grace to look ashamed. "They won't dare pester me here."

"Your scullery maid was out of coal, West. No food in the house. I could see my breath unless I was in the kitchen standing by the hearth. That girl was scavenging at the Haymarket for edible garbage."

Miss Clark's situation bothered me more than Healy's appropriation of the ducal residence, which was saying something.

"The lower orders are resourceful," West said, bracing a hand on the mantel. "I have been resourceful, too, but you show me no understanding whatsoever."

He was on his feet and all but begging for a thrashing.

"Cut line, or we are for the alley, where you will not last five minutes."

His chin came up. "I box, I fence, I ride to hounds. In all modesty, I must warn you that I can give a pretty impressive accounting of myself."

Spare me the bleatings of a blustering bachelor. I clipped him on his pretty impressive chin, a left cross, the sort of blow that at first seems negligible. Then the pain begins to radiate along the jaw, the teeth and nose join in, and a throbbing starts up in the brow and temple. Harry had taught me the left cross because it was an unexpected opening move and never had I used it to such excellent advantage.

"That is for Miss Clark, whom you left all alone to guard your empty, freezing larders. Unless you want more of same—for Hyperia who fretted terribly over you, for the staff here of whom you've taken shameless advantage, and for my own selfish satisfaction in teaching you some pugilism—you'd best get the apology over with and make a start on the explanation."

West rubbed his jaw, which was turning a pleasing shade of red. His gaze held wary surprise, and I was reminded that he had no brothers. The gentle art of horseplay had likely been denied him.

And that gap in his education showed.

"I am sorry. Never meant to inconvenience anybody. Meant to follow Hyperia down to the Hall in due course, but the press of business demanded my presence in Town. She hadn't been gone an hour before the tailor was at my front door—the man himself at my *front* door—and I knew the bootmaker would be right behind him."

And the hatter, glovemaker, wine merchant, gentlemen's clubs, jeweler...

"West, the trades must be paid. They've extended you credit *for the entire year*, and now you must pay them. You know they must be paid."

"I do know, true, but I was a bit vague on how much they had to be paid. Hyperia managed the household money, and thus the grocer and cheesemonger and so forth are all taken care of. The coalman fell on my side of the ledger, and he's an insistent sort. Caldicott House was staffed, and I didn't think you'd mind my biding here for a bit. It's so blessedly quiet, and I need that."

He was a good-looking specimen. Tallish, broad-shouldered, trim through the middle, hair styled a la Brutus. He cut a dash credibly enough. I could not see him impersonating a recluse.

"Do you need quiet or cash?"

Something speculative flickered through his eyes, a how-much-to-admit/was-that-an-offer quality. "Both, though the shortage of cash is pressing. I could do the usual pathetic things—sell the artwork, claim the pianoforte is no longer stylish, pretend to pant after heiresses—but those measures *are* pathetic, and they also lack imagination.

Every fellow bobbing in the River Tick attempts them. I am not in dun territory quite yet. I just need some time."

"So you thought you'd demonstrate your flare for bad manners and move in here without an invitation?" I could, in a grudging corner of my mind, admit that West had shown initiative of a sort—a near-criminal sort.

"I thought I'd..." He stared at the fire. "Well, never mind what I thought. You found me out, and now I suppose you will tattle to Hyperia."

"I have yet to hear the full explanation, West, and try as you might, you cannot paint me as the villain of this piece. You are living beyond your means, and when you could not prevail on Hyperia to solve that dilemma for you, you turned to subterfuge and duplicity."

I was laying it on a bit thick—West's means had been considerably reduced by a true felon—but I sought the full story, and he was being coy. Had he simply wanted to evade creditors, he could have jaunted down to Caldicott Hall days ago with Hyperia. The Hall was a ducal residence, and West had been invited to visit there.

He could have asked me for permission to tarry in Town for a few days at the ducal town house, claiming his entire staff deserved holiday leave. I would have seen such a request as blatant penny-pinching on his part, but assented. Future brother-by-marriage, victim of undeserved ill fortune, and all that.

"Not duplicity," West said, dropping his contemplative young philosopher pose by the fire. "I planned to tell you when I came down to the Hall. Mention that I'd imposed for a brief while, gone short of staff at home, and that sort of thing. You, though, must see wrongdoing instead of a man coping with exigencies beyond his control."

"I might see both if you'd tell me what it is that you're writing and how you think it will cure your lack of cash."

He went still. "Writing? You think I'm involved in a writing project?"

I was fairly certain, based on circumstantial evidence and my recent experience with Arthur's mountains of mail in the Caldicott Hall study.

"You claim to *need* peace and quiet," I said. "You have a gentleman's education and can thus read, write, and, to a limited extent, reason. Somebody has certainly been scribbling away in the past hour or two right at His Grace's desk. You can publish anonymously in most instances, thus preserving your gentlemanly credentials while taking coin for your creation. You have ink on your fourth finger, though we know ledgers and bank drafts aren't the reason."

I settled into Arthur's seat, which was still warm from West's prolonged occupation of it. "You chose to work here in the study," I went on. "A quieter venue than the library, warmer, and housing many fewer distractions. His Grace's studies are set up to comfortably facilitate great quantities of reading and writing. Ergo, you are trying to write your way out of debt."

"You are scarifying, my lord. Positively scarifying. Hyperia has the same ability to notice a few details and then tell a fellow that his mistress is playing him false. She was right—Hyperia, that is, not the mistress—but a sister ought not to notice such things, much less speak of mistresses. Scarifying."

"If you criticize your sister one more time in my hearing, I will black both your eyes. What is your magnum opus?"

West took the chair opposite the desk. "A play. *Tom Jones* brought forward sixty years. A coming-of-age tale on the surface, but satire if you look more closely. When one goes short of coin, one sees how little value is truly placed on standing and heritage. They all want money—the bachelors, the bankers, the strumpets, the matchmaking mamas. At least the tailors and strumpets provide some value."

Coming of age indeed. "Is this play any good?" I expected harrumphing and pawing in response, but West's smile was wry.

"I hope so. It's funny, in parts. Bit, um, autobiographical in a vague sort of way."

Meaning our hero's mistress had played him false, and his foolish behavior on the field of honor had seen him blackmailed, while the family fortunes had unaccountably dwindled?

I had to admit that West had had a hard year. He was trying in a bumbling fashion to both make sense of his situation and to address his obligations. Heaven knew I'd stumbled along that same path. Maybe I would black only one of his eyes…

"You won't finish the play reading the penny press, West."

"Oh, but I will. The penny press is merciless, and they spare nobody. Some of my best material derives from the doings of my betters as recounted by the scallywags and weasels of the fourth estate."

He spoke with a bit too much relish. "You keep your nasty little imagination off His Grace of Waltham and the Caldicott family, West, or I will break every one of your fingers." I was certainly propounding a great deal of violence for a man who'd pulled the only punch he'd landed in months.

Peace on earth and goodwill toward future brothers-in-law. "Though I suppose," I went on, "if I did give you a proper drubbing, Hyperia would commence breaking my toes."

The promised tray arrived with enough food for four hungry men. I chose a toasted cheese sandwich, still hot for once and good fare for a cold winter day.

"Don't stand on ceremony now," I said, gesturing with my food. "You've appropriated an entire residence. Purloining a bit of sustenance is well within your capabilities."

He took a beef-and-brie sandwich, also toasted. "Will you tell Hyperia?"

"She'll be proud of you. You are making an effort to honor your responsibilities. If you asked her for a loan, she'd cheerfully give you credit, but you haven't. She'll like that."

"I mean about squatting in the ducal town house. Mooching."

Perhaps you should have thought of that when you waltzed in the front door and lied to the butler. "I will not knowingly mislead your sister about anything. If the topic comes up, she will hear the truth from me." The sandwich was luscious, from the melted cheese to the perfectly toasted bread.

"And if the topic does not come up?"

"Then I would advise you to raise it with her, West. On this earth, I have not met a better friend than Hyperia, nor a better mind for parsing through options, possibilities, might-have-beens, or should-have-dones. She has the kindest heart paired with the keenest insight. Lying to her is pointless and stupid."

West poured out two mugs of steaming mulled cider. "You are far gone, my lord. Hopelessly so. I assume you intend to propose?"

"Eat your sandwich. I assume you will get back to work when you've had your fill. I'm off to see a man about a recent delivery to the village, and by this time tomorrow, God willing, we will both be safely at the Hall. Before I decamp on my afternoon rambles, I will pen a note to that effect to be delivered to your sister by flying express."

We finished our meal in silence. After I'd dispatched a message by pigeon to the Hall, I left West sitting at Arthur's desk, pen in hand, foolscap on the blotter. He looked as happy as I'd seen him in recent months. I hoped for his sake—and his tailor's—that his play became the sensation of the New Year.

CHAPTER ELEVEN

Whitechapel lay about five miles east of Hyde Park, past St. Paul's, past the City, east even of the Tower. I made the journey by phaeton, despite the cold, and used the time to consider what exactly I sought from Mr. Thomas Mears.

Answers, of course—who had ordered the bell for Waltham village—and context. When had the order been placed? Had a date certain for delivery been agreed upon, or had it been happenstance that the other bell had arrived before mine?

I was lucky, in that the journey lasted little more than an hour. I had no intention of tarrying on the premises. Darkness would soon be falling, and London's East End after sunset was no place for a stray lord in his fancy equipage.

"I'm here to see Mr. Mears," I said to a clerk who occupied an enormous desk just inside the door. The premises had been a coaching inn in an earlier century, and I suspected the desk was a legacy of those origins. The front door had been decorated with a handsome wreath and the exterior lintel swagged with pine boughs.

The interior, with its exposed-brick walls, bore a resemblance to an austere chapel long since abandoned by the angels.

"Who might I say is calling, sir?" The clerk was tidy, dark-haired, and wearing fingerless gloves. He did me the courtesy of rising as he questioned me.

"Lord Julian Caldicott." I passed over a card.

The clerk studied the card, which was a bit rude of him, while I took in my surroundings. I'd been here previously, nearly a year ago, and honestly did not recall much about the place.

Not well done of me, to let the reconnoitering lapse, a sad testament to the state I'd been in.

The foyer rose to two chilly stories, while the building itself stood at three and meandered back from the street along a side alley. Most of the establishment was faced with staid brown brick, a sensible choice given London's smoky air. Seven tall mullioned windows across the front were doubtless intended to let in what meager light the London winter skies afforded.

A pungent metallic scent cut through the pervasive sulfurous aroma of Town in winter, suggesting that casting went on apace, despite the approaching holidays.

"Is Mr. Mears expecting you, my lord?"

"Unlikely." I hadn't planned to make this call until I'd left the Hall and had the entire morning to consider the matter.

"Please come with me." The clerk bustled off, and I followed him from the frigid foyer through one of several doors and into a labyrinth of corridors, across a metal walkway that ran above a stiflingly hot foundry area, and back into more orderly corridors.

We entered a room that might have been any gentleman's estate office. I did not recognize the place, nor did I recognize the man who rose from behind his desk.

"Hampton? Who have we here?"

"Lord Julian Caldicott, sir. He does not have an appointment, but would like a moment of your time."

"Of course." The smile was commercially cordial. "I believe we cast a tolling bell for his lordship, and it was only recently delivered. Would my lord like a cup of tea?"

Whoever this fellow was, he knew his business, and he was polite. He was not Thomas Mears, though there was a resemblance about the eyes and mouth.

"No tea, thank you. The purpose of my call is brief, and I do appreciate your seeing me."

The clerk withdrew on a half bow.

"My lord dealt directly with Thomas Mears, I gather," my host said. "We always trot out the master founder himself for the nobs. I'm his son, Charles. I trust your bell is satisfactory?"

"I honestly don't know. The bell hangers have yet to work their magic. Based on appearances, I anticipate complete satisfaction." I hadn't asked Sigafoose how the denizens of Hop Bottom had reacted to the arrival of their bell, but I could not see them objecting.

"We always aim to please. Papa won't be in until the New Year, so do allow me to assist you." He gestured to a pair of comfortable wing chairs positioned near the hearth.

I took one. Mears took the other. He was young, brawny beneath his fine tailoring, and had likely served out an extended apprenticeship to his father, before embarking on a tour of duty among the ledgers and solicitors. Did he spend hours a day on correspondence while longing to get back to the heat of the foundry?

"I come on a somewhat peculiar errand," I said, wishing I'd rehearsed this part of the call. "Waltham village, as you apparently know, has been without a church bell for years. I sought to address that oversight and thus ordered a bell about a year ago. My request was not urgent, but when I learned the bell would be delivered before Christmas, I was pleased."

"Bells make the holidays merrier, whether it's sleigh bells, bell carols, charity bells, bells accompanying the glee on the corner... We do like our bells at Yuletide."

A tolling bell fulfilled none of those cheery functions, and yet, Mears had a point. A bell was rung for a purpose—to summon worshipers, summon the watch, hail a houseful of guests in to dinner. Bells told us to act, to pause and reflect, to take notice.

To mourn or rejoice.

"As it happens," I said, "I was not the only person determined to rectify Waltham's lack of a bell. Another specimen arrived, very like the one I ordered, and that other bell is slated to be hung in our tower. The bell I ordered will be donated elsewhere. I am curious about the provenance of the bell that arrived first."

Dark brows drew down. "I recall something about this. We reasoned that one of the smaller parishes in your vicinity was also enjoying the generosity of a benefactor. Perhaps you set an inspiring example, my lord."

Not possible, given that I'd told no one I'd ordered a bell, not even Arthur. He would have suspected morbid motives of me, and he would have been correct.

"Perhaps I did, and I would like to thank whoever followed my example. I know what I paid for my bell—worth every penny, of course—and this second bell was indeed quite the holiday beneficence."

Mears tapped a finger on the upholstered arm of the chair. He was doubtless weighing the consequence of refusing a courtesy lord's request over the lapse in confidentiality involved in revealing the identity of one customer to another.

"Let me have a look." A shrewd response. If the other customer was the archbishop's auntie, as opposed to some grouchy old squire, that changed the complexion of the situation.

He opened a glass-fronted bookcase and finger-stepped through pasteboard files, removing one from the middle of the row. He leafed through the contents, his air of puzzlement increasing.

"We haven't a name, my lord. This is most unusual."

"How can you take a substantial order from a customer without a name?"

"The whole matter was dealt with by correspondence. The customer placed the order with a very precise written description of the desired product—I gather it was to resemble the previous bell in many particulars—and payment was sent in advance. We often take a deposit, particularly for larger jobs, but never demand payment in full before casting."

"Might I have a look?"

He passed me the file, which held only a few pieces of paper. A brief letter requested a bell and described it in some detail, no sender's direction stated. The bell was to be delivered to Waltham village at least a fortnight before Christmas and a bell-hanging company retained to position it.

A different hand had kept a schedule of progress, the last entry noting that the bell had been safely delivered a few days earlier.

"How did you contact your customer?" I asked, studying what few pages I held.

"We did not. They sent us the order and a bank draft made out to bearer for the full amount. We did the work. We delivered the bell. Unusual, my lord, as I said. England is not exactly awash in bell foundries, so we have customers from all over the realm and even across the seas. The distant customers usually fret that we've forgotten their orders, that we'll send the bell to the wrong village of Knowles, that sort of thing. They ask for reports of progress, while this customer... A trusting soul, I'd say. Old-fashioned, but then, the squires and curates know we're an old-fashioned company."

"You suspect this order came from gentry?" I stared at the initial letter, trying to will it to tell me something. The order had apparently not come through the mail, but had instead been delivered by a hand I had no chance of identifying.

Mears shook his head. "I can't say gentry ordered the bell, my lord. I know only that the bell went to an estate village here in the Home Counties. We have plenty of peers hereabouts, but for all I know, the mayor of Paris ordered that bell."

I wanted to crumple the damned anonymous letter and toss it into the fire, which would be pure foolishness.

"Well, thank you for as much as you've been able to tell me. I don't suppose any other bells have been ordered for delivery to Waltham village?"

"Not that I know of, my lord."

I was disproportionately disappointed with the interview. The answer to my Christmas conundrum was supposed to stare up at me from the page—a name, an explanation, a simple why-didn't-I-think-of-that solution.

Instead, I saw a bell described very much like my own save for the angels on the canon, an amount noted, and a date requested. *With All Due Respect...* No signature.

Bah and fiddlesticks. I proffered the file to Mears and then snatched it back. *With All Due Respect* indeed.

"My lord?"

I rose and surrendered the file. "Checking a detail. Happy Christmas to you and yours, Mears, and may all the bells ring for joy on Christmas morning."

"We live in hope, my lord."

A skinny boy led me back through the corridors and across the raised metal walkway, and then I was paying another skinny boy for having guarded my phaeton.

"You gave me a shillin', guv. Charge is a penny. Tuppence if you're gone 'alf the day." Dark eyes, unruly dark hair, ankles showing above his tattered boots. Honor bright as a new penny.

"Your Christmas token, lad. Go someplace warm and eat something hot for a change."

He grinned, revealing the beautiful teeth of a child whose diet included very little sugar. "Thankee. Hot cross buns and a toddy, and I'll bring extra for Ma and the girls."

He was off like a rabbit on the heath, and I climbed onto the chilly bench. "Away we go, horse. You haven't been standing a quarter hour."

The beast moved forward, and we waded into battle with London traffic as darkness began to fall. I nevertheless made a stop on Ludgate Hill and produced for examination a simple pearl ring I'd borrowed from Hyperia's jewelry box. The adornment was an unprepossessing gold circle, but the pearl had a lovely pinkish hue, and I knew the ring fit its owner well.

That errand also took less than a quarter hour, and when I urged the horse homeward, I had the satisfaction of one mission accomplished. Ordering a ring for Hyperia was a hopeful gesture, and in this at least, the present holidays were an improvement over last year's version.

I wasn't in full possession of all my faculties, I wasn't married to the woman I adored, and I hadn't yet won the battle to become the Waltham duchy's trusted steward-at-large. But my circumstances were improving, and I was even making progress in the puzzle of the secret Father Christmas.

With All Due Respect. The D in *Due* had been the same D as in *Do enjoy Philadelphia.* The same D as in Christmas *Day* as penned in the note to Mr. Blentlinger. The exact same.

Either the gifts were all from the same giver, or the curious coincidences had extended to include idiosyncrasies of penmanship, and that I did not believe for an instant.

"What was the best gift you ever received?" I asked Healy West as the ducal traveling coach rocked along the frozen roads.

"The best gift? You mean, like a *Book of Common Prayer* with my name on it or a pony?"

"Better than a pony." Now that I knew my competitor for top-anonymous-elf honors was one person, I was determined to take the competition into more innings.

"Nothing is better than a pony," West said. "I still recall my first, and he was, of course, the best equine ever to trot through creation. Wasn't keen on cantering, and I think that's why Papa bought him. I named him Forsooth."

"Shakespearean of you."

"My pony is Ladon," Atticus said, "except he's not really mine, but he can gallop."

Atticus sat once again with his back to the horses, having lasted not one tollgate beyond London up on the box. Outside the confines of Town, the day was bright and bitter.

Good skating weather and terrible for my eyes. "Think, West. Some gift or benevolence other than a pony struck you dumb as a boy, some magnificent surprise."

West considered Atticus, who was once again thumping the bench with a heel. "Papa took me up to Town when I was seven. We did the usual things—the menagerie, a hack in the park with me up before him, Gunter's. I recall that excursion very fondly. To have the old man to myself for a time, no mama or Hyperia intruding, was wonderful."

"His Grace did something similar with me," I replied, having forgotten the trip until West had spoken. "I gather each child was taken to Town individually with either Her Grace or the duke, according to gender, for fittings and boots and ices and, weather permitting, a sail on the river. What I recall about the river is the stink. We came in summer, and the tides were sluggish, and Papa thought my reaction hilarious."

"The river still reeks in summer," West said. "London is growing like topsy, but nobody has thought how we'll deal with all the resulting sewage and trash. Subterranean rivers and Roman brick works can only handle so much."

Atticus looked fascinated by that remark.

"Leander won't have a country lad's sense of wonder about London," I said. "He has dwelled here and has unhappy memories of the place. I'm looking for a special gift that will truly impress the lad and welcome him to the family."

Atticus looked away, and I realized too late how my words might cut a boy who had no family, a boy who had been welcome only where he could work for his keep.

I dropped the subject and regretted bringing it up in present company.

The horses eventually slowed as we approached another village. We were one change away from home, though I felt as if I'd spent eternities in the coach, jostled and chilled, despite heated bricks fitted into the floor periodically and a hamper still mostly full.

"Toy soldiers?" West suggested, as if he'd been musing on the question for miles. "Leander's papa was a soldier, if what Hyperia has told me is true."

"Harry was a soldier." Also a rascal, ducal heir, and a damned fine brother most of the time. "Alas for me, the Caldicott Hall nursery already boasts an embarrassment of riches in the miniature military ranks. Every army you can think of and a few you've never seen mentioned outside the history books. I will give the matter more thought."

"You don't have the Scots Greys," Atticus said. "Not really. You have cavalry on gray horses, but the uniforms are wrong. Uncle Kerrick said."

Kerrick was not the boy's uncle, though in the same manner that Aunt Bertha was universally Aunt Bertha, and Aunt Crosby was universally Aunt Crosby, I allowed the appellation to pass. To correct Atticus would be unkind, and for all I knew, his pride was already smarting.

He lacked a proper *last name*, for pity's sake. Would that Father Christmas could give him one and a happier past to go with it. I shoved that gloomy thought aside and returned my mind to the instant question.

How to top a pony—an elegant dapple gray pony—in the great anonymous Christmas gift sweepstakes?

"Leander likes stories," Atticus said. "Not *Aesop's Fables*. He knows those off by heart because his mother read them to him. Big stories like *Much Ado About Nothing* and *Hamlet*. *Hamlet* has a duel in it, and a talking ghost. Miss Hyperia says Hamlet wanted to lose the duel, which is stupid."

"Hyperia reads Lamb's versions to the boys?" West asked.

"Probably the copy Her Grace bought for me, though I was old enough to read them for myself." Charles and Mary Lamb had tried to keep the flavor of Shakespeare's Elizabethan prose, while sanitizing the worst of the earthiness. Compared to the originals, the resulting stories had sometimes been brilliant adaptations and other times made for very odd literature.

"The fate of the realm does not rest on coming up with a perfect gift," I said, "nor is Christmas yet upon us. The subject can be put to rest for now."

"The fate of my tummy rests in that hamper," Atticus said, though with West along, the boy would not eat without first being given permission.

"I'm a bit peckish," West said, "and good food... should not go to waste."

Atticus had joined in on that chorus, and they shared a conspiratorial smirk that excluded me. West opened the hamper, and Atticus sidled along the bench to peer into it with him.

"As buried treasure goes," West said, "these shortbread biscuits certainly qualify. I see we also have some ginger biscuits. Delightful."

"You'll ruin your nooning," Atticus retorted, swiping the packet. "I'll look after the biscuits."

"You'll eat every one," West said, making a fake grab for the goods. "Rogue, thief, brigand."

"You look after the cheese toast sandwiches. The guv'nor can't be trusted around them."

"I will make you a bargain," West said, locating the sandwiches. "I'll trade you one-half a cheese toast sandwich for ginger biscuits."

"One biscuit for a whole sandwich."

They haggled with all the mock intensity of good actors having a good time. I smiled indulgently and pretended to boredom, relieved that the awkward topic of how to spoil my nephew was behind us. I made the mistake of lifting the window curtain and got a stab of brilliant sunshine in the eyeballs for my trouble.

Ruddy, rubbishing holidays. I was loath to return to the sniping and bickering at the Hall's meals and daunted by Arthur's mountains of mail. That trivial annoyances such as these weighed on my spirits made me even more disgusted with myself.

That honest, ragged boy guarding my phaeton in Whitechapel reproached me for my moodiness, as did my own common sense.

And yet, the question still circled in my mind: What gift was more impressive than a pony? What would create lasting memories for all of Leander's remaining days? Something precious, enduring, and dear?

"I have to use the jakes," Atticus said as the coach turned into the yard of the local inn. "Haven't gone in forever."

"You go at every change," West said. "You slow us down with your sightseeing."

"You ain't never been told when to piss and when to hold it all day. I gotta piss."

Another peek into life in a poorhouse. "I'll get out," I said, tugging down my hat brim and donning my blue specs. "But be quick, or yonder hooligan will eat all your shortbread."

"I'll guard the hamper," West said, taking a bite of a biscuit. "Away with you, brigand."

"He won't eat them all," I said, unlatching the door. "Out you go."

Atticus scrambled down, and I followed, bracing myself for the inevitable throbbing that even my spectacles could not protect me from when the day offered bright sunshine on snow.

"Around there," I said, gesturing to the right. "And do not think to sully a snowbank like a common ne'er-do-well. Use the facilities."

Atticus executed an elaborate, wrist-twirling bow and jogged off around the corner of the inn.

The boy increasingly troubled me. I'd taken him on as my tiger because he'd been completely wasted as a general dogsbody in the Makepeace household. When everybody else save Hyperia had been against me, Atticus—small, fierce, and ostensibly powerless—

had guarded my flank. He was bright, eager to learn, and trustworthy.

He deserved more from life than hard work and harder luck. He for damned sure deserved a last name. I had had Leander's surname changed to Caldicott by the simple use of a deed poll and some coin. Atticus's situation was more delicate, in that he was no family connection whatsoever.

As these thoughts racketed through my mind, I watched the bustle in the coach's innyard. Our tired team was led away, harness jingling in the frigid breeze. A fresh team, all bay, no white markings, were led prancing and curvetting up to the coach. The hostlers worked with the precision of an artillery squad and with a good deal less profanity as the horses were backed step by step into position.

"I'm going to be a coachman when I grow up," a young girl said, tilting her head to peer up at the box. "Like him!" She pointed to John Coachman, who saluted with his whip as if the child were some passing dignitary.

She whirled and clapped her hands, which caused the off-leader to take a few nervous steps and an old hound dozing on the inn's long wooden porch to look up from his nap. The dog took in the scene at a glance, considered the girl for a moment, then put his chin back on his paws.

Dear old thing. He'd probably been watching coaches come and go for years. Dogs had been my friends in Spain, alerting me to noises I could not hear, scents I could not smell. Nobody kept watch like a dog, or was quite such a comfortable...

I wanted to whirl and clap my hands. "I'll get him a dog. A noble hound. Man's best friend and child's best playmate. Doesn't have to live in the stable, can even keep a lad company in the playroom."

Atticus came around the corner of the innyard at a trot. "C'mon, guv. Mr. West will eat all the biscuits if we don't keep an eye on him."

I mentally saluted the old hound and hoisted Atticus into the coach.

"Count them," I said to Atticus. "Count the biscuits, and West will owe us a forfeit for every one he pilfered while on guard duty."

"For that insult," West said, dramatically clutching the parcel of cheese toast, "you shall starve. I ate a mere half dozen."

"Six!" Atticus dove for him as the coach lurched forward, and the result was a lot of crumbled biscuits, though Atticus assured us they tasted just as good smashed to bits, perhaps even better. By the time we reached Caldicott Hall, the lad was complaining of a bellyache, and I had made a mental list of places where I might procure a friendly, mild-tempered, trustworthy hound.

Happy Christmas to all.

"Not to be critical," Aunt Bertha said, setting down her spoon. "But this soup could be hotter. Potato soup should be hot or cold, not warm, and this offering definitely qualifies as warm."

"Not to be critical," Uncle Terrence muttered, "but why must every meal be ruined by your liberal servings of discontent, Bertha Higgins? It's winter, in case you haven't noticed, and food gets cold on its way up from the kitchen."

Theodoric Pettigrew slurped his serving noisily, which I supposed was meant as a reproach to both combatants. At the foot of the table, the duchess tucked in silently, while Kerrick busied himself buttering a roll.

Ginny had once again pleaded fatigue—my sister was no fool—and Hyperia looked resigned to more four-course skirmishing.

I had been home from London for a matter of hours, and I was ready to travel the whole distance back to the metropolis on foot, if only to escape the inevitable dyspepsia such bickering engendered.

"Winter is no excuse," Aunt Bertha replied, brandishing her spoon. "God made warming pantries for the very reason you state. The kitchen goes to all the trouble to prepare passably acceptable fare, and that fare is more palatable if served as hot as intended."

"The warming pantry," Aunt Crosby noted, "is located off the formal dining room, on the other side of the foyer and half the length of the house away. That venue serves much larger gatherings and needs a warming pantry."

For her, that was a nearly pleasant observation.

"If you would use your mouth to eat, Bertha Higgins," Terrence said, "instead of to complain, your food would not get as cold."

"Enough," I said, though Uncle Terrence had a point. "The soup is delectable. My compliments to Mrs. Gwinnett. I understand preparations for the Boxing Day fete are coming along nicely."

That was a pitch straight at Her Grace, and she caught the conversational ball neatly. "Most satisfactorily. The young people are tasked with decorating the assembly rooms, the cake raffle has six donations confirmed, and the baskets are airing in the gallery."

"What goes into the baskets?" I asked when nobody else seemed inclined to support the cause of polite discourse.

"Yarn for knitting," Her Grace said. "Some lace, especially if the family includes a new baby or a young lady, tins of tobacco and tea, a bottle of brandy—medicinal, of course—jars of honey and jam, some of Mrs. Gwinnett's holiday sweets, a few coins for the children, scented candles, scented French soap, a bit of this and that."

A bit of practical luxury. "Do we ever include storybooks?"

Hyperia smiled at me. "Excellent suggestion. Families without small children can pass them on to relatives or friends. We can have some sent down from Town."

"A *Book of Common Prayer* would be my choice," Aunt Bertha said, pushing her empty soup bowl away. "Etiquette manuals are also becoming quite popular. One ought to know how to behave in the presence of one's betters."

"*One* certainly ought," Uncle Terrence muttered.

And so it went, until Hyperia excused herself prior to the dessert course, pleading an obligation in the nursery, Kerrick was eyeing the clock, and Squire Pettigrew had—I was certain—kicked Terrence under the table twice.

Not hard enough, apparently.

"In my day, the holidays were merry," Uncle remarked, apropos of nothing. "We didn't spend the month of December lamenting the temperature of the soup."

"In your day, you were hardly ever sober," Aunt Bertha rejoined. "And your day has yet to entirely pass. And as regards the food, this syllabub could do with a dash more nutmeg."

"Nutmeg is dear," Pettigrew said. "More dear than cinnamon. A dash will do."

"But one also needs to dust each serving as a garnish," Aunt rejoined. "One wants to *display* the nutmeg, a slight extravagance as *un hommage* to one's important guests. I would not expect a man to understand."

"Mrs. Gwinnett's menus are devised to nourish and please," I said, "not for ostentation. My syllabub was delicious." Not delicious enough that I was tempted to have a second serving and thereby delay the exodus of the ladies.

They decamped, eschewing gentlemanly escort because only Her Grace and Aunt Bertha were to gather around the teapot. That left me with Pettigrew, Kerrick, and Uncle Terrence.

How had Arthur hosted supper after supper, Sunday after Sunday in the country, and even more frequently in Town, in company such as this? Granted, Bertha, Terrence, and Crosby were particularly accomplished at sniping and skirmishing, but their skills were hardly legendary.

"I'm off t'see tae m'wife." Kerrick bowed to the remaining gentlemen and left me quite on my own. He'd done host duty for the two days I'd been gone to London, so he'd earned compassionate leave, if nothing else.

"My regards to Ginny," I said. "Sledding tomorrow, I'm told."

Kerrick groaned, struck a hand to his brow, and left.

"A good lad," Pettigrew said. "Honestly frets about his missus. I could use a digestif, my lord."

I brought the decanter to the end of the table closest to the hearth and set down three glasses.

"We need Bertha to tell us the nose fails to impress," Terrence said, "connoisseur of fine spirits that she is."

I poured out three drinks. "The nose will impress. His Grace keeps a very fine cellar. To happy holidays, gentlemen."

We were supposed to drink a health to the king and queen, then the Regent, my old regiment, Pettigrew's old regiment, various race-horses Terrence recalled fondly, and so forth. Both older fellows repeated my toast and sank into chairs. I took the duchess's seat, though I felt once again surplus to requirements.

"Bertha's getting worse," Terrence said. "I know I say that every year, but she passes all bounds now."

"You goad her," Pettigrew said. "If you agreed with her, she'd fall back and regroup. Though I suppose then Crosby might ride in with reinforcements. This is excellent brandy. His Grace doubtless paid dearly for it."

Money again. "I believe this was a gift from some French *comte*. His Grace sent the man some merino sheep, which are still some-thing of a rarity in France. The *comte* knows his roses and apparently his brandy."

Pettigrew studied his drink. "If the *comte* survived what that lot did to their aristos, he's either very lucky or very shrewd."

"He bided his time in England," I said, "and waited for the Bour-bons to restore titles in a futile effort to pretend the past fifty years of French history can be ignored."

Talk turned to politics, which was a blessed relief, and an area where Terrence and Pettigrew were in surprising accord. The crown had best watch its step, according to them, because John Bull had not sent his sons for the past twenty years to subdue the Corsican only to watch those same sons starve for the sake of Prinny's art collection.

In its own way, the conversation was just as wearying as the aunties' carping. True, peace was proving a challenge to a nation that had built its empire by bloodshed, but it was still peace. I need not fear to lose Kerrick or Ginny to roving French patrols. My nightmares didn't include thoughts of Leander or Atticus being conscripted at the age of twelve.

"We're wearing the lad out," Squire Pettigrew said. "Best seek your bed, young man. Leave the serious discussions to your elders."

The serious drinking. "I will do just that." I rose and bowed. "Gentlemen, good night. Sleep well."

I certainly hoped to, but first I had to tend to a chore I'd been dreading since the coach had pulled up to the Hall's front door hours ago. Another chore I'd been dreading. I took a carrying candle from the sideboard and let myself into the positively frigid corridor.

The temperature was so disobliging that Her Grace had given orders no footmen were to be on duty in the corridors overnight, and the porter in his nook by the front door was to be kept supplied with braziers and blankets.

I entered Arthur's study, prepared to spend some time building up the fire. Instead, I found a cozy haven, candles already blazing, and Hyperia busy at the desk.

CHAPTER TWELVE

"Darling lady, whatever are you doing?" Hyperia wore a pair of spectacles on her nose. They made her look serious and scholarly, and also a little more like me.

Human. Vulnerable to imperfections of the body and mind, though on her the effect was adorable.

She rose and approached me. "I'm glad you're back, Jules. I couldn't greet you properly with Healy looking on, but I am very glad you're back. Thank you exceedingly for bringing Healy to the Hall. He told me about taking up residence at the ducal town house."

She led me by the hand—hers warm, mine cold—to the wing chairs in front of the fire. Before she could sit, I scooped her into my arms and seated myself with her in my lap.

"Better," I said. "How did Healy explain making himself an uninvited guest at the town house?"

"His excuse was economies. Caldicott House is never without some staff, while his house could be all but closed until spring. He mentioned leaving a maid in residence, and I went very spare with him over that. A footman might have done, but a maid? He owes the girl a raise for not abandoning her post."

I laid my cheek against Hyperia's crown. "She had nowhere to go, Perry, and no means to get there. Fresh from the shires, would be my guess, and ripe for misadventure in the big city. Your brother can be something of a dunderhead." As could I, but I hoped my dunderhead-edness redounded mostly to my own inconvenience. "If all Healy sought was to close his own house, he could have come down directly to the Hall."

"He said he did not want to impose, and when I pointed out to him that he made no sense—cozening his way into the town house was more of an imposition than embarking on an expected holiday visit at the Hall—he explained that he's writing a play."

West had taken my advice and admitted his foolishness to his sister, which was encouraging. "He said as much to me. While I would rather he had asked permission to use the town house, and I find his treatment of the maid execrable, I do applaud his sense of enterprise."

"You do?" Hyperia snuggled closer. "I'm relieved, Jules. Healy means well. He means to be responsible and so forth, but he hasn't much practice at it, and his plans are unconventional."

I could hardly judge him for that. The way Hyperia and I were cuddling in the ducal study was unconventional in the extreme. "Did you offer to make him a loan to cover the immediate bills?"

"I did, but he said as soon as the rents are paid at the end of the month, he'll come right. He let some of the Michaelmas payments wait until after harvest, and fortunately the harvest was good. As soon as the steward has the rents in hand, Healy will tend to the trades."

He was cutting it very close, but then, many respected families did. "Tell him next year he shouldn't forgive an entire quarter's rent. Make the tenant pay something such that he's motivated to not disappear after six months' grace. If the tenant pays a little something, then he's walking away from his own coin, and few of us do that willingly. He will also owe less when the full sum comes due, and that's another reason to stay the course."

She closed her eyes and nuzzled my neck. "You can't explain that to him?"

"He will listen to you. He resents me." I was aware, despite nuzzlings to the contrary, that six feet away, epistles and reports sat on Arthur's desk in stacks half a foot high. I was more aware that I had missed the simple affection Hyperia so generously shared with me.

A more dutiful man would have deposited the lady in the opposite chair and gone to work.

Fatigue and gratitude made me weak. "I paid a call on the Whitechapel Bell Foundry while I was in Town."

"Do we know who the mysterious benefactor is?"

"Yes and no. We know the same person is behind the bell, the bank draft, and the pony."

She opened her eyes and studied me. "This vexes you?"

"Puzzles me. I cannot seem to leave a puzzle alone." I gathered Hyperia closer and spoke the next words near her ear. "I've been half tempted to inquire of Her Grace as to my paternal antecedents."

Hyperia sat up, narrowly missing my chin, extricated herself from my lap, and took the other chair, toeing off her slippers and tucking her feet under her skirts.

"This paternal antecedents business vexes you, doesn't it, Jules?"

Arthur, Leander, Harry, everybody from Squire Pettigrew to Young Jamison knew who his father was, everybody except me—and Atticus.

"I sat at supper tonight, listening to Terrence and Pettigrew fence with the aunties, and I thought: Somewhere an old man is being difficult, and what troubles him is not his gout or cold soup, but the fact that he has a son who doesn't know him. In the alternative, even Her Grace might not know who my father is for a certainty, but she can certainly narrow the field."

"And then you will attack the possibilities as if solving a puzzle and go about waking dogs that have been sleeping for nearly thirty years?"

"I might go visiting cemeteries, Perry. Time grows short, if my father is still alive."

Hyperia crossed to the desk and took a shawl from Arthur's chair. She draped that around my shoulders and kissed my cheek.

"Ask your mother what she knows. Just ask her, Jules. Once a question gets hold of you—who purchased the bell, where has the missing heir gone, who stole the prize hound?—you don't let it go until you've found not just any answer, but the right answer. Her Grace might think you already know who he is. She might not realize what you suspect. Just as Healy should have spoken to you and me directly, you should put your questions to your mother."

I rose, the shawl around my shoulders. "And if Her Grace flies into a rage, insulted by my impertinence?" Or more likely, refused to tell me anything?

"Then you give her time to reconsider and know you tried, but she will not fly into a rage. She will likely be embarrassed. In her day, a lady's duty was to produce an heir and spare, which she did, as well as daughters. She was free to frolic by the relevant rules of that time. We are more closed-minded toward wives exercising their freedom now, and she probably fears you will judge her by current standards."

Hyperia offered sound counsel as usual, and yet, how exactly did I ask my mother with whom she'd committed adultery? After the previous duke's death, Her Grace had permitted herself a flirtation or two, but adultery during coverture was a different matter altogether.

"I will give the matter more thought," I said. "I was supposed to spend this hour sorting the past two days' mail, but instead I burden you with my concerns. Not well done of me."

"Jules, I burdened you with my fears regarding Healy. You braved the elements, flew up to Town, sorted him out, and brought him to me. Thank you."

She kissed me again. I was on my feet and ready for her, and we indulged to a degree that would have made the kissing boughs blush. Desire became a sweet, low note, like the tolling of a distant bell across the dark countryside.

I was learning to merely observe such stirrings. To welcome them as signs of improving health, and to attach neither hopes nor fears to them. My manly humors had taken some sort of drubbing when I'd been captured by the French, or perhaps lingering melancholic tendencies robbed me of physical passion.

I was increasingly confident that my malady was temporary and that improvement would continue, provided I was patient.

"We must stop," Hyperia said, sighing and leaning against me.

"Why?"

"Because I grow so muddled when you kiss me like that, and being muddled disagrees with me."

A curious admission. "You describe kissing me in the same terms you might use for strong spirits."

"You take my point, then." She stepped back and patted my chest. "You are a patent remedy without compare. I will dream of you, Jules, and they will be pleasant dreams indeed." She went up on her toes and kissed me again, a little nighty-nighty, something-to-think-about kiss. "Until morning."

She took up my carrying candle and wafted from the room, leaving streams of possibility and wonder in her wake.

"To horse," I muttered after goggling half-wittedly at the door for a long moment. "Once more unto the damned chair..."

But when I took up my post in the chair that didn't fit my backside, I found that not only was the mail organized—reports, estate correspondence, personal correspondence, bills, and other—but each item that required a reply had acquired a note card summarizing the contents and directing the response.

Brief thanks for thorough work, nothing of note in the report.

Condolences should be sent on the passing of Lady B's aunt, who was approaching the hundredth year of her age.

Grant requested two-week extension.

Based on the handwriting in evidence, the elf responsible for this great efficiency was my own dear Perry. Whether she'd sought to hide from the elders, spare me bailing against a deluge, or alleviate boredom, she had granted me that wonderful, unexpected gift I'd been maundering on about in the coach.

A lovely surprise, a gesture of such insightful kindness that its warmth would linger in my heart for all the rest of my days. Kisses and confidences were delightful, but I'd be a fool not to marry the woman who'd spun the straw of ducal correspondence into the gold of consideration and loyalty.

Christmas was yet a week away, and December had already been one of the longest months of my life. Aunt Bertha did not trim her sails one iota, while Aunt Crosby grew quieter and quieter, a darkly disapproving presence who took a sniffy leave halfway through as many meals as she finished.

Pettigrew ate heartily and did his part at the whist table, while also interrupting Uncle Terrence's recollections until Aunt Bertha interrupted Pettigrew, and Aunt Crosby interrupted Aunt Bertha, and so it went.

If a silver lining could be said to apply, it was that I was finding my sea legs with the mail. I knew which stewards would summarize a month's business in the final paragraphs of a monthly report and which put the only important bits in the first paragraph. I had my rote replies memorized, though for form's sake, they had to be written in my hand, not merely signed by me. I marked bills to be paid, and a clerk filled out bank drafts for my signature.

I cherished the hope that by the time Arthur returned late in the New Year, I'd have his duchy in hand. I would hug him soundly upon his arrival, give him time to settle in, then fling the lot of it at his handsome head, and light out for some region unknown to the Royal Mail.

When I completed my daily shift in the epistolary salt mines, I went dog-shopping. I met the long-bodied, stubby-legged Welsh herding dogs, the gamekeeper's retired retrievers, and a mastiff raised by a distant neighbor who claimed to have sold two puppies to the august and much revered Duke of Severn earlier in the year.

I loved dogs, but I wasn't shopping for myself. I was shopping for Leander. The younger herding dogs were too energetic, the retrievers too venerable, the mastiffs too enormous. Severn, who had been held captive in the same French garrison where I'd been imprisoned—was known to be something of an eccentric, and heaven—and I—knew His Grace had his reasons.

After several days of diligent searching, I still had no suitable candidate, and Christmas was but a week away. I laid my plight at the feet of Mr. Blentlinger, the local livery being a nexus of news and gossip, and Blentlinger eyed me curiously.

"You are looking for a dog, my lord, and a dog might well have been looking for you. Take a peek."

I had already paid my respects to the ponies. I followed Blentlinger down his barn aisle and out into the winter sunshine.

"That 'un showed up two days ago. No collar, nothing. Has manners, I'll give him that. Doesn't come into the barn unless invited, and when I offer him a bowl of scraps, he's polite about it. Bit skinny, though. Nobody recognizes him. Missus thinks somebody let him out of a coach for a run and then took off without him."

The creature was good-sized and sturdy with a thick, fluffy coat. Not huge, not excessively energetic.

"He looks like a cross between a collie and an Alsatian." Plenty of teeth, upright ears, a plume of a tail, a compact sort of strength, and the aspect of a smiling cousin to the wolf.

"He looks like a dog," Blentlinger said. "Not the sort for a London swell, not exactly a hunting dog."

"And certainly not a lapdog." A common, handsome, healthy canine. "You've made inquiries?"

"Asked about at the inn. I let the beast warm up from time to time by the parlor stove. He's hardy, and he don't expect much, but that dog was somebody's pet not long ago."

"You don't want him to guard the stable at night?"

Blentlinger snorted. "This is Waltham, my lord. Nobody wicked enough or desperate enough to steal a horse in this village."

I looked at the dog, who was already looking at me. The friendly wolf was also intelligent.

"Here, boy." I held out a hand, and the creature rose and gave it a sniff. He did not bound forward in an unseemly display, nor did he sulk as if he'd not heard me.

"Sit."

He sat with all the dignity of a prince.

"Lie down."

Down he went, gaze upon me.

I walked off a few paces, struck by how closely the dog watched me. "That'll do."

He came to my side and lay down.

"Away!"

The beast bolted to the right in a fast circle halfway around the snow-covered green.

"Come by!"

A quick pivot, and he was circling left.

"Steady," I called, and the dog's pace moderated. A few more commands had him panting at my side. "Good boy. Good, well-trained boy."

"A herding dog, then," Blentlinger said. "Who'd have thought? How did you know the commands?"

"Learned them in Spain from an old sergeant, then learned the Basque equivalents for a bit of work in the hills. Those are the basics, and every shepherd in every language embroiders on them in his own style."

"He's no puppy, then." Blentlinger's tone was admiring, now that he'd seen the dog work.

"He's not too old, not too young, not too big, not too busy, and he's a gentleman among canines. I do believe my Christmas luck has changed. How much do you want for him?"

"He's a stray, milord. No charge. He's cost me exactly three bowls of scraps that would have gone to the midden or the chickens."

My new friend probably wasn't stray in the usual sense. Drovers would bring herds to London from as far away as Scotland, turn their dogs loose, and take a coach home. The dogs were expected to make their own way over hundreds of miles while mild weather lasted.

This fellow had missed the good traveling weather, or perhaps he'd had enough of chasing sheep the livelong day.

"You come with me," I said, scratching a silky ear. "If you were mine, I'd name you Lucky, but choosing a name will be for your new owner to do."

The dog easily kept pace with Atlas as I returned to the Hall. I gave the canine into the gamekeeper's hands under orders for strict secrecy, rather than risk the grooms gossiping to the dairymaids, who chatted up the footmen, who passed the time with the nurserymaid.

Lucky was to be my consolation round in the anonymous Father Christmas sweepstakes. I had only to keep him out of sight for a week, and victory would assuredly—and finally—be mine.

At supper that evening, I was in a particularly fine mood. Lucky— perhaps Leander would name the dog Lucky himself—had been dropped into my lap, a fine beast, at no charge, as if to remind me that good fellows who persisted against the odds did come by an occasional reward after all.

My sense of satisfaction was soon eroded by the company at the table. We were a full complement, save for Healy, who'd claimed an inchoate head cold, which I suspected was in the nature of a scene involving swords, ringing declarations, and heroic derring-do, with trouser roles. Healy claimed the whole business of stage humor was more complicated than it might first appear.

Much like running a duchy, perhaps.

"Not to be ungrateful," Aunt Bertha said as we finally reached the dessert course, "but I see we are to have syllabub again for our sweet. If Mrs. Gwinnett has so few recipes as that, I will happily give her the benefit of my wider experience of fashionable cuisine."

"I like syllabub," Ginny ventured from the duchess's left hand. "In Scotland, we are less apt to serve anything with lemon, though I daresay our raspberries are the finest in the world."

"It's the light," Kerrick said. "Goes from short days to long in a matter of weeks. Gives the berries excellent flavor. My grannie had a cordial recipe—"

"Nevertheless," Aunt Bertha said somewhat loudly, "one must admit that the same dessert in less than a fortnight shows a want of imagination. Not to be too particular, but there are dozens of fine sweets suitable for a winter supper, and that Mrs. Gwinnett has no more regard for the consequence of His Grace's table than to return again and again to the simplest offerings—"

Pettigrew tossed his napkin on the table. "Be damned to you and your consequence, Bertha Higgins. You fear nobody will notice you unless you are hurling verbal darts. We notice you, you infernal woman. We have always noticed you. We notice you even if you have no children, no husband, no fawning brothers, or doting papa. We noticed you just fine on your own merits, but a mere gentry lad back from the wars wasn't good enough for you. Eat your syllabub and be grateful for it."

Ginny was staring, the duchess looked weary, and Uncle Terrence, for once, had nothing to say.

"You skimp, Theodoric Pettigrew," Aunt Bertha retorted, "and you penny-pinch because you let your only daughter marry a wastrel. Your guilt over that mistake drives you to leave her as much security as you can. The wastrel will go through her inheritance just as he went through her settlements, and that is not a dart—that is the plain truth." She smacked her palm on the table like an auctioneer knocking down a hotly contested item.

"Fat lot you know, Bertie, my girl. I've tied the whole up in a trust, and I add to that trust every month. His Grace has agreed to serve as trustee should I die."

So there hung in the air, as did decades of sentiment and frustration.

"Excuse me," Aunt Crosby said, in what was becoming a frequent addition to the gustatory dramas. "The manners at this table have gone begging. Theodoric is right, Bertha, that your carping has reached unbecoming frequency and intensity, and at least Miss Mandy's wastrel loves her. Bertha has a point too, Theodoric. We cannot be laying up treasures on this earth at the expense of finer feelings and a few creature comforts."

She pushed wearily to her feet, before any of the gentlemen could hold her chair, and departed at a dignified totter.

The duchess recovered first and directed a look at the footman trying desperately to appear invisible by the sideboard.

"Please take Aunt Crosby some syllabub and a pot of weak gunpowder with all the trimmings in a half hour or so."

"Yes, Your Grace."

"She prefers China black," Aunt Bertha muttered.

"Not at this late hour." That came from Ginny, and as gently as anybody had said anything in the past quarter hour. "If you all will excuse me, I must ask my husband to see me up to the nursery. Duty calls."

"Of course, my dear." Kerrick held her chair, and they, too, abandoned their syllabub.

"Well, I must say..." Bertha glanced around the table, her air one of injured dignity. "I must say indeed. I do feel a megrim coming on."

Pettigrew rose to hold her chair, and a look passed between them I wished I hadn't seen.

Frustration, despair, longing, resignation. I'd thought Pettigrew was devoted to Mandy's mother, but the story was apparently more complicated.

"Miss West," the duchess said, "let's leave the gentlemen to their port and politics. I have Christmas baskets to fill. Perhaps you'd care to join me. The gallery will be chilly, but the peace and quiet welcome."

"I'll join you," I said, bolting to my feet. I held chairs for both ladies. "Terrence, Pettigrew, I leave the decanters in your capable hands."

Both old gents looked more morose than pleased, but I simply could not tolerate a postmortem discussion of the evening's unpleasantness. The ladies and I traversed the frigid corridors, the kissing boughs creating odd shadows on the floorboards and the cloved oranges giving the whole house the scent of an outsized fruit cellar.

"I will plead fatigue too," Hyperia said at the top of the steps. "Sledding wore me out."

Hauling the sleds up the hill had done the same to me, to say nothing about the ongoing protest from my eyes, and yet, the evening presented an opportunity for time alone with my mother.

"Good night, darling girl," Her Grace said. "Dream of the New Year."

Hyperia curtseyed, and I bowed, which was ridiculous, and she disappeared into the shadows.

"Why not light her to her room, Julian?"

"She would have asked me had she wanted that courtesy. Sometimes a lady needs solitude."

Her Grace moved off toward the gallery. "You and she are becoming friends. That's good. The hearts and flowers are nice, too, and necessary for a time, but one must at all costs be friends with one's spouse. You are not to unpack the baskets after I pack them. Your father always did, claiming his arrangements were aesthetically superior. He did it to vex me, and then he'd apologize under a kissing bough."

Some affection underlay her tone and no little wistfulness. "You will never be like the aunties," I said, holding the gallery door for her. "Put the notion from your head. They are unhappy old women, and they were unhappy young women. I would bet my saddle on it."

The gallery was less arctic than the corridor. Both hearths were lit, but the room was large, with twelve-foot ceilings, and would take several days and strategically placed braziers to heat.

"You'd bet your saddle," Her Grace said, "but not your horse, though you'd win the bet. Crosby in particular was as disappointed with holy matrimony as Bertha was disappointed with the lack of it. We'll start over there."

Three dozen wicker baskets, large enough for market day duty, had been set out on trestle tables. Each basket had a curved wooden handle forming a semicircle above it, and from the highest point of the handle's arch, a miniature kissing bough dangled on ribbons of red, gold, or green.

"Whose idea were the kissing boughs?"

"Miss West's. She has a very artistic imagination. We'll see how her little addition goes over in the village. I quite like it."

As did I. "Is there unrequited romance between Bertha and Pettigrew?"

"One might call it that. You start at that end. Put a wool scarf in the bottom of each basket. The color doesn't matter, but do fold it neatly."

The color would not matter, because the feel of the wool, softer even than pure merino, was so sumptuous. The hues were subdued, suitable for any member of the family to wear to divine services, but the luxury was undeniable.

I folded a lovely green specimen. "Pettigrew was in love with Bertha, and she scorned him?"

"Pettigrew was in love with Bertha, and she told him she wasn't about to marry a clod-hopping boy from the shires. He scraped together enough coin to buy a captain's commission and served with distinction in the American colonies. When he came into his inheritance a few years later, he renewed his addresses, and Bertha again gave him his congé."

One by one, I folded the scarves and arranged them in their baskets. Her Grace followed me, topping each scarf with muslin sachets filled with lavender.

"Was Bertha's mulishness fortunate for the squire in the end? I understood him to be devoted to Mandy's mother."

"He was loyal and faithful to her. He wanted sons to inherit the family acres. When one's own parents have gone to their reward, one begins to wonder who will be on hand to look after one in one's dotage."

"Mrs. Swinburne being a case in point."

"So she is."

Mrs. Swinburne, happily contemplating a reunion with her daughter in the spring, no thanks to me. We finished with scarves and sachets and moved on to jam and honey. The jars were a pint each and probably constituted a year's worth of sweetness for the poorest families.

"The squire married well and happily enough," I suggested, "and Bertha realized she'd let her biggest fish swim away?"

"I don't know what Bertha realized, but when Pettigrew was bereaved, he did not seek her out. She took up the habit of visiting the Hall, and we took up the habit of inviting Pettigrew to supper when Bertha was on hand, but they never resumed their flirtations. They barely spoke at first."

"Perhaps Pettigrew fell out of love."

"Your father thinks Pettigrew tired of her games. At that point, the squire had been married to a woman he respected, even if he hadn't been head over ears for her, and he had a daughter to raise. Bertha's insecurities yet plagued her, and waiting for her to gather her courage... He moved on, was how your father put it. We don't grow too old for romance, but we grow too wise for outright foolishness."

Tempus fugit. I was glad I'd ordered a ring for Hyperia, very glad.

"That explains Aunt Bertha's situation, but what of Aunt Crosby? Was Uncle Tommie really so bad as all that?"

Her Grace paused between rounds along the baskets. "Thomas was older than Crosby and had for the longest time declared that he would not marry simply to provide more unnecessary insurance policies for the ducal succession. Then Arthur came along, and Thomas was no longer the young buck just down from university. You do the tins of tea."

"While you do what?"

"Spools of lace."

"Entire spools?" Why had I never noticed how lavish the Hall's Christmas baskets were? Or perhaps Her Grace was making a special effort this year?

"I well understand, Julian, that some of the families will sell the contents of their baskets. The lace might appear at a friend's stall in the little market in Hop Bottom or be sent to a cousin to sell in her shop. That is none of my business. My business is to give the gift and hope it's enjoyed in some manner. So yes, entire spools. We can afford it, while dear old Mr. Sigafoose is probably rationing his coal and praying for an early spring."

Because I was Lord of Reports, Invoices, and Mail of That Ilk, I had reason to know that Sigafoose was well supplied with coal. Of coin, though, he had little, which was typical of curates all across Britain.

"Two tins of tea per basket," Her Grace said. "One black tea, one green tea."

"Are you suggesting Uncle Tommie put his foot in parson's mousetrap and had reason to regret the decision?"

"Crosby certainly regretted marrying him, poor dear. She was young and retiring, easily swept away by Thomas's charm and station. She soon realized the error she'd made. I thought your father would have explained all of this to you."

I started on my tea rounds. Her Grace had ordered from Twinings, and the quality would be excellent.

"Papa and I never reached the chatting-over-the-port stage. When I was down from university, he usually asked about my studies or my finances. Ancient family history didn't come into it, and Uncle Tommie's colorful past was referred to in only passing generalities."

I might have missed the expression on my mother's face, except that I looked up to check the time on the clock over one of the mantels.

She had a length of white lace wrapped around her finger and was staring at it as if the delicate stitchwork aroused bittersweet memories.

"Thomas was a rascal and a rogue," she said. "The genuine variety. Claudius could be annoying, but Thomas had a petulant streak. I didn't see that at first, and each year, he seemed to grow more charming and outrageous. Harry was a lot like him. They both had an appetite for risks, for brushes with scandal. As a younger woman, I found that boldness attractive, I regret to say. Harry adored him, of course. I enjoyed Thomas's company too, for a time. Claudius was amazingly tolerant of his brother, but then, Claudius was no saint. You're sure your father never explained all this to you? He said I wasn't to fret about it."

"*All this?*" Had Uncle Tommie overstepped with a royal princess? His behavior put me in mind of Pettigrew's assessment of Bertha—annoying, even outrageous, for the sake of garnering attention. Every schoolyard I'd passed through and every army camp had been full of fellows employing that strategy.

The duchess let the lace trail off her finger. "Never mind the details, Julian. Suffice it to say that Thomas broke rules and lived to regret it. His tale is old news, and we have present holiday revels to enjoy."

Any attempt I might have made to steer the conversation to *other* old business—say the details of my paternal pedigree—would have to wait for a moment when Her Grace was not scowling at imported lace and dismissing the past as irrelevant.

I added another tin of tea to the basket at my elbow. "We have holiday revels to endure."

Her Grace tossed a spool of lace into the same basket. "Just so. If Miss West is ever to become the hostess at the Hall, she'll need to know what sort of traditions she'll inherit."

"Old ghosts and unrequited love make for odd holiday fare."

"Tend to the tea, Julian."

I would have to ask Lady Ophelia for a full recounting of those ghosts. Godmama knew all the scandals, and yet, she'd never brought up Uncle Tommie's peccadillos with me. For all I knew, she numbered among them, though I doubted she would have poached on another woman's preserves, did that lady object. I speculated that she and the late duke had at least flirted, but she'd neither verified nor denied my theories.

Her Grace and I made a dozen more rounds of the baskets before she took her leave of me, another lady who hadn't asked for my escort through the drafty corridors.

I remained behind, glad for the solitude and for the time with Her Grace.

I was doing better with my holiday responsibilities. The mail was no longer the dreaded all-day ordeal it had been at the start of the month. Healy West had been sorted out, and as the tides of correspondence had ebbed, I'd become more conscientious about spending time with Leander.

And yet, two puzzles still vexed me.

Who was our Father Christmas, and who was my father? Hyperia had advised a blunt charge at the latter query, but the duchess had retreated with her usual adroit firmness from even a discussion of a late uncle's youthful indiscretion. Whoever my progenitor was, Her Grace was not making opportunities to discuss him, and dodgy family history could not be taken up with Lady Ophelia by mail.

I wandered around the beribboned baskets, moving a sachet here, a pair of beeswax candles there, or rose-shaped bar of French soap there.

Where else could I look for clues as to my antecedents? With Arthur's blessing, I had read the old duke's diaries and found little of interest. Much business, some fatherly humor, some husbandly fondness.

I was rearranging the cloved oranges on the end basket when it occurred to me that Harry had been a spy before he'd gone to war. As a little boy, he'd been a compulsive eavesdropper. In early youth, he'd graduated to hoarding recondite snippets of churchyard gossip. In the military, he'd been able to predict what orders were coming down even before the dispatches arrived.

He hadn't told tales, but he had liked knowing what others did not know or wished to keep hidden. Nosy, one might say. Inordinately and inconveniently curious.

Which, Harry's ghost reminded me, might well have been what had resulted in his death. That and my own imprudent curiosity.

What a hopeless thought. Don't pursue it. Don't let it pursue you. Bid Hyperia good night.

On that cheering inspiration, I left off fussing with the baskets and was soon letting myself into Hyperia's sitting room. She had not waited up for me—she'd truly thrown herself into the joy of sledding with the children—and she was far gone in slumber when I entered her bedroom.

My darling was curled beneath the covers, snoring gently. I pulled the quilt up around her shoulders, kissed her cheek, and retreated to the sitting room. I could climb in with her, after I'd tended to my ablutions and changed into nightclothes. Slip through the little passage and share some sweet dreams...

I was pondering possibilities when it occurred to me that I was in Harry's old sitting room, surrounded by *Harry's old journals*. Somewhere in their depths, I might find the clues to the past I sought. I would have to do a lot of reading and doubtless content myself with oblique references and obscure allusions.

If I had to wreck my eyes to find the truth, I'd consider the effort a fair bargain. I closed the door to the bedroom, chose the earliest volume I could find, and sought my apartment. In the morning, I would start reading through my brother's entire personal literary legacy.

He'd of course already done the same with any journal of mine, and that thought gave me the sort of comfort and joy known only between devoted and reciprocally nosy siblings.

CHAPTER THIRTEEN

I plowed through the next morning's correspondence, eager to tear into Harry's journals. The hour had nonetheless advanced past noon before I moved to a wing chair in front of the fire and embarked on my literary search. Harry had been ahead of me at university, and his observations made for interesting, occasionally insightful, and often slyly hilarious reading.

A certain future duke had all the charm of a gouty mother superior. A marquess's darling nephew was a wizard at chess but a dunce about his tutor's pretty daughters. A friendly barmaid dubbed Amadea was mentioned in terms both wistful and worshipful. When Harry had occasion to refer to me, I was always "old Julian" or "old Jules" or, rarely, "dear old Jules."

By Harry's standards, I was a dreary soul indeed. My scholarship was thorough but plodding, my literary tastes staid, and my appreciation for solitude positively backward. Old Jules was doomed to wear a bishop's miter, in Harry's opinion. The next term, Harry predicted that old Jules would end up teaching classics to spotty university boys.

As I read through these pages, I sensed both my brother's affection for me—he lamented the tedium of my looming fate—even as I also sensed a creeping disdain. At least when he'd written this journal, Harry had found me boring and something of an embarrassment.

And yet, he noted my accomplishments too. "Old Jules took another first. His Grace will be pleased." Toward the end of the first volume: "Jules has the respect of the dons, heaven help him. A rigorous mind according to Plumley and a scholar's academic integrity, whatever that is. One can hardly credit that we are related."

In truth, I'd been shy. The boisterous confidence of the typical Oxford scholar had eluded me, and that same scholar's usual entertainments hadn't interested me. I'd kept to myself and my studies by default, there being little else to do at university if a course in debauchery held no appeal.

Could Harry have been *jealous* of my bookishness? The mind boggled, and yet, the evidence—

A tap on the door had me closing Harry's tome. "Enter."

"Beg pardon, my lord." Young Jamison half bowed and set a tray on the raised hearth. "Miss West said you would need some sustenance."

A glance at the clock confirmed that the hour for the midday meal had come and gone. "Miss West is right as usual. What's on offer?"

"Lentil soup, beef-and-cheddar sandwiches, and a request from the stable for your lordship to pay a call on the horses, if you can spare a moment."

"Do we know who sent that request?"

"'Tweren't the lad, sir. He's in the kitchen learning to knit. Undercook says idle hands are the devil's workshop, not that I see the lad idling much. Knitting does keep the knees warm."

Jamison was cheerful, hardworking, and well-liked, but he was also a complacent soul. "Jamison, *is Atlas colicking?*"

"I certainly hope not, my lord. Gracious, you do set store by that horse, as is known to all. Colic can be serious of a certainty."

The food was hot, I was hungry, and yet... if Atlas was in distress,

I wanted to know the particulars. If he was looking at all peaked or off, if he was listless...

In my mind, he was "just" a horse. A convenient, if expensive, means of covering ground or transporting goods.

In my heart, he was a friend, a fellow soldier who'd known me in my darkest hours and guarded all my confidences. I had taken care, in my last will and testament, to ensure Atlas became Arthur's responsibility, just as Arthur had specifically charged me with looking after Beowulf in Arthur's absence.

"Bank the fire please, Jamison. I'm for the stable."

"Yes, sir. Mind you bundle up. Wind is fierce today, and Mrs. Gwinnett says we'll have more snow before Christmas."

"Won't that be jolly." More hauling sled-loads of children up hills, more bright sunshine on sparkling white landscapes.

Stop it, old Jules. I lectured myself all the way to the stable, about gratitude and humility and borrowing trouble, but with every step, I also prayed.

Don't put my Atlas through this. Don't make me shoot my horse. Not at Christmas. Not ever. I will climb four mountains of mail per day for the next year, but please... not Atlas.

My dear horse was lipping hay contentedly when I reached his stall. He looked at me as if to inquire what foolishness had sent me out into the bitter elements and then sidled over to his half door. I rewarded his overture with a chin scratch followed by some ear scratches.

"We had him out for a few hours this morning," the head lad said, eyeing the disappearing pile of hay. "Before the wind picked up. Days like this, the saddle horses are all happy to come in for their nooning. Plow stock likes it cold."

Daughtery was lanky, ageless, and possessed of the softest hint of a brogue. Horses loved him, and his grooms sang his praises even while they grumbled about horses being cosseted like royalty.

"Atlas seems quite content. Did you send for me, Daughtery?"

"Aye, milord. We have a new arrival, and none of the lads seem to know where he comes from. I thought perhaps this was another one of your lordship's Christmas gifts."

"*Another* pony?" Blentlinger had promised me discretion about the pony, but among the shire's ranking equestrian professionals, discretion was apparently not the same as secrecy.

"Not a pony. Come have a look." He led me between parallel rows of loose-boxes, each one housing a contented equine. The stable was warm enough, thanks to those horses, some of whom wore blankets and all of whom had full water buckets and ample fodder.

"We put him here," Daughtery said, "the weather being so frigid." He opened the door to a space off the saddle room that served as both a workroom and a place to pass an idle hour. One of the junior grooms was oiling a pile of harness in the corner farthest from the parlor stove. Two others were playing cribbage on the warmer side of the room.

The aroma would have done a cavalry officer's heart good. Peat, leather, horse, and hay, blended in a fragrance as delicate and comforting as the nose on well-aged brandy. The brick floor was swept, braided rugs added a homey touch, and the worktable held day-old newspapers as well as some pamphlets on equine care and feeding.

Even here, a kissing bough hung from the main crossbeam. The mistletoe sported not a single white berry, suggesting various maids, laundresses, dairymaids, and village ladies had visited the Hall's stables.

I needed a moment to realize why Daughtery had brought to me a space usually reserved for the staff. A puppy was curled up on an old horse blanket folded before the parlor stove, a Spaniel from the looks of it. White with brown spots and some flecking.

A puppy. Ballocks. "There was a note." I was not asking a question.

Daughtery withdrew a folded piece of paper from an interior pocket.

For Leander Caldicott, to be presented to him for naming on Christmas Day.

Complete with the telltale flourish on the capital D in *Day.*

"A puppy." The little beast was thumping his tail against the horse blanket before even properly opening his eyes. Once he'd yawned, stretched tail-high, and settled back on his haunches, he faced me with the requisite adorable pink tongue and bright, happy expression. "That is a damned puppy."

"I dunno as the creature is damned, my lord," Daughtery said. "Seems rather friendly to me."

Play at the cribbage board paused, and the lad with his pile of harness was watching me curiously.

"I cannot compete with a *ruddy, wretched puppy.*" A Spaniel puppy, all silky ears and wagging tail. A cute, warm, wiggly, sweet puppy. I thought of mature, dignified, well-trained Lucky and wanted to throw every kissing bough at the Hall into the flames.

Old Jules was once again the loser in the Christmas token sweepstakes.

"Keep him fed and warm," I said, passing the note back to Daughtery. "If he's not keen on exploring the snow, give him an empty stall to use for his latrine. Be sure to keep him out of sight if Leander comes down to pay a call on the horses."

"Of course, my lord." Daughtery let the puppy lick his fingers. "It's a lucky little boy who gets his own puppy for Christmas. They'll grow up together, the pup and the child. The lad will delight in teaching the pup a few tricks, and the pup will delight in playing with the lad. Can't do better than a puppy for making a child smile."

"Delight on every hand," I muttered, collecting an apple from a half barrel by the door. "If anybody sees Father Christmas, please tell him I'd like a word in private." All three men regarded me as if I'd been at the toddies. "Happy Christmas, gentlemen."

I quit the workroom and returned to Atlas's stall.

"I need a good gallop," I said, taking a bite out of the apple and passing the rest to my horse. "A hard, fast gallop to someplace with no bells that magically show up the day before mine, no generous bank drafts from mysterious benefactors, no dainty gray ponies, and most assuredly no *rubbishing* puppies."

Atlas ate his treat, dropping juice and apple bits into the straw. When he'd demolished my offering and realized no more would be forthcoming, he returned to his pile of hay.

I readjusted my scarf and headed back into the stinging wind. Nobody save Blentlinger and the gamekeeper knew of Lucky, and Blentlinger had been exhorted not merely to discretion, but to silence. Given the weather, I doubted the gamekeeper had stirred from his cottage since Sunday.

"Rubbishing puppy."

I returned to the Hall and to Harry's journals. Old Jules wasn't taking any firsts as Head Elf, but perhaps I could still find some hints of family history lurking between the pages of my late brother's journal.

I was skimming Harry's recounting of his first summer house party—his first understanding of the origins of the term *merry widow* —when it occurred to me that I'd overlooked evidence already in hand.

The anonymous benefactor was one person, based on the consistency of the penmanship in the notes and letter. I hadn't tried to match that penmanship to anybody at the Hall, but as Top Mail Wrangler, I could do just that.

I contented myself with that brilliant, if belated, insight and went back to Harry's assessment of the virtues and drawbacks of trysting in linen closets.

Christmas, with its feasting, caroling, and greenery adorning the inside of the Hall, would come on a Wednesday. The greatest benefit to me of the approaching holiday was that no mail would be delivered. Twice the usual load would doubtless arrive on Boxing Day, but on Wednesday, I would be faced with no epistolary straw to spin into gold.

I focused on that boon when Mr. Sigafoose exhorted the congregation to keep gratitude foremost in the mind in the midst of the season's busyness.

"Be grateful," he said from the pulpit, "for what warmth and shelter we have, for what health we have, for what time we have with loved ones. Be grateful that soon the days will grow longer and the bitter cold will be behind us. Bestir yourselves to gratitude, and the season truly will be merry and bright."

"There endeth the true lesson," Hyperia whispered beside me. "He's a dear, Jules, though he must be the oldest curate in a cassock."

"He claims the humbler calling suits him." Sigafoose presided over services fairly often, Vicar being prone to calls upon his bishop in London, his daughter in Portsmouth, his other daughter in Brighton, and his three sons scattered about the Home Counties, two vicars and a curate.

The service concluded, and Sigafoose took up the traditional post at the foot of the church steps. The day was neither too bright nor too cold, merely wintry, and thus Hyperia and I had taken the sleigh to services. Her Grace, along with Terrence, Pettigrew, and Bertha, had chosen the warmer confines of the coach.

Kerrick and Ginny had pleaded a sleepless night—another sleepless night—and Healy West was enduring the most prolonged head cold in the annals of modern medicine. Aunt Crosby had signaled her intent to enjoy a quiet morning at the Hall by avoiding the breakfast parlor altogether.

"Would you like to drive us home?" I asked Hyperia as we waited for Bertha to finish instructing Sigafoose on the scriptural references that would have enhanced his homily.

"Yes, but I might get us lost."

"Lost all the way to Town?"

Hyperia smiled graciously at Mrs. Blentlinger, who'd waved to her across the churchyard. "All the way to Paris. I vow our elders bring such tremendous stamina to their bickering. How do they do it, Jules?"

"Why do they do it? There's Sigafoose, with his tiny cottage and his tiny salary, and he exudes contentment and good cheer most of the time. I grumble more in a day than that man has likely grumbled in his whole life."

"You are merely vexed because you have been bested by a puppy."

And by a pony, a bank draft, and a bell. "You must admit, I have been bested by an excessively adorable puppy, not just any stray canine." Though what was I to do with Lucky? A gamekeeper did not need a herding dog, and the sheep pastures on the home farm were such modest acreage, Lucky would be wasted there too.

For that matter, what was I to do with the bay pony?

"Let's sneak away," Hyperia said, pitching her voice low. "If we leave before the coaches, we'll have better going."

Mrs. Blentlinger foiled our attempted escape, prosing on at impressive length about the cake raffle—up to nine cakes!—and Mr. Blentlinger's new fiddle, a holiday gift given early so that he might practice before the Boxing Day fete, don't you know?

We did know, having been regaled with the same recitation the previous Sunday and the Sunday before that. We knew. We smiled. We nodded. We sank so low as to plead that Atticus was likely getting chilled, though the boy sat in perfect good cheer on the bench of the sleigh, swaddled to the ears in three lap robes. One coach after another departed, until eventually Mr. Blentlinger took pity on us and demanded his wife's escort back to their home.

"Jules," Hyperia said, gesturing with her chin, "what do you make of that?"

The churchyard was once again a deserted expanse of trampled slush. The church doors were closed, but around the side of the building, away from the green and the shops and the livery, Sigafoose stood in close conversation with a lady whose face was hidden by her bonnet.

"That's Miss Winters," I said. "I recognize the blue cloak."

Sigafoose and Aunt Crosby's lady's maid appeared impervious to the cold and were standing quite close.

"Good heavens."

While we watched, Sigafoose hugged Winters, and she hugged him back. The embrace wasn't quick enough to be a mere holiday gesture, but neither was it furtive. They had hugged before, those two. Had apparently been hugging for quite some time.

"We might be seeing the reason Conrad Sigafoose has been content with a curate's post long after he was qualified for his own vicarage."

"Oh, Jules." Hyperia laced her arm through mine and leaned on me ever so gently. "That is sweet and sad. My heart would break if I could see you only a few times a year and then have only moments with you."

Good to know. As we watched, the embrace ended, and Sigafoose and Winters proceeded arm in arm toward the lych-gate.

"I have an idea, Perry. Might you circle the green a time or two with Atticus? If you pass Miss Winters on the lane, offer her a lift to the Hall. I won't be but a moment."

"What is this idea?"

"I intend to abet the course of true love." I kissed her cheek. "You know, happily ever after, love, and laughter. That sort of thing?" One small step in the direction of holiday generosity that I could take without fear of being bested by the unseen purveyor of puppies, ponies, bells, and bank drafts.

"Don't tarry in the cold, Jules, or Healy won't be the only one under the weather."

I did not tarry. I took up a post at the corner of the church, and after Sigafoose bid farewell to Miss Winters, I waited for him to see me. I expected he'd be nonplussed, if not embarrassed, to know his embrace had been witnessed, but he was all smiles.

"Sigafoose, do I mistake the matter, or have you just parted from a lady of whom you are more than passingly fond?"

"Very fond indeed, my lord. Profoundly fond, and I am pleased to note that she returns my sentiments." He rocked on his toes like a giddy boy. "Miss Winters and I have been great friends for many years."

Such great friends that Sigafoose had denied himself advancement in the church in the hopes that Aunt Crosby would continue to impose on the Hall's hospitality from time to time. Miss Winters had probably been loyal to her employer for the same reason.

An awe-inspiring example of true devotion. "Sigafoose, would your prospects brighten if I offered to pension you in the New Year?" I named a sum that would allow the man to take a wife, at the very least. He and his love would not live like royalty, but they could be snug and happy.

His jovial demeanor faltered. "A pension? My lord, what would I do with a pension?"

Did he not want to marry his great friend? "Enjoy security in your sunset years."

"A pension? Well, that is most unexpected and, as it turns out, unnecessary. My dearest friend has just had the best news. The very, very best. Might you keep a confidence, my lord?"

Not if it involves rubbishing puppies or perishing ponies. "Of course."

"Miss Winters is soon to come into an inheritance. Not a vast fortune, but a tidy sum. A tidy sum indeed. The solicitors have been crossing all the t's and dotting the i's, and when they finally looked over the family tree from top to bottom and branch to branch, dear Ann was the only heir still extant. I call that a miracle, my lord. A third cousin at some remove, a complete stranger, and my Ann—Miss Winters, rather—becomes an heiress. My happiness on her behalf is without limit."

He meant this. He was overjoyed, ebullient, and beaming. "Do you plan to court her?" Forward of me to ask, but I would hate to see such devotion thwarted by a misguided excess of humility.

Sigafoose's gaze went to the bell tower. "One must not be too hasty."

"Sigafoose, you are not the shepherd boy pining for his goose girl. Make hay while the sun shines and all that."

He rose up on his toes again and rocked back. "My lord has a point, and thus I tell you, again in strictest confidence, that when certain obligations have been tended to, my Ann has agreed to make me the happiest man in creation. We might well be the first couple to put that glorious new bell to a nuptial use."

That *other* glorious new bell. "I won't offer congratulations prematurely, but I will be the first to do so when matters have been formalized. If you're to take a wife, though, you will need more coin than a curate commands."

The sleigh had gone around the green twice with Miss Winters now ensconced beside Hyperia, and one wasn't to discuss finances on the Sabbath, and my feet were cold, and yet, I had my doubts about this third cousin/stranger. Miss Winters's inheritance might truly be a well-timed coincidence of the happiest sort.

My faith in coincidences was at low ebb.

"My lord is very generous, though I must refuse on the grounds that I have no need of coin. I've been careful, my expenses are modest, and Ann's good fortune will be ample for our needs. We'll have the legal fellows set up the trust so her money remains under her control, but funds will not be an issue."

What a wonderful, humble, nigh saintly man. Why did I want to plant him a facer? "Will you at least let me gift the happy couple with a year rent-free at the cottage Mrs. Swinburne now uses? She'll be vacating in the spring, and the new curate will want quarters close to the church."

Take the damned cottage, please.

"I suppose he will, and I cannot expect Ann to dwell in a made-over summer kitchen, can I? She would, though, bless her, and we'd be happy."

He was happy, deliriously so. Virtue-rewarded, dreams-come-true, patience-of-Job-vindicated *happy*.

"We're agreed, then," I said. "You'll have the use of the Swinburne cottage for a year without rent. If the bride has no one else to escort her up the aisle, I will happily appropriate that honor."

"Would you, my lord? Would you truly? Ann would appreciate that. I appreciate that. My cup runneth over, to a degree even the psalmist could not fathom. Happy Christmas, my lord, and I hope to see you on Boxing Day."

He all but danced off, the wind whipping his cassock around his ankles, a man in transports.

I was not in transports. On the one hand, I was delighted for him and agog at the strength of a love equal to such patience and fortitude as he and his Ann had shown. On the other hand...

I was dogged by the nagging suspicion that on this occasion, the mysterious benefactor had galloped past the post before I'd left the starting line. As an aspiring assistant to Father Christmas, I was an utter failure.

Again.

I climbed into the sleigh when it made its next pass around the green. With Atticus fidgeting beside me on the bench, I smiled politely while Hyperia recounted Miss Winters's tale of extraordinary Yuletide good fortune.

CHAPTER FOURTEEN

Aunt Bertha, like an artillery crew firing off a shot to gauge wind and range, embarked on her usual carping over the Sunday afternoon roast.

"Not to state the obvious, but potatoes are a pedestrian accompaniment to a decent cut of beef. I've always said so, and while I know root crops are an inevitable penance on winter menus, carrots are more colorful and nutritious."

Mrs. Gwinnett's version of mashed potatoes included sour cream and grated cheese as well as chives and dashes of subtle seasonings. I had hallucinated about her potatoes when in captivity, and the generous portion I'd put on my plate was nearly gone.

My experience in the churchyard had left me chilled and frustrated, and my obligations since divine services had included a mandatory session of throwing a ball for the rubbishing Spaniel puppy. I had not ridden Atlas in days, and a light snow had begun to fall as we'd sat down to our weekly feast.

I could not and *would not* tolerate disrespect toward Mrs. Gwinnett's potatoes.

"I invite the company to play a game with me." Because I tended to hold my peace at meals, my announcement earned the attention of the whole table. Even Healy hadn't dodged the Sunday repast, and Aunt Crosby was still in her seat halfway through the meal.

"Games at a formal meal are ill-bred," Aunt Bertha observed. "Not done, even during the holidays, which have not officially commenced."

"This is a family supper," I countered. "Far from formal, and you will lead us in this game, Aunt Bertha. The rules of play are simple. We each say something nice or mention one thing for which we are in that moment grateful. I am grateful, for example, for Mrs. Gwinnett's *luscious, steaming-hot, hearty, exquisitely flavorful potatoes.*" I took a bite while the whole table watched.

"Delicious. I learned this game," I went on, "when I came home from Waterloo and all my good spirits felt as if they'd expired on the battlefield with so many of my friends. When I'd despair, which was moment by moment, I would challenge myself to think of one thing that was good, wonderful, sweet, and positive. I would write it down. By the end of the day, I'd have quite a list."

These people, most of whom I considered family, were looking at me as if I'd put forth a decree that we must all take ship for Cathay.

"You all recall the state I was in," I said. "Jumping at shadows, unable to appreciate a decent meal, my conversation a procession of gloomy monosyllables, when I could converse at all."

I hadn't intended to remind anybody of the poor condition I'd been in a scant year ago. Kerrick in particular was watching me closely, as was Hyperia.

"Go on, laddie," Kerrick said, winking at his wife. "I know certain exhausted parents who could use a few rounds of this game."

"I'm fond of dogs," Pettigrew said. "I am grateful, rather, for the old hound who kept me company when Mandy went off to East Anglia. Beast went with me everywhere, and I admit he heard a few unrepeatable sentiments from me. Never told a soul. Bertha, you are to lead us in this game, I believe."

"Yes, Bertha," the duchess said. "Give us an inspiring example."

Bertha picked up her fork and considered her plate. If she managed to turn this simple exercise into another vehicle for her complaints, I'd toss her out into the snow.

"I am grateful," she said at length, "for memories. For some memories." When she raised her gaze to Pettigrew across the table, she was neither smiling nor frowning.

"I can second that," Healy said before Pettigrew could respond. "Grateful for memories of the holidays with my parents, who were particularly fond of Yuletide. I'm also grateful for the footmen who keep the library so toasty. Aunt Crosby?"

"How can you be grateful for a hound, Mr. Pettigrew?" Crosby asked. "Smelly, loud creatures with invariably muddy paws. Their tails alone leave a path of destruction, and when they bark, half the shire hears their incessant noise. Cats are so very much more dignified."

"Now, Crosby," Bertha said reprovingly. "Follow the rules. I did."

"Very well, then. Shawls," Aunt Crosby said, gathering both of hers closer. "At this time of year, I am exceedingly grateful for shawls."

"Teething babies," Ginny said. "A teething baby is a healthy little creature embarking on the important business of growing into a rambunctious child. I am grateful for teething babies, also exhausted."

Kerrick lifted his glass in her direction, and so it went on around the table. Aunt Bertha refrained from further fault-finding, and we even managed our mince pies without hearing criticism of the spices, the presentation, the sherry folded into the whipped cream, or the recipe used to concoct the dish.

Healy offered to read from *Twelfth Night* for the elders in the library—an acceptable diversion even on the Sabbath—and Hyperia and I slipped off to her parlor.

"How far have you read?" she asked as I tossed a square of peat onto the fire.

"Through university and into Harry's careening-about-London

phase. Harry has made the decision to join up. He's dithering between a captaincy and a major's post, and finding something to dislike about every regiment that has available openings."

She rearranged pillows on the sofa. "You suspect he truly did not want to serve?"

"I suspect he was waiting for me to finish my studies, because he knew that I, as the extra spare, would be expected to buy my colors. He waited until I'd made my choice, and then he followed suit so to speak."

Hyperia wrapped her arms around me. "It all grew complicated, didn't it, when he died? The motives and the memories?"

I held her familiar shape and warmth, breathed in the floral fragrance she favored, and was comforted.

"Complicated, and also simplified. Harry is gone. Nothing I can wish, pray, promise, or do will change that. Rereading his journals makes me miss him, but also reminds me that Harry and I were very different creatures, and that difference was sometimes a burden for both of us."

Harry had not, in fact, evidenced as much liking for me on the pages of his journal as I had attributed to him. Though he was the spare, he grumbled frequently, as an older sibling would, about his juniors. Resentment sat just beneath the surface of what he admitted, and yet, he'd gone to Spain in part to protect me, as I had gone to protect him.

I searched through the shelves for the next volume of his memoirs, the one that chronicled Harry's transition into the military, his officer's training, such as it was, and his first experiences of battle on the Peninsula.

"Sometimes," Hyperia said, tossing a pillow into a wing chair, "I didn't like Harry very much. He had a bit of Aunt Bertha's ability to see what could have been improved, in his never-very-humble opinion."

"He had all sorts of ideas for how I could have been improved." I found the journal I sought, the penultimate in the series. Once Harry had begun spying in earnest, he'd resorted to a cryptic personal calendar and ceased journaling.

"One does not improve on perfection," Hyperia said, appropriating a corner of the sofa and fishing in her workbasket. "I shouldn't say this, but I have wondered if Harry even knew how to be happy. Jolly, yes. Flirtatious and boisterous and funny, but his happiness was always a question, in my mind."

The discussion was unusually frank, even for us, and both a relief and a sadness. "Harry made a hash of matters with Leander's mother," I said, taking the place in the middle of the sofa. "He died knowing the child had not been well provided for, and he died having disobeyed orders and knowing that because he'd done so, I had as well. I contemplate his death with a great deal of guilt, but also... puzzlement. What the hell was he doing? He had a child..."

Perhaps this was the question at the root of all my investigating: Why had Harry left camp that night? What had been so important that he'd abandoned the safety of the camp, abandoned *me*, and all but invited the French to take him prisoner?

And as far as I knew, Harry might have left behind half a dozen children, five of whom were now struggling in abject poverty. I had not known my brother as well as I'd thought I did, and that gave his absence a fresh coat of sorrow.

Hyperia extracted her embroidery hoop from her workbasket. "Jules, do you ever wonder if Harry was working for the French?"

"Yes." The admission was disloyal, also honest, and with Hyperia I had vowed to be honest. "He was as fluent with languages as I am, cannier about people, charming and bold, like Uncle Thomas. Bold to the point of risking his life."

"All soldiers risk their lives." Hyperia smoothed her hand over satin rose petals and shiny green leaves. "I am angry with Lord Harry. For his sake, you risked your life and your honor. For his sake, your reputation has taken numerous beatings. I'd say that evens the score between you and his memory."

I wrapped my arm around her shoulders. "Harry would understand your ire. If he was a double agent for the French, I don't want to know about it. More likely, he was involved in some bit of intrigue that made for strange bedfellows."

She took up her needle, which sported golden thread. "Such as?"

"We always knew who the enemy was in a general sense, but in specific instances, pragmatic considerations sometimes prevailed over politics. Wellington's soldiers were not paid timely, and thus the sums owing grew to enormous proportions. The French wanted the lot of it when the pay wagons finally rolled, while Spanish Bonapartists and royalists alike wanted English soldiers to get their packets."

"Because that coin would be spent in Spanish taverns, brothels, and markets, while the French army survived by pillaging."

"Bonapart called it foraging, but yes. In that instance, Spanish guerrillas distracted the French patrols looking for the paymaster's convoy of wagons, and Spanish Bonapartists let the distractions serve their intended purpose despite being tasked with thwarting the guerrillas."

That was the tale as far as I and my fellow intelligence officers had made it out. The men had been paid at long last, the French frustrated, and the Spanish of every loyalty indirectly enriched.

"Then Harry might have been following some obscure set of orders when he left camp?"

"Possibly." But not likely. He would have warned me of his departure, however vaguely. I considered the journal in my lap and opened it to the first page. A folded sheet of paper slid out, the late duke's handwriting in evidence.

"What's that?" Hyperia asked, poking her needle up through the fabric.

"One of His Grace's letters, probably from Harry's university days. Papa was forever exhorting us about diseases and drunkenness. His advice was sound, and he applied it with a light hand." I tucked the letter between the pages of the journal. "I don't feel much like reading more of Harry's commentary just at the moment."

Hyperia put aside her embroidery between one stitch and the

next. "You were telling the truth at supper, weren't you? You made lists, every day, moment by moment, and read them over and over."

My eyes had been worse then. I'd had to print the words letter by letter, using the light of only two or three candles in a darkened room. "I still have my lists."

We stayed like that, half embracing on the sofa, while the snow came down, the day darkened, and I pondered my brother's demise. Harry had not resisted capture, but had, in fact, wandered straight into a French patrol's waiting guns. By design? Because he'd sensed I was on his trail and about to blunder into the same patrol? He'd left camp for a compelling reason.

Why, Harry? Old Jules, in his dogged, dull, and dutiful way still wanted to know why.

I slept badly that night and woke up cross—more cross than usual.

I rose on Monday, the twenty-third of December, annoyed with the late Lord Harry, annoyed with Arthur—a less conscientious duke would have had far less mail—and annoyed with myself. I had been putting off an inevitable if somewhat difficult conversation, and needed to address the oversight.

"I intend that you shall have your own mount," I said to Atticus as I tossed the ball for the puppy. The creature gamboled across the trampled snow—I had appropriated the yearling paddock for this discussion—and, ears flapping, tail wagging, the puppy brought back the ball.

"I have me own mount," Atticus replied. "Nobody else rides Ladon, and he's only driven to market if Halifax needs a rest."

"Ladon has been a good teacher," I said, tossing the ball yet again. "You've done well with him and learned a lot from him. You none-theless need a steed who can manage a course of jumps and canter more than fifty yards without getting knackered. Ladon's getting too old for such expectations."

Atticus climbed the first fence rail and watched the puppy root about in the snow. "Ladon's younger than you, guv."

"In horse years, he is much my senior. The truth is, I have on my hands an excellent mount for a half-grown boy and nobody to put him to use."

"Give him to Leander. Lee's always bangin' on about the cavalry and his papa were a soldier. You won't get him off that pony except to pee or play with his puppy." No rancor colored that observation, no jealousy. Atticus was simply sharing the wisdom of an older child regarding one of his juniors.

"I had intended this pony for Leander, to be honest, but somebody has provided another mount, smaller, better-suited to Leander's shorter legs and uneducated seat. I'm giving you my first choice, though the beast would have been largish for Leander's present dimensions."

"You're going toplofty on me, guv. Lee will be tall, like his sainted papa and you and the duke."

The little dog found his treasure and came trotting back as if he'd located the crown jewels beneath the snow.

"I am not giving you Leander's castoff, Atticus. I could have sold this pony for a goodly sum, could have turned him over to the grooms as Ladon's understudy. I am giving him to you in fee simple, absolute."

Atticus pretended to make a swipe for the ball in the puppy's mouth, and the puppy dodged away. "What's 'at mean? Free, simple, resolute, or whatever?"

"This pony will not belong to the estate, or to His Grace, or to me. He will belong to you, not only to ride, but also to own."

Atticus pulled off a glove and dangled it before the puppy, who dropped the ball at the sight of a possible new toy. The glove, of course, went back on Atticus's hand, while the ball was neatly snatched from beneath the canine's nose.

"Why?" Atticus asked, tossing the ball straight up into the bright morning air and catching it, while the puppy parked on his haunches and watched intently. "Why give me a valuable creature?"

Because I'd fallen asleep wondering how many other by-blows Harry had left behind to fend as best they could in a mean and contrary world. Because I'd claimed to want children, and here was a child in my care whose prospects I could improve.

Because no little boy, no child of any description, should feel as if he was a tolerated happenstance rather than a treasured boon from heaven.

"I'm giving you this equine as a challenge and an inspiration. You will be expected to look after him, to groom and feed him most mornings, muck out his stall, and keep an eye on his health."

"I do that now with Atlas, though sometimes he won't lift his feet for me to pick out his hooves. What aren't you tellin' me, guv?"

Canny little blighter. He fired the ball across the paddock with particular force.

"The rest of the offer goes like this: Once you've broken your fast and tended to your responsibilities in the stable, you will spend some hours in the schoolroom. If you want a gentleman's education, I'll see that you get it. French, Latin, ciphering, and history, for a start. Botany, Greek, and literature can come later, and you'd do well to take an interest in the pianoforte. If you'd like, we can also arrange some drawing lessons, but one can only learn so much in the course of a morning."

The puppy was tiring. His explorations were less energetic, and when he found the ball this time, he brought it back and dropped it at Atticus's feet.

"And how to shoot," Atticus said, stroking the dog's head. "You said when I have the English and French well in hand, you'll teach me how to shoot."

"I did say that, and now I'm saying you'll have professional instruction, if you wish. Tutors, a music master, a drawing master, and so forth." To impose a governess on the boy was an outlandish notion, both because he didn't need one and because he'd be insulted by the very thought.

Another hard toss, with the puppy trotting after it. "But no pony, unless I take up with the tutors?"

"The pony will be yours regardless of your decision regarding educational opportunities. The pony is also not your Christmas token."

Atticus squinted up at me. "Ruddy big not-my-token, guv. What are you playin' at?"

He asked the vernacular form of *why*, again. "I could tell you that you've been a good boy, but it's more that you will be a good man. A good man with some means and education can have a greater impact on the world than a good man without resources."

"Here's a pony, and I'm welcome in the schoolroom? What's the rest of it?"

I heard in his tone that I'd blundered tactically. To him, a lad who'd survived the poorhouse on native vigor and the occasional slice of buttered bread, the schoolroom was not a purgatory to be endured, but a privilege reserved for his supposed betters.

A gift horse in addition to a gift pony aroused Atticus's considerable capacity for suspicion.

"Why does there have to be a rest of it?" I asked as the puppy found his ball, bounded a few steps in our direction, then slowed to a tail-wagging walk.

"There's a rest of it," Atticus said, "because you think like that, guv. I think about what's for nooning, and you think about the week's menu. Maybe intelligence officers have to range wide in their pondering, or half dukes do."

And yet, Atticus was asking me what the true price of his pony would be, a question that looked far beyond his next meal.

"You will still have a great deal of liberty, particularly in fair weather. Liberty to read, to roam, to ride, or to study what catches your interest. I'm told most boys go through a phase of collecting bugs, but I never felt the need. You will no longer have responsibilities belowstairs, if you embark on the course I propose. You will have your own quarters in the nursery suite. The tutors won't hover over you every minute, and I will expect some independent scholarship of you. You might eventually decide that you'd like to try German or Italian, for example."

"You'll make a gentleman of me?"

"Would that be so bad?" We were lobbing the *why* questions back and forth, and I had a premonition that this graduate of the poorhouse might make a formidable solicitor.

"Just doesn't make sense," Atticus said. "I'm good with the horses. Daughtery said so."

"I am good with horses myself, as is His Grace. That did not mean we were to be grooms."

I was being logical, and logic was not always the most convincing argument. "I want you to have options, Atticus. His Grace, the duke, grew up knowing he was bound for the title—nothing he could do about it. Lord Harry was the spare, and again, that precluded him from many avenues that might have made him happier. I went for a soldier, as Harry did, my other choices being diplomacy, letters, or the clergy, and I was suited for none of the above. You, my good fellow, will have far more numerous options."

"Jamison would tell me to stop frettin' and be glad I don't have to clean any more muddy boots."

"There's a bit more to it than muddy boots, young sir. If you attend to your studies now, you will have more freedom for the rest of your life." Freedom to make his own way not just in name but equipped with the resources to make that freedom meaningful. Freedom to starve had been his from birth, poor lad.

I could certainly do better by Atticus than that, and yet, he hesitated.

"Jamison will still give you advice if you become more of a scholar." Though Atticus apparently perceived that his change of station would have repercussions. "He might, in fact, give you more advice. Daughtery will still correct you if you leave a lead rope on the ground, and Mrs. Gwinnett will still turn a blind eye when you purloin the occasional biscuit."

What I could not explain was the urgency of the situation. If Atticus declined my offer now, then season by season, trading the lot of a junior groom for that of informal ward would become harder and harder, not only because Atticus would fall further behind the expected gentlemanly curriculum, but also because his loyalties to the other grooms and staff would bind him ever more tightly to his muck fork and boot polish.

"May I think about it, guv?"

May I, not *can I*. A few months ago, he'd had no idea of the distinction.

"The morning after Twelfth Night, I want an answer. You can continue on as you have been, as my tiger and a junior groom, complete with your own mount, or you can embark on a proper education."

He tossed the ball to me, though the puppy continued to watch him. "Don't tell anybody, guv. I want to think in private."

And he wanted to think at length. A barrister, then, rather than a solicitor. A lord justice eventually, perhaps.

"One sympathizes with the need for quiet reflection. We'd best return the puppy to his blanket."

"I'll be sure he has fresh water." Atticus picked up the panting little Spaniel. "Happy Christmas, guv."

He did not sound particularly happy, and maybe that was for the best when confronted with such profound change. It occurred to me to remind him of what would remain the same.

"Atticus, when I go investigating, I will still expect your aid and support, just as I rely on Miss Hyperia to aid and support those ventures."

"You'll need a tiger?"

"On occasion, or a charming boy to fly a kite with me when I need an excuse to spend an hour in Hyde Park, or a lad to accompany me on what appears to be a quiet hack. One cannot be specific, but

I'd be a fool to give up such a valuable ally in the face of pressing riddles."

He brightened somewhat as the puppy tried to lick his chin. "You're not a fool, mostly."

"Such lavish praise will give me the flutters. Get the dog inside and think about what I've said."

He saluted and marched away, the puppy in his arms.

Atticus would doubtless consult with his familiars, and they would give him wise and kind counsel. Between now and January seventh, the boy might change his mind several times, but I was hopeful that he'd choose the schoolroom over the stable.

The choice had to be his. That mattered to me.

I returned to the Hall, my eyes already protesting the day's sunny outing. The day's correspondence awaited.

"Lord Sisyphus," I muttered. Atticus would love the mythological tales, and he was such a gifted mimic, he'd learn languages more easily than most.

As I settled myself in Arthur's chair and did an initial sorting of the pile of letters stacked in the middle of the blotter, I realized that for the first time that holiday season, I had offered a gift to somebody that had not immediately been rejected, topped, or rendered irrelevant.

I had finally won a round against the mysterious benefactor—and a very important round. Feeling somewhat cheered by that observation, I got to work wielding the figurative muck fork for which my education and station had suited me.

CHAPTER FIFTEEN

For reasons known only to Father Christmas himself, Christmas Eve saw the delivery of a mere dozen bits of mail. Two brief reports—first paragraph/last paragraph affairs—a few invoices, holiday greetings from Lady Ophelia, some parliamentary whatnot, and a small package sent by express from Town to my attention.

A month earlier, I would have needed an entire morning to win even so paltry a skirmish. I considered using my unexpected liberty for a jaunt to the stable, but the grooms had insisted on taking over the puppy's exercise sessions.

I wished them the joy of that task. More interesting work awaited me in Hyperia's sitting room, and there I did go. On the way, I had to dodge a dozen footmen and maids intent on bringing long ropes of pine boughs into the house, replacing the kissing boughs that had been denuded of all of their berries, and exchanging shriveled cloved oranges for fresh.

As I reached the landing on the main staircase, a pair of under-footmen nearly smacked me in the face with the top of a six-foot-long fir tree.

"Beg pardon, milord," one of them said. "Not used to hauling trees about."

"The custom is German." I dodged around waving boughs. "Our dear queen has taken to setting up holiday trees in the royal residences." The smell was quite pleasant, though the mess and bother were considerable.

"We're being fashionable, then?" the second footman asked. "Setting the trends?"

"Or indulging the duchess's whims." Which might have been in honor of Arthur, who was deep in the heart of Christmas tree territory. "Carry on, and mind you try not to knock over anything valuable."

"Wouldn't dream of it, milord, assuming you don't consider Young Jamison valuable." They went grinning on their way, and I, in good enough spirits, went upon mine. To my delight, Hyperia was alone in her cozy parlor, though the room had never struck me as cozy when Harry had been in residence.

"Jules, greetings. Are you fleeing the Royal Mail again?" She sat by the reading table at the window, the late morning light finding fiery highlights in her hair. The table beside her held a tea service for one. I kissed her crown and poured out, steam curling from the cup.

"I was given a light sentence in mail jail for once, though I assume I'll pay for that boon come Boxing Day. Share a cup with me?"

She gestured to the opposite chair. "Of course. The elves are very much in evidence this morning, and I retreated in defense of my wits. The duchess took Aunt Bertha into the village to meet with the Boxing Day Committee, and Aunt Crosby pleaded the need to see to her own correspondence. Healy is pacing about the library and muttering, and Kerrick took a breakfast tray up to Ginny and hasn't been seen since."

"You have been gathering intelligence." I added a dollop of honey to the jasmine green tea and passed cup and saucer across the table.

"One must," she said, "though I haven't any notion what Squire

Pettigrew and Uncle Terrence are about. The squire flew down the drive in the sleigh, Terrence beside him, and they were arguing about some horse race."

"Off to root through old Jockey Club form books, would be my guess. Only holy Scripture will do when debating who came in second in the 1797 Witless and Wanton Stakes."

"Is there such a thing?"

"Not that I know of, and unless you consider the whole of a London Season. How is it you've made this room less Harry's and more yours?"

"I changed the curtains. Harry preferred forest green to my burgundy, and I moved this table closer to the window."

She'd done more than that. The table was graced by a pea green lace runner in the middle of which sat a bouquet of pink camellias. The sideboard had a matching lace runner and bouquet, and the candles on the mantel—unlit at present—were also green and set straight into shining brass holders.

The escritoire was tidy, the pillows on the sofa arranged just so in shades of cream, pink, and emerald. A pretty cloisonné music box that I'd last seen in the music room of Healy's London residence added another touch of brightness to the mantel.

"Harry would approve of the changes, even the pink flowers." He would grumble about fripperies and fussing, but Harry had genuinely liked women and appreciated the grace and beauty they'd brought to his life.

"He's on your mind today?" Hyperia took a sip of the tea and passed the cup back to me. "Finish it. I've already had two cups."

"I came up here hoping to read to the end of the next to last journal. The rest of the week will be busy, what with the usual feast, then the Boxing Day nonsense in the village, and calls, and the big market on Saturday... It doesn't seem right that we'll have no reception at the Hall, but I suppose that's for the best." Traditions were merely that, rather than immutable laws handed down from heaven.

That I would miss having the entire shire larking about the ballroom, miss the noise and revelry, was to be expected.

Hyperia rose and retrieved Harry's journal from the sideboard and her workbasket from beside the sofa. "You liked all the nonsense and riot when the Boxing reception was here."

"I was a boy the last time the Hall hosted such festivities. The memories are happy, albeit characterized by headaches and dyspepsia. Harry was always trying to goad me into outlandish behaviors—shooting peas through a straw from the minstrel's gallery to see who could pot Mrs. Vicar's bonnet—and nobody was punished for high spirits. Mayhem was his native element, and Yuletide was allowable mayhem."

"While his journals are not exactly merry?"

"Not generally." Though Harry had offered humorous commentary in many places. "Nor have they shed any light on my paternity."

Hyperia kissed my cheek, patted my shoulder, set the journal beside me, and took up her embroidery. The whole sequence took her less than thirty seconds, but conveyed support, a touch of command, encouragement, and a gracious yielding to my need for privacy.

I had read in silence for the better part of an hour—Harry was both eager to leave for Spain and sorry to quit his Town indulgences—when I turned a page, and Papa's letter once again fluttered free. I picked it up this time and, after a moment's hesitation, decided that by right of the Lord of the Mail, I was permitted to read such a brief epistle.

The missive turned out to be addressed not to Harry, but to Her Grace, and that was just the first of the surprises it contained.

My darling duchess,

This letter is by way of apology first and overture second. You must believe me when I say that I blame myself for our current contretemps. Had I been a better husband, a faithful, dependable, considerate husband, you would not have been so easily tempted. I am most unhappy with my brother, and he with me, but he was only able to prey upon your loneliness and discontent because I had so bitterly disappointed you.

I apologize for my transgressions, dearest Dot. I have the great good fortune to be married to the only woman in England who was willing to consider a union with me despite my title, rather than because of it. I have been lamentably slow to realize how blessed I am in my wife, and Thomas was lamentably quick to take advantage of my stupidity.

Thomas has convincingly apologized. He told me that you were reluctant, that you both regret the whole business, but you could not regret your actions, my darling, as deeply as I regret mine. If it is your wish to live apart, I will bide up in Town, and you and the children can remain at the Hall. I would ask for the sake of appearances, that we occasionally manufacture displays of public cordiality. On my part, they will be expressions of genuine and abiding regard.

In the alternative, I offer you this: My assurances as a gentleman (I can hear you growling, my dearest), a peer, and a man who knows he has bungled badly that the child will be loved and raised as my own. That I will be as doting a papa upon this next addition to the nursery as I have ever been to our other offspring, and that nobody—not the buffoons in the Lords or the spite-mongers in Mayfair—will ever know that this child is anything but the beloved fruit of a contented and devoted union.

I am asking you to put the past behind us, to give me another chance, Dot, and to let me show you that I can be not a perfect husband, but appreciably better than I have been.

All my love,
Claudius

I read the letter from start to finish, stared hard at the signature, then read it again, and still the significance was hard to grasp. When in doubt...

"Perry, might you look at something for me?"

"Of course." She set aside her hoop and took the letter. As I watched from across the table, her expression shifted from dismay to puzzlement. "His late Grace is all but groveling."

"For Papa, that is abject terror barely concealed behind abject remorse. The villain of the piece appears to be Uncle Thomas." *My father.*

She set aside the letter. "You do resemble him. You have the Fennington nose, but about the eyes and chin, you are a Caldicott."

Which meant I resembled the late duke, too, but more nearly... Uncle Thomas? "Tommie was never particularly interested in me, not that I could sense. I was a child to impress with his jokes and card tricks and otherwise too serious for his tastes. He was avuncularly affectionate, but he and Harry were more temperamentally alike. Both spares, both fond of the ladies, both up for any mischief."

"If Thomas is your father, then you are absolutely a Caldicott, Jules. You would qualify for the succession had Thomas been married to your mother."

This observation, while true, brought no joy. Uncle Thomas had poached on *his brother's* preserves. The duke had cast his own sibling as a predator, taking advantage of the young duchess's fury and broken heart to lure her into infidelity.

"Jules, what are you thinking?"

"I'm thinking that when we are dispirited in a certain regard, any distraction can entice us. Drink, danger, debauchery... Those follies might have some appeal in the usual course, but when they promise to hold demons at bay, they gain an insidious allure."

Hyperia came around the table and climbed into my lap. "The duchess was young, and she'd already presented Claudius with his much-vaunted heir and spare. He was clearly playing by rules that hurt her, and she decided to hurt him back. Her strategy apparently worked. Claudius did not grow a halo, but he stopped taking her for granted."

Interesting analysis. "Not quite as she intended it to work, because here I am, a very great complication when viewed from a certain perspective." I carried Hyperia to the sofa and settled into what I thought of as our cuddling corner. "I thought Uncle Tommie a capital old thing when I was young, but as I went off to school, he became tedious. Not in the same league as the aunties or Uncle Terrence, but somebody I did not want to sit next to at supper."

"The same stories, the same jokes?" Hyperia suggested.

"And they weren't that amusing the first time."

We remained on the sofa for some while, until Hyperia retrieved her needlework, and resumed working while sitting beside me.

I rummaged around in my mind and sorted through reactions.

I had an answer. I was the son of Dorothea, Her Grace of Waltham, and Lord Thomas Caldicott. Uncle Tommie hadn't *felt* like a father, but then, Claudius had fulfilled that role in my life. In every regard, the late duke had been a loving, devoted, interested, and caring parent to me.

He and my mother had clearly settled into some sort of truce, and by the time I was old enough to assess their marriage with any detachment, even I could see that Claudius and Dorothea were fond allies. They'd come through their war and made peace with each other, if not with Uncle Tommie.

"Poor Aunt Crosby," I said slowly. "She was doubtless married to Thomas before she realized that her sister-by-marriage had sampled his dubious charms first." Distasteful didn't begin to describe...

"And Crosby had no children," Hyperia pointed out, holding her hoop at arm's length. "Her son or grandson might well have become the duke."

Hyperia, who did not want children, would notice that. "What a ruddy muddle. What a ruddy, rubbishing... I am all at sea, Hyperia, and I suspect I will be for some time."

Uncle Tommie had not set the sort of example to inspire filial admiration. I hadn't even truly liked him and had not sensed any particular liking on his part for me. Perhaps I'd been an embarrassment to him. I should have been a walking reproach.

I and my Fennington nose.

"You want to go for a gallop," Hyperia said. "The lanes should be safe enough."

"I either go for a gallop, or I fear you will find me swimming laps in Mrs. Gwinnett's holiday punchbowl. I cannot credit... Uncle Tommie. Of all the possibilities, he wasn't on the list."

"*Nor should he have been.* Give Atlas a kiss on the nose for me."

I got to my feet, abruptly craving cold, fresh air. "You don't mind that I'm abandoning you?"

"You are not abandoning me, Jules." Hyperia rose as well and took my hand. "First, you have to know I don't care who your father was. Second, the old duke loved you and raised you, and you doubtless loved him. That's a blessing, Jules. Think of all the times he took you up before him in the saddle, all the times he admired your schoolwork or scolded you for being naughty. You had at least one good father, and that's more than many boys with a regular provenance have."

Hyperia's pragmatic, logical sentiments comforted me. She was right: I had much to be grateful for. "Is there a third?"

"Third, I love you, and this letter doesn't change who you are. The sole result might be that we can look upon Aunt Crosby more compassionately."

"True." *We* could. The two of us, a pair united in love and mutual support. I had very, very much to be grateful for.

Hyperia kissed me on the mouth, turned me by the shoulders, and gave me a friendly shove toward the door. "Gallop safely."

A contradiction in terms, given the footing. "I'll see you at luncheon."

"Mind the elves, and no swimming in punchbowls."

I crossed the few steps back to her, hugged her hard, kissed her fiercely, and left the ruddy, rubbishing letter sitting beside the pink camellias on the pea green lace runner.

≈

Despite the bright sunshine, despite the lanes being slushy and muddy between frozen shady patches, despite all the tumult of recent weeks, the magic of time on horseback fortified me. Atlas and I held ourselves to extended canters rather than true galloping, and the sensation of mud flying behind us, the stinging wind whistling past our ears blew away a considerable quantity of cobwebs.

The mail, the grumbling elders, the uncertainty of Atticus's future, and even the bittersweet nature of Yuletide memories all receded to more manageable proportions.

"Grumbling over the dratted mail is how I fret that Arthur won't come home," I informed my horse as we turned up the path that led to the stable yard. "If I become too adept at mucking through that pile of straw, then Arthur might abandon us for good. Not logical, but the theory lurks in my mind anyway."

Atlas paused to paw messily at a slush puddle, flinging mud and wet snow all over the lane.

"Spring will come. I take your point. Walk on, naughty beast."

After a few more splashes with the other front hoof, Atlas deigned to comply.

"My tokens arrived from London," I told him, simply because I enjoyed talking to my horse. "I did not get you a particular gift, my friend, but I hope good care and ample fodder will suffice." He'd have a bran mash tonight with plenty of apples and a generous tot of molasses. Feasting at Yuletide wasn't only for the formal dining room.

We slopped into the stable yard, and I patted him soundly on the neck before swinging down.

"He was overdue for an outing," Daughtery said, taking the reins over Atlas's head. "Mrs. Swinburne says more snow tonight, and those clouds to the west agree with her."

High, wispy mare's tails. "I vote tomorrow," I said, having acquired in Spain some ability to predict weather. "Before noon, but tomorrow."

"Don't tell the lads. They'll start placing bets. More bets. Happy Christmas, my lord."

"Happy Christmas." I patted Atlas's rump as Daughtery led him off and promised myself, even if we had to trot sedately along the fence lines, I would not go so long between rides again. In the same spirit of renewed determination, I paid a call on Beowulf, Arthur's personal mount. He was a grand, dignified gelding who would shame the puppy with his eagerness where apples were concerned.

I had initially been religious about taking Bey out along the usual bridle paths at the same early hour Arthur had favored, but I soon realized the grooms envied me that privilege. In their way, looking after Bey was a means of demonstrating loyalty to the absent duke, whom they held in the very highest regard.

My availability to ride Beowulf had strategically ebbed, less mail had piled up, and the stable yard was happier for my sacrifice. I collected two apples and found Beowulf dozing, hip cocked, in his capacious corner stall. His quarters had two windows and an attached run, the equivalent of the ducal suite for equines.

"I come from the east bearing gifts," I said, paring the apple into quarters. "The least you can do is look interested."

I was not the right purveyor of sweets, but Beowulf was a gentleman. He ambled over to his half door and took a treat from my hand.

"You miss him too," I said, scratching a hairy equine ear. "We'll continue to guard the castle in his absence, but it's not the same without him, is it?"

Beowulf butted my chest with his nose. I fed him the rest of the apples and got my fingernails thoroughly dirty scratching him in several favored locations while he ignored my sentimental nonsense.

On this chilly, bright Christmas Eve, I missed both of my brothers, and the old duke, who'd been banned from appointing himself Lord of Misrule when I'd turned ten. Mama, the staff, and my siblings had all rebelled against ceding that much authority to so dodgy a character as His Grace of Waltham, and Papa had good-naturedly handed his scepter over to wee Ginny, who'd declared sweets mandatory at every meal.

Though Harry had likely whispered that suggestion into her ear.

I gave Beowulf a final pat on the neck and had just emerged into the nigh blinding sunshine when I realized what detail about Papa's epistolary olive branch had been bothering me since my first reading of it.

Why had that letter fallen into *Harry's* hands? The document was ancient, the ink fading, the paper yellow with age. The contents did not in any way affect Harry's standing in the ducal succession. Why had *Harry* known more about my paternity than I had? Why had he kept that knowledge from me? Out of kindness, out of his compulsive need to hoard secrets, or perhaps because the old duke had entrusted him with the knowledge?

I would never know, because Harry was no longer extant.

I had an answer to my original query—Lord Thomas Caldicott was my biological progenitor. That information was, upon reflection, more disappointment than relief. Yes, I was a Caldicott, as Hyperia had pointed out, but only by means most unfortunate.

And that revelation had left me with more questions. Why? Why hadn't either parent enlightened me? Why hadn't Arthur, or had the truth been kept from him too?

Be careful what you wish for, old Jules.

A happy yapping in the yearling paddock distracted me from what could easily become brooding. Atticus and another figure were tossing the ball for the Spaniel, who gamboled after his prize with more exuberance than grace.

I had to squint and shade my eyes and approach the paddock to make out the fact that Atticus's companion was Aunt Crosby. She clapped her hands and called to the puppy and made a great fuss over the little beast when he dropped the ball at her feet.

More fussing ensued and praise and patting.

Good for the old girl to get some fresh air and sunshine, good for Atticus to see her as something other than Aunt Crosspatch. I left them to their noise and activity, determined to reread Claudius's letter until I had it memorized. Somewhere in the old duke's words lay more answers, or hints, or something that would settle my sense of having stumbled into a thicket of misperceptions rather than onto the truth.

Uncle Thomas. I could not credit it, but the tale made sense, given the actors in question.

Aunt Crosby passed Atticus the ball and stroked the puppy's head, until Atticus hurled the prize again and the puppy streaked after it. Aunt called encouragement in a surprisingly loud voice. I turned my steps for the Hall, sure of at least one thing: Aunt might detest dogs in the theoretical sense. She was nonetheless putting on a fine show of enjoying the puppy's company, though that might be for Atticus's sake rather than the dog's.

Luncheon was a quiet, enjoyable affair, what with Pettigrew and Terrence off to consult Pettigrew's library of racing forms, Mama and Aunt Bertha in the village, and Healy deep in the throes of his denouement.

Aunt Crosby had pleaded a need to rest in anticipation of the evening feast, leaving me with Hyperia, Kerrick, and Ginny.

Ginny sat back from an empty plate. "I feel as if we four should play whist now strictly to reacquaint ourselves with the game as a pleasant pastime rather than a pitched battle at the card table."

"Let the old dears bicker among themselves," Kerrick said. "The day may come when even that is lost to them." He exchanged a look with Ginny that spoke volumes about passing decades, love, and family.

"If I haven't said it before,"—I raised my wineglass in their direction—"I'm saying it now. I am delighted that you and the children joined us at the Hall for the holidays. You make the whole company brighter, and you remind us that family, even squalling and squabbling, is a gift." I gestured in Hyperia's direction. "As are dear, dear friends who can be counted on in times of adversity as well as times of celebration."

"The two occasions," Kerrick murmured, "often bearing a close resemblance." He and the ladies joined my toast, and we lapsed into a contentment that might have put Kerrick and Ginny in mind of the moments when a crying infant dropped off to blessed, quiet, peaceful sleep.

We put period to a platter of ginger biscuits and shortbread with a concluding pot of tea, the meal having been light in deference to coming attractions.

"I'm for a nap," Ginny said. "You lot must think I am the most napping adult ever to stumble forth at midday in my dressing gown, but I vow to you, I sleep little and badly at night."

Kerrick rose and held her chair. "Was the same when Declan was a baby. Days and nights mixed up, the nursery coming to feel like our natural habitat. That's partly why we made the journey—to get a needed change of scene—and also to dodge the rigors of a Scottish winter, of course."

"Oh, right," Hyperia said. "This balmy English weather is nigh boring to one of your Viking standards."

Ginny kissed her husband's cheek. "Miss West knows a fraud when he struts about in his kilt. You take a chill so easily, my love, that—"

He kissed her back on the mouth. "Don't be tellin' tales, darlin' wife, or you'll not have your Christmas token of me."

They took themselves off, still flirting and bantering, and Hyperia watched them go. "I envy those two, but their situation also exhausts me vicariously."

"One takes your meaning. I think the whole parenting marathon steals up gradually, with the baby sleeping a great deal at first and then less and less, and besides, Kerrick and Ginny could turn a lot of the baby's care over to a wet nurse and staff. They choose to man the nursery oars to the point of exhaustion."

Hyperia smiled at the plate of biscuits. "They do seem to nap at all hours, don't they?"

"Shamelessly devoted to their rest." I helped myself to another ginger biscuit. "Perry, why did Claudius's letter end up in Harry's possession?"

She took another sweet for herself. "That question crossed my mind. Your paternity was none of Harry's business. Arthur, as heir and then duke, should have been put wise, I suppose, but Harry...? And he never said anything to you, never hinted or dropped confusing allusions into late-night conversations?"

"He could be cryptic," I said, thinking back, "but he was cryptic about his own affairs, his trysts and informants and obligations. I can't think of any occasion when he alluded to my irregular circumstances. I consoled myself with the hope that he didn't know."

And yet, Harry had clearly resented me from time to time, though I'd also resented him.

Still did. I castigated myself over those mixed feelings less and less of late.

Hyperia broke her shortbread in two and dipped half into her tea cup. "Harry continues to confound and vex from the grave. It isn't fair, but I suppose that's part of death's bad reputation. The whole of a person's life cannot be put in order, try as we might. I miss my mother terribly, and I know Healy does, too, but what's to be done about it? Not one thing."

I patted her hand. "You don't miss your father?"

She munched the soggy half of her treat. "Papa was around longer, and older when he expired. He was ill and in pain, and if we allowed him enough laudanum to dull the pain, he was asleep. Death became his friend, as the saying goes. This is gloomy talk for Christmas Eve, Jules."

Honest talk. "Maybe if we express the gloomy thoughts, they don't plague as badly."

She studied me over her tea cup. "I wonder what gloomy thoughts Aunt Bertha hasn't been able to express. If somebody said to her, 'You should have had a doting husband, six robust children, a thriving reputation as an herbal expert, and the ear of the king's physician on all matters of botanical medicine,' would she stop her incessant fault-finding?"

"She might, at least for a time." We pondered the possibility in silence. "Or maybe she needed a napping partner."

Hyperia, with whom I had passed some very agreeable hours in slumber, beamed at me. "Perhaps she did. Does the knowledge of Uncle Tommie's role in your life leave you feeling gloomy, Jules?"

I rose, because even the modest meal had left me feeling sluggish, and more tea and sweets would not improve my mood.

"Not gloomy so much as bewildered. I'm put in mind of a particular summer when Wellington was beginning to angle into northern Spain. That's when the French should have come for us, should have commandeered every able-bodied mercenary and mule and put us to rout once and for all. They dithered. They moved camp. The regional generals corresponded among themselves, and they moved camp again. Every British officer was confounded by a sense of missing the whole picture."

Hyperia finished her biscuit and stood. "Missing the whole picture how?"

"Were the French waiting for reinforcements? Was Napoleon himself preparing to take matters in hand? Were the Spanish royalists turning up fractious and frustrated with their French overlords? What in blazes was afoot? The generals were merely squabbling among themselves, each protecting his own fiefdom, but we had no idea the business was that easily explained."

"And you feel the same befuddlement now? I can explain what in blazes it took for the duchess to conceive you, if that would be helpful."

"Please do," I said, offering my arm when we reached the corridor. "I'm vague on the details."

Hyperia kept her powder dry until we were beneath the kissing bough in the main foyer. This octagonal entrance space qualified as a thoroughly decked hall. Swags of pine, red and gold ribbons, dashes of holly, wreaths, cloved oranges—the whole lot was deployed in fragrant, chilly abundance.

When Hyperia had maneuvered me beneath the fresh mistletoe, she unleashed a volley of kisses that nigh knocked me flat.

"I thought *I* was supposed to ambush *you*, Miss West." I smoothed my hair down where she had disarranged it and straightened my cravat. The lady, by contrast, was still tidily composed but for a becoming flush to her cheeks.

"That was to remind you of my earlier point, my lord."

"One's memory has gone frolicking in the snow. What earlier point?"

"I don't care if your father was Dick Turpin. I love *you*."

"Thank you. Thank you for that impressive declaration, for being here, for reminding me that I am not my antecedents. I love you, too, madly."

She slipped her arm through mine and escorted me up the stairs. "You want to read that letter again, don't you?"

"Of course. I'm missing something, Perry. I know that feeling well, and I ignore it at my peril."

"You don't want Uncle Thomas to be your papa. I can understand that."

"I don't want him to have been my father, I don't want Harry to have kept the secret from me, and I don't want to have been kept in ignorance of my own situation by people who claimed to care for me... I cannot believe that Harry, much less the old duke, would do that to me." I could not believe that Uncle Thomas, who had been neither shy nor discreet, would never have acknowledged me in some regard.

As for Mama, her pride came into it, and also, perhaps, a conviction that I was better off learning the details of my situation from His Grace or his lordship.

As we reached Hyperia's suite, the questions hopped about in my mind like March hares, as if I were at the beginning of an investigation rather than at the end.

"Here." She handed me the letter and sat on the sofa. She did not perch in my lap or take my hand.

I brought the letter over to the window and reread it, though the contents had not changed. "I can't see it," I muttered. "Whatever it is that still bothers me about these words, I cannot see it."

"Then read Harry's last journal," Hyperia said. "You often solve a riddle by looking at it sideways, Jules, and there might not be a riddle to solve."

"This letter should have been mine to keep, Hyperia, not Harry's." That fact alone would drive me to Bedlam, and yet, Hyperia was right: The most irksome conundrums usually had to marinate in my brainbox for a time, until some seemingly random fact or connection jostled loose an insight that put an answer within reach.

"Take your mind off the past, Jules," Hyperia said, patting the cushion. "Tell me about the next week. Do you collect quarterly rents on Christmas Day?"

I knew the answer to that question. "I do not. My grandfather kept to the Lady Day, Michaelmas, and Midsummer quarter days, but he believed that transacting business on Christmas was unseemly. He was similarly of the opinion that attempting to collect rents on Boxing Day would be pointless, because tenants were neither at home nor sober. Our stewards gather up the rents on December thirtieth, which struck Grandpapa as the least riotous of the twelve days."

"And you agree with him?"

"The late duke,"—who should have been my father, who had felt unquestionably like my father for much of my childhood—"pronounced the twenty-seventh Sore Heads Day, so I suppose the thirtieth makes sense to me. We've recovered from Christmas itself by then and aren't yet in the grip of the New Year nonsense."

I stared hard at the letter in my hand, scanning it from top to... *The date.* Dates mattered, and this date mattered very much. An odd fizzing sensation prickled over my nape.

"Perry, I see it."

"What do you see?"

"The issue is not the words, the problem is *the date*. Some Lord of the Mail I've been. I missed the date." I did not recall crossing to the sofa nor deciding to sit thereupon, but somehow my backside ended up on the cushions. "Look at the date."

In his tidy, slashing scrawl, Claudius, His Grace of Husbandly Remorse, had dated his white flag.

Hyperia frowned. "You weren't born yet, but... ah. Well, then. That does put a very different complexion on the matter."

"Correct. I was not born yet. More accurately, *I hadn't yet been conceived*. That letter is dated nearly a year before I appeared in the earthly realm."

She folded the epistle and passed it back to me. "You are not the cuckoo. You are proof that the duke and duchess reconciled."

The feel of the letter in my hands changed, from an old clue to a somewhat distasteful mystery, to *my brother's* legacy, *his* curse, and *his* truth. A holy thing, also painful, fragile, and poignant.

"No wonder Harry resented me. I was legitimate. He was not." No wonder the duchess had seemed focused on Harry—he had a burden to bear neither Arthur nor I would ever share. A burden that could have well turned us against him.

"No wonder nobody told you," Hyperia said. "Harry was ahead of you in line for the succession, and had you been a different sort of fellow, you might well have hated him for that. The duke and duchess doubtless hoped the whole matter would never come up, and their hopes have been sadly justified."

Because Harry was no more. Even as I had that thought, the logical question crowded in behind it: Had Harry been careless with his life because, in his own mind, he'd never deserved the status of spare? Had he taken himself off the chessboard from some silent sense of guilt?

"I am relieved," I said, "to know that Claudius was, in fact, my father, but sad—so sad—for Harry and Her Grace."

"Not for Claudius?"

"Not for Claudius." He'd been a fool, and made amends, but he'd also admitted to putting the whole sequence of events in train. Marital relationships weren't that simple, of course, but I was viewing the man as a father, not as a husband.

"You aren't done fretting over this, are you?"

I tucked an arm around her shoulders, and she cuddled up in blessedly familiar fashion. "I was so certain, Perry. I heard my parents discussing what I knew to be me. The sort of conversation a child should not hear, because he can make sense of the words but not the context. The duke said Her Grace must put the past behind her.

"He didn't stop there. 'So the little brat is not my son in the biblical sense. I am fond of him, I am more than passingly fond of you, I understand the motivations of all concerned, and we have agreed to leave the past behind us.' *I* was the little brat, the youngest son, Sprat the Brat, and so forth. I wrote down what he said before I forgot it, and I reread the words many times, though initially, all I understood was that I wasn't Claudius's son in his own eyes."

I recalled all too vividly the sick, empty confusion that revelation had caused, the utter shock and the certain knowledge that I must hide my reactions at all costs, especially from the eagle eyes of my own dear mama.

"Claudius alluded to Harry, not you."

"Apparently so, which is why Harry had that letter and why my mother didn't reveal the whole of it to me. One must not speak ill of the dead—Harry or his father. The irony is, I do resent Harry, terribly, but for dying, such that I've moved up the line of succession. I'm quite clear on that."

Hyperia hugged me, and I held her with an overwhelming combination of gratitude for her presence and relief. So much came clear... Harry's reckless nature, driven partly by guilt—he was a bogus spare, but not entirely so—his protectiveness of me, his appetite for other people's secrets, driven by the secrets he himself carried.

"I hope," I said, "that wherever he is, Harry is abundantly happy.

Surpassingly ecstatically happy."

I could not say the same for Uncle Thomas.

"Jules, when did you overhear that conversation? The one about the brat who wasn't you?"

I gazed out the window and saw that the cerulean sky was now streaked with high, thin clouds from the zenith to the western horizon.

"Winter." But that wasn't as accurate as I could be. I swallowed around an inconvenient constriction in my throat.

"The occasion was Yuletide, Perry. Their Graces were making a final inspection of the Boxing Day baskets, which were in the library that year. I was lurking among the plays, pretending I didn't have a raging bellyache, and it was Christmas damned Eve."

That odd prickling raced over my nape and arms for the second time, cold and unsettling. Then the sensation subsided into a hollow ache, for my mistaken younger self, for my parents with their myriad regrets, for that other boy, who had been my brother in every meaningful sense.

For the heartsore former soldier, who'd come to the Hall last Christmas and had to blow retreat one more time.

"In future, Jules, when you think of Christmas, don't think of that bewildered little boy struggling under the confusion of overheard secrets. Think of kissing boughs and baskets full to bursting and sledding and toddies and carols in the music room. Think of the love and never let it go."

Memories and anniversaries being inextricably bound, I would continue to associate Harry with Yuletide, of course, but I would also try to focus most on Hyperia's list. To that end, our activities on the sofa for the next quarter hour would have denuded every kissing bough in the Hall of its berries.

I added that quarter hour to my treasure trove of holiday memories, placing it atop the mental heap like the golden star placed atop one of the royal Christmas trees, and there it would stay for all the rest of my days.

CHAPTER SIXTEEN

We did justice to the Christmas Eve feast, with even Aunt Crosby cleaning her plate. Bertha, for once, sent compliments to the kitchen, though she glowered pointedly at Squire Pettigrew all the while.

Peace on earth could take varied forms.

As I watched Terrence escort Aunt Crosby to the family parlor after the meal, I thought again of how difficult any visit to the Hall might be for her and of how delighted she'd seemed when she was playing with Leander's puppy.

She, who professed to detest dogs.

"Jules?" Hyperia slipped her arm through mine. "Would you rather join us for tea than gather round the port and cigars?"

"I detest cigars. They give me dyspepsia." I wasn't that fond of port either.

"Then have Kerrick preside in the dining room. You come with us. We'll let you pretend to read the paper while you doze by the fire. Tomorrow will be long and busy."

I looked over my shoulder at Terrence and Crosby making a slow progress down the corridor. The meal had clearly tired Crosby, and Terrence's expression was a mixture of affection and worry. Memories came back to me of small moments—Aunt Crosby choosing green tea over her preferred strong China black. Aunt finishing only about half of her meals, wearing two shawls rather than one. Arriving without an invitation, despite being a great one for protocol and decorum.

And then there was the little coincidence of when I'd encountered Miss Winters in the servants' hall, just after my unsuccessful sortie to Mrs. Swinburne's cottage—Miss Winters, who'd claimed to have just come in from admiring the starry, starry night.

"Aunt Crosby has been letting Bertha run on at tiresome length," I said, "when in previous years, Crosby took on the task of keeping Bertha in line."

"I beg your pardon?" Hyperia followed my gaze. "Aunt Crosby?"

"She loves dogs, Perry."

"She does?"

"She loved that rascal Thomas too. I'd bet the whole lot of Christmas baskets on it."

Hyperia tugged me through the parlor door. "What are you going on about?"

I'd been focused on the conundrum of my paternity, which had turned out to be a puzzle relating to Harry's paternity, but the mystery of our anonymous Father Christmas had been swirling in the depths of my mind too.

"Crosby always demands Uncle Tommie's old rooms, but this year, she wanted—she needed—warmer quarters." And that departure from a pattern maintained over the course of years decided me on several points. "I know who procured the bell, Perry, and who is sponsoring Mrs. Swinburne's reunion with her family, and who is behind the pony and the puppy and Miss Winters's windfall."

Others were joining us in the parlor. Hyperia and I moved to the window while the ladies took seats closer to the fire. Young Jamison arrived with a lavish tea tray, a sprig of holly affixed to his lapel.

"One person did all of it, Jules?" Hyperia asked quietly.

"With the aid of an ally or two, one tired, dear person accomplished all of that, and I must have a quiet chat with her." While there was still time. "If you'd keep the other ladies occupied around their scandal broth, Aunt Crosby and I have a few things to discuss."

Hyperia's smile was puzzled, but she marched forth to admire Young Jamison's boutonniere and offered to pour out.

I positioned myself near Aunt Crosby, who was waiting for Bertha to finish fussing with the pillows on the sofa.

"Auntie," I said, bending close to Crosby's ear, "you have been naughty."

She gave no indication that she'd heard me. "I married a Caldicott, young man. One learns by example all about naughtiness."

I put an arm gently around fragile shoulders. "Tell me all about it, that I might be instructed by your wisdom."

She came along easily, and we appropriated the pair of reading chairs near the opposite hearth. The duchess gave us a passing glance, and Ginny noted our defection, but Hyperia asked Aunt Bertha about her favorite holiday treat, and Aunt Crosby and I were allowed our privacy.

"What gave me away?" she asked when I'd positioned a footstool for her just so, and she'd rearranged her shawls at length.

"The puppy was the purveyor of the final insight. You professed to hate dogs, but I saw you in the yearling paddock, and you no more hate dogs than I hate my horse."

"Your Atlas is a splendid creature. Young Atticus adores him."

"Where did you meet Atticus?"

She readjusted the drape of her larger shawl to cover her knees. "In the playroom. The boy Leander is quite taken with Atticus, and Atticus, though older, is unused to being admired. They engage in exactly the sort of bloodthirsty play you and Harry used to delight in."

I was abundantly, sorrowfully aware that I might not have another Christmas with dear Aunt Crosspatch.

"I have learned of Harry's irregular antecedents, though the truth was only recently made plain to me. For you to be around us—around him—must have been painful."

Hyperia brought us each a cup of jasmine gunpowder tea, then retreated. Aunt Crosby held hers cradled in both hands.

"The whole business predated my marriage to Thomas, but he hadn't told me of it. To him, it was the past, a closed chapter. He was so fond of the boy, though, and he and I were not to be blessed with children. I regarded that as divine retribution for Thomas's cavalier behavior, but failed to see why I should be punished as well." She took a sip of her tea. "Thomas and I put each other through some hard years, Julian. Mean-spirited, difficult, trying..."

"What changed?"

"Dorothea kept inviting us to the Hall, and she was so gracious, and so clearly indifferent to Thomas as a man. She and Claudius had mended their fences, and to an extent Thomas was right—the whole business did not concern me. That Thomas would fail to inform me of the situation was his attempt to save face before a younger wife. I could understand pride. I am not the most perceptive creature, but I do understand pride."

She was very perceptive. "You knew we needed a bell."

"Both your father and my husband were buried without a death knell. The leading family in the shire, and we buried them without alerting the angels to their passing."

Did the angels know Harry had joined their ranks? I would hazard they did, given Harry's nature. "You sent Miss Winters to leave Mrs. Swinburne a bank draft, and you arranged for Leander to have a pony and a puppy. I suspect Uncle Terrence was your minion in those undertakings." Hence, his skulking about the hedges.

"Terrence can be discreet, on rare occasion. You should know I've arranged for more than a pony and a puppy. The boy is Thomas's grandson, and I am in a position to see that he'll not want for anything. I will also leave him Burnside Manor and ensure his inheritance is in good condition when it passes to him."

A perceptive, generous woman. "You needn't. Arthur and I will do right by the boy."

"*I* shall do right by the boy in his grandfather's stead, young man. He's a very bright lad and worthy of the legacy."

Leander would be a wealthy little fellow, one day all too soon. "Are you the reason Miss Winters has come into a sizable inheritance?"

Aunt smiled, revealing a mischievous side. "Those two, pining from afar. They tried to be careful, but every time I'd visit at the Hall, Winney found an excuse to deliver some bit of lace or embroidery to the vicarage. When I made my duty visit to Mrs. Vicar, I never saw the results, because they somehow ended up in the curate's cottage instead. Most curious."

"A matchmaking Lady Father Christmas," I said. "Curious indeed."

"I owe her, Julian. Winney is a second cousin of some sort on my mother's side, a lady fallen on hard times. I simply arranged matters such that she needn't be quite as patient."

"And you love dogs."

"Who cannot love a dog? I wanted the boy to have a companion. He's alone in the world, which should not be possible in a ducal household, but we well know it's not only possible, it's entirely likely. Thomas was in some sense raised as an only child, his older, smarter, handsomer brother set apart from him. I only came to see that when Arthur was raised in the same tradition. I don't care for it, though that probably makes me a radical."

I wanted to hug my radical aunt. "You are very forgiving." Perhaps that was another gift of approaching death. One reconciled oneself to one's humanity and to the humanity of others.

She finished her tea and set the cup back on the saucer. "I am forgiving *now*. Thomas wasn't entirely to blame for what occurred, I know that. Dorothea was a young, lonely, embittered spouse, and Thomas was angry with Claudius over some financial matter. Claudius had increased Thomas's allowance and situated him comfortably on a good property, but Thomas expected more. Claudius expected Thomas to grow up. We all make mistakes, and Claudius was no saint as a husband."

She studied the group across the room. Ginny was regaling the ladies with some tale about Kerrick on the wedding journey, and all was merriment and fond laughter.

"Dorothea and I," Aunt Crosby said softly, "live with regrets. I come here as a sort of reminder that I have blundered too, but also because Dorothea invited me when any other woman would not have. Besides, being furious and affronted is a great lot of work."

"We could ask Bertha about that, though she and Pettigrew seem to be negotiating a truce. Do I sense that you enjoy watching Terrence bluster?"

"Mind your own business, young man. Terrence has been privy to the family secrets and held his tongue."

Discretion in his case might have been the better part of devotion. I decided to be direct rather than discreet. "Have you consulted the physicians, Aunt?"

"I am in the very pink."

"You are putting your affairs in order." I knew the look. With the late duke—*my father*, the late duke—I hadn't had enough experience to sense a preparation for final partings, but I'd made the preparations myself and seen many a soldier do likewise.

Aunt Crosby was unwell. She might recover, she probably would not, and her life had been difficult in some regards. Lonely.

She fussed with her shawls. "One should always have one's affairs in order."

We weren't to discuss particulars. Very well. "One should also be rewarded for taking an entire neighborhood's Christmas in hand and not expecting a word of thanks. I do thank you, and I have a gift for you."

"I have everything I need, Julian. Truly, I do."

"I beg to differ. You will come with me and for once without being contrary." I rose and offered her my arm. She came along—

Aunt Crosspatch indeed—and we found Young Jamison at his post in the corridor. I gave him a few instructions, and he bustled off double time.

"I have no use for a pony, Julian. I know my Christmas list has put you a bit out of countenance, but I assure you that was pure coincidence. The bell, Swinnie, the pony... I was merely tending to the logical tasks."

I escorted her to the music room, which was toasty enough and quiet. "You did a thorough job of reconnaissance and took the logical steps based upon your observations. I will have to be very clever in subsequent years if I don't want you beating me past the post again."

Though we might not have subsequent years.

"You most assuredly will, but then, the Caldicotts tend to cleverness. Witness, you arranged for Theodoric's ancestral pile to get a thorough cleaning, such that he has lost his best excuse for discouraging callers. Ingenious of you. Bertha will storm his gates if he doesn't extend her an invitation before Twelfth Night. If this gift of yours does not soon—"

A tap on the door silenced her. Young Jamison came in, Lucky trotting at his heels.

"Your gift," I said. "His provisional name is Lucky, and he is a thorough gentleman."

Aunt extended a pale, veined hand. "Lucky?"

As if he had indeed heard his name, the dog came forward, sat on his haunches, and sniffed delicately.

"Not Lucky," Aunt said, stroking his head. "This is a dignified creature and so handsome. Fortunatus, I think. Lucky by another name. One hopes he's house-trained."

"That he is," Jamison said. "Knows all the tricks. Sit, stay, lie down, come, shake hands, roll over, and more than that. He'd make a proper footman, though we aren't normally called upon to bark very often. Shall I take him up to your room, milady?"

"A good suggestion," I said before Aunt could protest. "A short tour of the side garden and then upstairs with him. Fortunatus will need a water bowl in some obscure corner of his quarters, and somebody should find the dog a leash."

"Julian, that beast has no need of a leash. He has herding skills in his pedigree. A leash would be an insult to his dignity."

Jamison grinned, suggesting that Mrs. Gwinnett's seasonal potation was much in evidence belowstairs.

"Away with you, Jamison," I said, "and I will see her ladyship to her apartment."

Aunt Crosby made a final little fuss over the dog, who accepted her affection cheerfully, and then we were making a very slow progress through the house and up the steps.

"I was dreading this Christmas," I said as we paused on the landing. "Thinking I had to somehow measure up to Arthur's standards, guard all the traditions, soothe all the ruffled feathers, and present myself as the good-humored exponent of all that is worthy about the Caldicotts."

"You always did enjoy a challenge, young Julian."

"I wanted a mission. I wanted orders to follow, maps and objectives, and that's a fine way to manage in time of war, but this is peace, and my strategy has failed utterly."

We started up the steps even more slowly, with Aunt Crosby leaning heavily on my arm.

"Not failed utterly, my boy. That's a fine canine you got me. Bertha and Pettigrew are in better spirits, and Terrence has agreed to escort me home next month. I gather you and Miss West are quite in charity with one another, and I have managed to make a few memories with Thomas's grandson. Perhaps I will not be remembered exclusively as Aunt Crosspatch or Aunt Crotchety. All this, mind you, before Christmas itself."

Never had I traveled so slowly through my own house, nor with such a bittersweet sense of time passing.

"I plan to offer Miss West an engagement ring."

"Winney and I have a bet going. See that your young lady says yes before sunset on Twelfth Night."

"The sun sets so early this time of year." We arrived by glacially sedate degrees at her parlor. I held the door, lit the sitting room candles, and nodded to Miss Winters, hovering in the bedroom doorway.

"The sun sets early," Aunt Crosby said, "but the sunsets are gorgeous. Winney, we are to have a dog, a fine, handsome, mannerly fellow. My Christmas token, courtesy of his lordship. What do you think of that?"

Miss Winters allowed as how a canine on his manners was a fine addition to any household, and then she shooed me out the door as if I'd been young Leander, intent on showing off my new spinning top to all and sundry.

I stood in the chilly corridor, happy, sad, and everything in between. I had found Aunt Crosby before we'd lost her, and that joy was mine to keep until I, too, could sincerely admire the fire and beauty of winter sunsets, despite the cold and approaching darkness.

I stopped by my room, retrieved a small package, and returned to the parlor, where only my mother and Hyperia remained. The duchess excused herself, waved off my escort, and hugged me in parting.

"Happy Christmas, Julian," she said. "And to you too, Miss West. Very happy."

Duchesses did not wink, but they smiled in a certain knowing fashion. Thus fortified, I closed the door behind my mother and prepared to offer Hyperia her Christmas token along with—again, forever, and for always—my heart.

"Let's take a tour of the public rooms," Hyperia said. "All must be in readiness for the great day tomorrow."

A perambulating proposal wasn't quite what I'd intended, but a gentleman did not argue with the woman to whom he was about to offer marriage for the third or fourth time.

"All of me is in readiness for a sound night's sleep," I said, offering my arm. "I don't suppose...?"

She peered into the music room, which at Yuletide was a public place. "We need our rest, Jules."

We left the warmth of the music room and moved toward the gallery. "As it happens, darling Perry, I sleep best with my arms around you."

She preceded me into the gallery, which had lost some of its chill by virtue of two roaring fires. They would be continuously stoked through Christmas Day to ensure that on Boxing Day, should the stray neighbor drop by, the room would be comfortable.

Hyperia stopped before a portrait of my late father with a young, solemn Arthur standing beside him, Arthur's little paw on Papa's shoulder.

"Of the two," she said, "Arthur looks the more serious."

"He was and is the more serious, but I hope he's not feeling very serious at the moment. I, by contrast..."

Hyperia moved on, and I began to sense that she was eluding the moment. Eluding *me*.

"You gave Lucky to Aunt Crosby, didn't you, Jules?"

"He is to be named Fortunatus, and yes. She clearly enjoys canine company, he's available for the post, and they seemed to get on famously. Not as famously as *we* get on, but well enough."

"And the rest of it? The puppy and the pony and whatnot? Did Aunt Crosby admit her role?"

"My membership in the loyal order of anonymous Yuletide benefactors forbids me to say."

Hyperia's next stop was the duchess surrounded by her daughters, a stair-step arrangement of pulchritude, mischief, and affection. "Your mother makes it look so easy to be always gracious and dignified."

"She has had her lapses in dignity, as we well know. Perry, are we in a footrace?"

My darling turned and regarded me with Mama and my sisters smiling over her shoulder. "Jules, I'm having misgivings."

I kept a pleasant expression on my face, I hoped. "About?"

"Not about you, but about..." Hyperia waved a hand at the generations of rogues and belles surrounding us. "I am merely gentry. You might well be the duke one day. You probably will be, in fact, and that will make me..."

I wanted to take her hand, to hold her to me physically. I put my hands behind my back instead. "The duke's dearest beloved. I've been thinking."

"You do that a lot."

"I want the Boxing Day revels returned to the Hall. I understand that Mama was in mourning for a time, and Arthur is not on hand to weigh in on the decision, but I am quite clear in my own mind, and for now the decision is mine."

Hyperia moved closer to the nearest hearth. We were burning coal in the gallery for now—hotter than wood and in need of less frequent replenishing—though the scent of pine boughs competed with the ubiquitous coal smoke. A great trove of roping was coiled beneath the windows in readiness for a flurry of last-minute decoration on Christmas Day.

"You are telling me," Hyperia said, "that you are your own man, and I can be my own woman—my own sort of duchess."

She made a pretty, worried picture silhouetted against the hearth. "When have you been anything else but your own woman? I told you when I went off to Spain not to wait for me. You most assuredly did. I came home in complete disarray of body and mind, and you insisted on showing Society that we were yet cordial. You abet my sleuthing, and worse, you encourage it. Half the time, you have the insights that solve the riddles. You have Arthur, Banter, Lady Ophelia, and Her Grace quite sorted out, and Leander and Atticus adore you."

"That matters? What those two boys think?"

"It matters to me, and to you, too, and that is why I know you will make a fine duchess. You see clearly and kindly, Hyperia. You see me clearly and kindly, and your honor supports me when my own grows tentative. I have a ring in my pocket, a lovely little ruby to complement your coloring and symbolize my love."

I extracted said jewel and held it out to her in the palm of my hand. "Toss it in the fire, if that will make you happy. You tell me that you love me, regardless of my antecedents, my legitimacy, the color of my hair, the state of my memory. I love you the same way, you goose. Ferociously, unstoppably. Be you gentry, queen of the shire, and everything in between, I love you, and I always will."

She peered at the ring. "Don't you dare toss that little beauty into the flames, Jules."

"Don't you dare toss our future away because of a little thing like a tiara."

"Have you *seen* your mother's tiaras?"

Shrewd of Mama, to show them to Hyperia now. Honest of her. "They are quite pretty. You are more lovely to me than any mere adornment, and I am asking you to marry me. I will keep asking until you send me away or cede the day. If you do send me away, I will ask by correspondence—I am quite proficient at wrangling mail now—and I will send pigeons and minions to plead my cause, and Kerrick to sigh and gaze about mournfully on my behalf, and Atlas to do the same."

My threats earned me not even a hint of a smile, which was appropriate, because they were offered in earnest.

"And Atticus, Jules? Will you recruit him to your cause?"

"He will harangue you without ceasing. I've offered him free run of the schoolroom, so be prepared to hear my praises from him in French, Latin, Cockney, and Greek."

"You did *what*?"

"The boy is bright and brave, Hyperia, and he has been loyal to me and to you. He deserves a chance. I can't change the cards life dealt him at birth, but I can add a few to his hand along the way." I hadn't anticipated that Hyperia would object to my decision, but she was clearly giving the matter thought now.

"People will say he's your by-blow, Jules."

"Would that bother you?"

The beginning of a smile hovered in her eyes. "Not in the least. He's like you in many respects. Thinks for himself, has his priorities in order."

I moved closer, the ring still in my hand. "You are my priority. Never doubt that. Don't marry me unless you will be happier for it, Perry. I hear myself say that and want to slap a hand over my own mouth, but my heart insists I speak the words. Your terms or none at all. What I have to offer, and what I cannot offer, are too... too odd a combination. You must be sure of your choice."

This was not the speech I'd rehearsed, not the soaring metaphors and carefully chosen snippets of poetry I'd delivered to myself in my cheval mirror.

And my spontaneous offering was apparently a failure. Hyperia blinked at the ring, then blinked again.

"So pretty and so... so typical of you. Nearly plain, but lovely. Elegantly understated."

Was that a yes or a no? "Please marry me. Ours will be an unconventional union, Perry, but we will be the most loving couple ever to make our own way through life. That much is mine to give."

She took the ring from me and held it up to her eye so that she viewed me through its circle, then slipped it onto her finger.

"It fits. You don't forget the details, Jules. I will marry you."

The fit of an engagement ring was not a detail. "The matter is decided, once and for all?"

"Yes. You gave Aunt Crosby the dog you would have kept for yourself. You are giving Atticus a choice about his future. You wanted to give all the elders their death knells and all the couples their wedding bells. Your gifts are unconventional, but they are loving, Jules. I dread the thought of being a duchess—your mother's slippers will be difficult to fill—but I am very clear that I want to go through life with you at my side."

Saved by a dog? "Atticus might decline my offer."

Hyperia stretched out her fingers, the ruby catching the firelight. "For a time, he might, but when he sees that Leander is learning some French, he'll reconsider. Where is some dratted mistletoe when I want to kiss my intended?"

"We don't need any mistletoe." I drew her into my arms and let actions prove the point. A great, soft unfurling began in my heart, of worries, hopes, dreams, possibilities, and burdens. Hyperia had given me her word, and she would never, ever break it.

We might be engaged for ten years or ten days. That did not matter. We had plighted our troth officially, and all the world would have to deal with us as a matched pair.

Happy Christmas indeed.

The ensuing days were busy to the point of pandemonium. We did move the Boxing Day revels back to the Hall—more pandemonium, complete with a biddy hen flapping around the minstrels' gallery while Leander gave chase. We had bellyaches and sore heads aplenty amid much jollity. Aunt Crosby grew rosier as the twelve days progressed. Aunt Bertha became nearly sweet, until she and Pettigrew were all but cooing while Terrence and Crosby pretended to be amused.

Aunt Crosby and I unwittingly started a local tradition. In subsequent years, anonymous Father Christmases regularly worked their magic. Old Mrs. Mayhew's ancient billy goat was succeeded by a robust young buck who set all the nannies' hearts dancing on Christmas morning.

The Kirkpatricks' farm became home to a new team of plow horses who'd shown up in the pasture unannounced. The assembly rooms were gifted with a new piano, though nobody would confess to hauling it up a flight of stairs on New Year's Eve.

Waltham and surrounds became home to an annual surfeit of elves, though by tacit agreement, Aunt Crosby, Hyperia, and I kept the origins of the tradition to ourselves. Mama doubtless guessed, and I was sure Pettigrew and Aunt Bertha had their suspicions. As for

Uncle Terrence, he took a different leaf from my book and proposed to Aunt Crosby on New Year's Day.

All quite lovely, though for me the entire holiday was joyous because I had become Hyperia's official fiancé. Our path to the altar was far from smooth, short, or easy. Our adventures in that regard tried us sorely and took us in many an unexpected direction, but those are tales for another time!